T0129486

FIGLIO DI CASSINO

SON OF CASSINO

WINFRED O. WARD

iUniverse®

FIGLIO DI CASSINO
SON OF CASSINO

iUniverse books may be ordered through booksellers or by contacting:

iUniverse
1663 Liberty Drive
Bloomington, IN 47403
www.iuniverse.com
1-800-Authors (1-800-288-4677)

ISBN: 978-1-5320-0426-1 (sc)
ISBN: 978-1-5320-0428-5 (hc)
ISBN: 978-1-5320-0427-8 (e)

Library of Congress Control Number: 2016914202

Print information available on the last page.

iUniverse rev. date: 08/27/2016

Dedicated to Annie

the adult world should forever hang
its head in shame at the terrible
unforgivable things done to the young"[1]

"Spike" Milligan
Diary entry 24 October

[1]   Milligan, Spike. *Mussolini: His Part in My Downfall.*
      Michael Joseph, 1978 (quotes from Penguin Paperback ed., 1980)

CHAPTER ONE

· ·

STEFANO CAPALDI LIVED IN a small village not too far from Cassino, which is about 90 kilometers south of Rome. The surrounding area was the site of the bloodiest battle in Italy during World War II. The village known as Capaldi consisted of only five families who were all related but not close. There are only five homes in the village and they were pretty much the same in shape and all made of the same material, massive twenty-two inch reinforced concrete. Stefano's was different in that it had a large second floor storeroom as well as a basement. The homes were definitely built to take anything except war.

The Liri Valley, in which the house, sat was a quiet and peaceful place and for the most part was dedicated to agriculture. Most of the plots were in the one to two acre category.

Stefano's farm was one of the most prosperous in the area and consisted of about three acres. Papa Stefano was a good farmer and a man of strict moral values until he went off to WWI. All of this is what was told to Stefano because he wasn't born until much later, in 1931. His family took care of the farmland with everyone doing their share, especially Mama. She carried more than her share but never complained. It seemed to Stefano that she was mainly the dispenser of chores.

It was only much later that Stefano realized that his father had deep symptoms of "shell shock", better known today as

1

post-traumatic-stress disorder. He was a tall man of bearing who was quite stern and un-smiling. Stefano was much different; he certainly was not tall and was usually smiling. His main distinguishing feature was his brilliant red hair which, along with his small size, led to a great deal of teasing. He admitted he had a "hot-head" but had lots of friends and was most times very generous.

Admittedly, Stefano hardly thought of Papa as a leading figure in his life, that position was reserved for his grandfather, Nonno. Those times when he did think of his Papa were usually associated with one of two things, his boots or his saber. He always held respect for Papa because he was his father but that's about as far as it went. There wasn't a great deal of conversation at home about Papa. Like so many other things in Stefano's life, he just wasn't talked about.

———————⌒———————

The scant memories Stefano had of Papa Capaldi came rarely. From stories he had heard he knew Papa had been a man of strength until he was injured in World War I and even then he was caring in his own way.

Stefano would shiver whenever he recalled the night he fell, landing with his hand in the fireplace. Papa had held him and tried to console him. Sitting Stefano in a chair Papa went to a cabinet and returned with an inkwell. He took Stefano's hand and reassured his son the best that he could. He took a piece of cloth, dipped it in the ink and began to paint Stefano's hand. Stefano jerked his hand back and yelled, "What're you doing?"

Stefano could recall Papa saying, "I'm trying to make the pain go away. Now be still."

The result was Stefano was fearful of the blackened hand even though it was attached to him. That night he pulled a little extra of the blanket up, wrapped it around his hand and stuck his hand deep between his legs. If he couldn't see it, it didn't exist.

Papa managed for the most part, but his war injuries seemed to make him susceptible to every ailment that came along. He owned a wonderful saber which he had carried into battle during the war. It was long, shiny and greatly admired by Stefano. Stefano often asked to hold the saber, but was admonished by Mama that he was too small. She was afraid he would hurt himself. Papa was too passive to stand up for his son. So the saber was admired from afar as it hung above the fireplace mantle.

Another special possession of Papa's was a pair of black shiny boots which he wore when he went into town and to church. He didn't go to church often, which led to heated "discussions" with Mama. Their few arguments centered on the subjects of the church and the administration of medication. One day Stefano watched and listened as Papa and Mama argued over the next dose of medicine. Mama's frustration showed on her face, her patience being tried.

"Woman, I don't want to take that stuff any longer. I don't like the way it makes me feel. Yes, the pain goes away, but it's like I go away too." There was a sad, pleading tone in his voice, but he acquiesced and rolled over on his bed. Mama lifted his head and held the medicine cup to his lips.

As she often did, Mama pleaded for him to get out of bed, but rationale had long since been lost on him.

He didn't move. He sighed and weakly said, "I'm not getting up." He was right, early the next morning he was dead.

Mama had to make tough decisions, but that wasn't new to her. The funeral would certainly not be one like that of a "Signore". There would be no new suit for the deceased or any elaborate casket. However, the viewing would be held. It was common practice for the funeral director to come to the home and prepare the body for viewing. Frequently the body was placed in a box of ice. They couldn't afford an ice cube, much less a big box of ice. Mama's only comment was, "Let's just pray the house will stay cool enough."

Papa was "laid-out" in the living room on a single bed while family and friends gathered around. Stefano wandered about the room trying to understand what was happening. His eyes were fixated on the black boots. He had never seen them have such a glistening shine.

The saber rested atop his father's body. He understood that Papa was dead, but didn't comprehend what that meant.

Stefano had rarely talked with Papa so the lack of communication presented no great change. Stefano's greatest sadness was derived from the looks on Mama's face. As a child he was trying to make sense of it all when suddenly he was whisked up by his sister, Marta. He was taken across the road to an uncle's home and from a window he watched the steady stream of people in and out of his home. Marta came fairly often to check on him, but evaded Stefano's steady stream of questions. He was allowed to come home during the wake which followed the funeral service. What he remembered most was how much food there was in the house.

In the years that followed there was little mention of Papa. But when Stefano thought of him, he always conjured up an image of black: black boots, black burned hand.

Following the service, Mama was upset, and not just at the loss of her husband. The priest had performed the regular mass for a Friday, not a funeral mass.

Stefano could recall her comment, "Such a lazy excuse for a priest. Maybe my dear husband was right, the church is for fools."

Signora Caspari dropped her coffee cup which shattered into tiny pieces on the hearth. Suddenly there was another pall in the house. All conversations came to an abrupt halt and all eyes glared at Mama. She quickly made the sign of the cross and said, "God forgive me." But Stefano could tell she was glad she had said it. He could see the twinkle of happiness in her eyes. He didn't understand it all but he knew that her expression made him happy.

CHAPTER TWO

. . . .

THE ITALIAN SUN IN the summer, hot as if it had a special fury, intensified the red of Stefano's hair. By midsummer he appeared to be wearing a bronze hat. He actually reveled in the sun. Never having shoes certainly was more tolerable in the summer.

Redheads in Italy were uncommon, so Stefano was often ridiculed by other children. This only served to make him more shy and withdrawn, but he thought a lot and was determined to do well at whatever the task. Within a period of eighteen months, he was the lone shepherd in the household.

There were days when Stefano was as happy as he could possibly be and would dream that things were going to be different, but they were basically the same as the day before, work and chores, chores and work. He had a lot of difficulty differentiating what was work and what were chores. It was usually Mama's call that would bring Stefano out of his reverie. Her calls usually carried an admonishment making him feel badly that he had neglected something. He felt as if he did as much as the next person in the household but it would be Nonno who would teach him to hold his tongue and his tongue would receive more food.

Alisha, the cow, always the obedient servant, seemed reassured by the tenderness of Stefano's hand as he reached out and rubbed her forehead. "Sorry lady but here we go one more time."

Alisha's shelter was an open-sided shed with dead grass as a bed. She certainly did more than her share of the work on the farm, but, *She never complains,* thought Stefano.

He completed the harnessing, and they proceeded to the field to be plowed. It was quite a sight, the huge Alisha followed by the tiny boy. The earth was packed and came up in large clods. From a distance it looked as if Stefano was dancing as he dodged the chunks. It was tough work for such a young boy, and especially tough on his feet. What kept him going was knowing that with the harvest it would be worth it.

Many of Stefano's pleasant daily memories would be about the bounty of food he had helped put in the basement. It was a kaleidoscope of colors from the canned fruits and vegetables, bright reds of the tomatoes to the brilliant yellows of the peaches. Then there were the wine casks which housed some of the best reds and whites in the area. Stefano took almost as much pride in the wine as did his grandfather.

Stefano had been allowed only rare sips of the house wine. Many people in the village tried to buy Nonno's wine, but he had always refused to sell. It had been compared to Gerva della Sala, the best known wine in the area.

Over the days, the villagers were determined they were going to maintain their homes and continue to live as they did before they heard the rumors of the German invasion. The families had not been close knit but were happy and peaceful. For the most part everyone lived in harmony and was in the same category, poor.

In the evening, after dinner, every member of the household assembled around the fire. The women knitted and Stefano could recall watching in fascination as his grandfather knit socks for himself. The males talked and talked and talked. It was mainly about pleasant times from the past and though it was not mentioned there was the question in the air, "Will things ever be the same?"

Every day on the farm was a new day of work and chores. Stefano had no difficulty getting to sleep, and usually he had great dreams. Lately though, it seemed his dreams centered on there being a difference in his life, but upon awakening the next morning he could never remember what the differences were.

The general meeting places in the evening were Stefano's home or Uncle Sandro's. Stefano and his cousin, Polombo would frequently sleep over at the other's home. Stefano was usually ready for bed by eight o'clock. Polombo always hoped Stefano would not be as restless as last time and let it be known, "Please go to sleep and stay that way."

Stefano was exhausted, but his head was filled with dreams of the past. Often his subconscious would rather dwell in the past than on the unpleasantness of the present. He longed for guidance, yet Papa was not able to provide it. After the death of Papa, Stefano's grandfather, Nonno, provided what he knew the boy needed.

Outside the sun was just rising over the peak of Monte Cassino, bringing morning warmth to the Liri Valley. Gradually the sun would burn away the morning mist and the wonderful views could be savored. To the east were several smaller ridges and to the northeast the glorious Monte Cassino with the gigantic Abbey sitting atop.

Nonno often told Stefano the history of the Abbey. It was on the mountain that St. Benedict established his first monastery, about 529 A.D. Fairly soon after Benedict's reign in 543 the Longobards of Zotone destroyed the monastery. Then it was rebuilt on order of Pope Gregory II, and by the 11th century Montecassion was the most prosperous abbot in the world. Under the reign of Abbott Desiderius, from 1058 to 1087, it rose to its glory with beautiful mosaics and world-famous manuscripts, the manuscripts that were produced by the more than 200 monks who lived and served there. Later Desiderius would become Pope Victor III.

The Abbey's edifice was damaged by an earthquake in 1349 and sustained a long period of decline over the next five centuries, before being restored again. Stefano little knew that the damage caused by the earthquake was nothing compared to what would happen during the present war.

_____

Grandfather Stefano, for whom the boy was named, decided that it was time for Stefano to take on more responsibility, after all he was five years old. "Tomorrow you will begin to go with me to take the sheep and goats to graze. It's time you learned to care for the animals."

The next morning it seemed that the thrill of being a shepherd had disappeared. Mama had to repeatedly call for Stefano to get up and prepare to go to the fields.

Each day Stefano and Nonno took the sheep and goats to the fields. It was here that Stefano learned about the nourishment of the land, the rotation of crops and animal care. He was also out from under his mother's and sister's skirts. He was small for his age, both short and thin. But he wouldn't let his size keep him from being a good shepherd.

Grandfather wanted to give Stefano as much leeway as he thought was safe. He could watch from a distance, watching the bobbing red head of the young shepherd.

There was one black day in his career as a shepherd. When he started school his sister, Marta, took the livestock to the fields and Stefano retrieved them in the afternoon. On that particular day, after school, he had been enticed by other boys to play a game of football. The temptation had been too great and he was quickly lost in the game. When Stefano returned home late in the afternoon, he heard his grandfather talking to Marta.

"Here is a box of matches. I want you to go to the fields and bring in the sheep and goats. When they have been secured in their shelter you are to set fire to the building."

"Nonno, truly you can't be serious!" responded Marta.

From outside the door, Stefano knew he was in trouble when he heard Nonno say, "I'm very serious. If your brother can't take care of the animals then we should not make them suffer. Burn the building."

Stefano came running into the room with tears streaming down his face. He grabbed his grandfather about the legs and yelled, "Please, Nonno, don't burn the animals. I promise it will never happen again. I was just playing and lost the time."

"The animals were not playing. They wanted water and you let their thirst continue. If an animal wants water it can't go to the well as you do. If you're to be their shepherd then it requires that they come first before your football."

At this point Stefano was beside himself with shame. He could see images of his favorite sheep dying in the fire. "Nonno, I swear on the Bible that I won't let it happen again."

Mama looked as if someone had slapped her across the face as she said, "Stefano, you do not swear on the Bible. What do you know of swearing?"

Nonno was not the passive one like Stefano's father had been. "Hush, woman. The boy has to understand, and if he is going to be able to handle his responsibilities as a man, maybe he can swear like one."

Mama's body jerked and she left the room. No one could see the tinge of smile at the corner of Nonno's mouth. He reached down and extracted Stefano from his legs.

"Very well, I will not burn the barn. However, you're to have no milk or water with your dinner. Do you understand?"

"Oh yes, Nonno."

It appeared to be foreordained that the pasta was very dry that night and each mouthful seemed to lodge in Stefano's throat. He knew better than to complain and was happy when the meal had ended.

In truth Nonno was a kindly old man who always had a moment to answer the incessant questions of his curious grandson. "Nonno, how long have you been coming out here to the fields?"

"Ahh, Stefano, I think I've been coming to the fields far longer than there has been dirt for the growth of the grass. I was coming out here daily before there were any animals on the earth. I guess that makes me coming out here since the fourth day of creation. So, I guess you could say I was ahead of my time."

"Oh, Nonno, you always have silly answers for me." They both laughed as Stefano slipped his small hand into the browned, aged hand of the only male figure in his life. That was the way they returned home every evening.

"You say they are silly answers, but they are answers to silly questions. We come every day because the animals must eat in order to help us eat in various ways. And it goes on and on in life so that life can go on. You and I have little other in our lives that we can do. I'm too old to do much except trim the vines and help a little with the farm, and you're too young to do much except learn how to do the things that you must do to help your mother and sisters to continue to exist."

"But I've heard you talk about being productive and you've explained what productive is, but I don't feel productive. Watching the sheep and goats eat grass is like watching water rise in the well: slow."

"For things to be useful they are not necessarily fast. Something may seem to grow slowly, but it's doing great things with its slowness. It's storing taste and energy for us. We work so we can take care of the animals and the land. Then we take it in and absorb that energy to help us do our work. It is the way it is. We are happy and we take care of each other."

Sometimes young Stefano was sorry he even asked a question. He would say that it always opened a philosophical lecture, though he did not know what philosophy was.

Over the next several days Stefano recalled much of what he experienced as a child. He could remember the peace and the tight family ties. The fact that they had land of about two and a half acres was the envy of several neighbors. The farmed area had harvest of corn, wheat, and various vegetables. The orchard contained apple, orange and nut trees. The fig trees provided delicious red and brown figs, the brown variety being Stefano's favorite. And then there was the vineyard where Nonno grew beautiful grapes used for the wine.

The unusual thickness of the walls of their home was probably the reason it was referred to as a little fortresses. The home was very comfortable, with the thickness of the concrete they remained relatively cool in the summer, and once a fire had been going in the fireplace for a few days the walls would absorb the heat and provide a smooth winter heat except during very extreme periods, which didn't come that often to their village.

Farming was a rough life. The women were responsible for the interior of the home and expected to do much of the work in the fields. Their days were long and exhausting. They were always dressed in the ubiquitous attire of head scarves, brown or black dresses and aprons, which served both to ward off dirt and as a makeshift basket.

To break the monotonous routine of life the young men often walked into town in the evening. They would meet in a local bar or grocery and play Briscola or Scopa. The games were easy to learn but difficult to play. Dictated by the fall of the cards, Briscola establishes a hierarchy among its players with a boss and under-boss.

The game prize was usually a liter of beer or wine distributed to the players by the boss with the under-boss' agreement. Rodolpho, a friend of the family and avid Briscola player, often invited Stefano to accompany him into town to watch. Through luck of the draw, Rodolpho was often the boss.

The thoughts of Rodolpho brought forth many fond and funny memories. Later in Stefano's life Rodolpho would be a great support to Stefano as he adjusted to the many changes that were to occur.

CHAPTER THREE

· ·

NINETEEN-FORTY WAS NOT A good year of philosophy for Stefano. Reality smacked him in the face right and left. He was eight, but in a period of eighteen months he aged in ways that far exceeded his years. Four major events put his world into turmoil.

Grandfather was 84 years old, but continued to go about helping where he could. He would prune and tie the grapevines and supervise the wine making. His wine was as if Bacchus was his assistant. He had long since turned the shepherding duties over to his grandson. Each day he went about his life and was happy for each hour. On more than one occasion he awakened in the morning somewhat surprised that he was still on the earth, happy to be on the right side of the dirt. He simply went along with whatever came his way.

He was busy setting a ladder against a large oak tree when Stefano stopped as he was heading to the well for water. He laughed as he spoke to his grandfather, "Nonno, Mama is not going to be happy with you. She says you're going to fall and break something."

"Ah, yes, Mama. Now you're going to be another old woman in the household. Nonno, don't do this. Nonno, don't do that. I listen to the women and I become an old fossil and then you can put me in a museum."

The grandson started to protest, "I'm not a wom…"

He felt the still-strong arms of the old man engulf him and a hand rustle his hair. "Go get the water like the man that you are. Nonno will be fine."

Stefano struggled to get the full bucket of water to the top of the well. He was resting the bucket on the edge of the well when he looked toward his grandfather in time to see him fall from the ladder. He dropped the bucket and rope down the well. He yelled for his mother as he ran to the old man.

"Nonno, Nonno, wake up."

There was no response. Stefano ran to the house screaming for help. His mother met him at the door. "Stefano, what is it? You'll wake the dead."

"Mama, Nonno fell from the ladder," said Stefano as he dragged her across the garden.

When she reached the body it was obvious that Nonno was dead. Mama reached down and gently closed his eyelids. Although Stefano was still confused about the life after death thing, he was well educated in the finality of the earthly process. He knew Nonno would no longer be with him. Immediately a hole was created in the boy's heart which wouldn't be filled by anyone for as long as he lived. There may be other loves but not like the one of Nonno.

Stefano ran from his mother, sobbing loudly. She walked back to the house and then across the road to inform Sandro that his father was dead. Stefano's wailing could be heard throughout the community. He had retreated to Alisha's lean-to and he broke into sobbing. As Mama approached his ear-piercing screaming returned.

She took him by the shoulders and shook him gently. "Stefano, stop the horrible screaming. What is wrong with you?"

"I'm trying to wake Nonno."

"No, dear, you cannot wake Nonno."

"But you said my screaming would wake the dead," sobbed Stefano.

She held him close. "Oh, my Stefano, you hear things differently than others sometimes. That is just a saying and you don't have the power to arouse the dead. Only God can do that. Uncle Sandro with God's help will take care of Nonno. Come, let's go in the house."

They started around the house, Stefano looked across the garden and started crying anew.

"Now what?"

"I dropped the bucket and rope down the well."

"Little one you worry about everything. No one will blame you for that. You did the right thing and we can get the bucket later. Let's have some milk and cantucci—biscotti. That is what Nonno would want you to do. Then you can go back to your chores." In Mama's mind chores were right up there with high mass in the order of importance.

Nonno was gone from the home, but he was not gone from Stefano's memories. It seemed that life was settling once again until one day sister Ilania, the middle child, was involved in a horrible accident on the farm. Somehow she had become caught in a piece of machinery that was working the land. Knife-like projections on the machine had penetrated her body in several areas. The medicine woman came to the house and did her thing. Stefano never could understand this old woman and her rituals. Ilania had been taken once to the doctor in Cassino, but it was this elderly, stooped creature who cared for the injured and sick in Cervaro.

A bed had been set up in the big room for Ilania. In this way she could be more under the constant watch of her mother. The old woman would come into the house and shuffle to the bedside. There she would wave her hands over Ilania while saying words or phrases that no one could understand. Then she would leave a potion with Mama, give assurances, and shuffle out the door. The potion was given as directed but Ilania didn't seem to get better.

Although her illness had been short, Stefano seemed to be kept unaware of how serious her injuries had been. It was as if it wasn't discussed, it didn't exist. She was a delightful little girl, three years older than Stefano. She stood out from the rest of the family where the men were tall and thin, the women were short and stocky. Ilania was short and thin. She and Stefano were harmonious and played well together, although she didn't seem to have much energy.

The Capaldi household was not one in which illnesses were discussed. In Stefano's mind nothing bad had ever registered about his sister. He was assured Ilania simply had to have more rest than he. When she suddenly died, Stefano was devastated. He wasn't told of what was happening but he knew that the people in his family who he loved were rapidly leaving him.

As if the deaths weren't enough to mess with the boy's mind, there were the constant rumors of what was happening and what could happen in the country. The Italian populace was growing more frustrated with Mussolini and his playing footsie with Hitler. One day Mama came home and gathered Marta and Stefano into a family conference. She was almost hysterical. "Signore Bellini told me today that Hitler may order gas be used on us."

Marta, with a puzzled expression, asked, "What do you mean, use gas on the people? Why would he do that?"

Mama wiped her tears with her apron. "Because Hitler is a mad man and from what I heard he is growing more desperate. He controls Mussolini and is desperate to prove he has control of all the people. Maybe he has heard that the Resistance is growing stronger." She was wringing her hands as she talked, only stopping long enough to wipe more tears.

"I think we will have to find some sort of tape. We will have to seal the windows and doors. It is sure that nothing could penetrate the walls. But the doors and window, I just don't know." She disintegrated into hysterical sobbing.

Stefano had never seen his mother in such a state, even when his father had died. The whole scene was frightening, but he wisely said, "That's pazzo—crazy—and I'm going to ask Uncle Sandro if it's true."

As he started out the door Sandro was standing there ready to knock. "Marta, what is wrong? Antonella told me she saw you running for home, crying."

Mama related what she had been told and looked at Sandro pleadingly. "That is total nonsense. To what purpose would he do that? Hitler wants us as laborers; he isn't going to harm his slaves. I believe someone is crossing gossip sources and is talking about what he has been doing to the Jews in Germany. Now put all of that silly gossip aside." Without further comment Sandro left the house, and mass gas attacks were never mentioned again.

One hot day six months later, Stefano was returning from the village, sweating copiously under the brilliant sun. The white cotton fabric of his shirt stuck to him like an iron-on patch. He kept thinking of a special treat that possibly awaited him at home. Often on such days his mother would bake a sweet as a surprise. He would take the gift, with a glass of milk, outside and sit under one of the big oak trees. There he would rest in the shade of the oak before beginning his chores. It was during these times that he had wonderful memories of his grandfather float through his mind. Sometimes Stefano even talked with his grandfather about whatever was bothering him. These weren't mental conversations, he spoke in normal conversational voice.

He looked up and said, "Nonno, I know I've told you this before, but today I saw one of Ilania's friends who looks so much like her. All of the old sadness came back. Why didn't they tell me she was going to die? If they didn't know she was going to die they surely knew she was sick. I get mad all over again when I think of that." It was a one-way conversation Stefano had had many times.

Mama had come upon him stood and listened. When she first spoke Stefano was startled. He hadn't heard her approach.

"Stefano, who are you talking to?"

"Uh, no one." He was too embarrassed to say what he was doing. He didn't think his mother would understand. "I was daydreaming."

As she turned, she said, "Give me the glass. You've dreamed long enough. Get busy with what you have to do."

Stefano stood, handed Mama the glass, and turned toward the field where the sheep and goats were grazing. He looked up toward a special tall, skinny cloud, smiled and said, "See, I told you Mama and Marta don't understand me."

CHAPTER FOUR

· ·

IT WAS A SATURDAY, the day that the Balilla or Mussolini Youth met in the square. It was very early, but already a few younger boys were milling about. Locals often laughed at the contrast between the stately constructed government buildings and the disorganized parading. The sun was well up, and the morning was bright and clear.

Although there was no newspaper or radio in the Calpaldi household Mama had heard enough about Balilla through word of mouth or rumor mill. She wasn't able to read or write, but she was able to listen and quickly able to reach her own conclusions, sometimes too quickly.

The square in Cervaro had a board where the daily newspaper was posted. When Mama was in town she would stand near the board and listen to the comments of those who could read. She often asked pointed questions.

That morning she listened as a man read about the latest wonders created by Mussolini—a new apartment building in Rome—a new superhighway.

When the man stopped reading, Mama asked, "So, what's he done for Cervaro?"

Signor Ricci proceeded to give a mini-lecture on the great things the leader was doing for the country and its citizens."

Mama gestured frantically, "Great things? You speak of blocks and concrete. Last week you read of some meeting between the fat man and that madman Hitler. What good can come of that? It is only the rich liberals who think that Roman stooge is good. Watch my word, Hitler will be telling us what to do before this is over."

The man was looking over his shoulders as Mama spoke. He waved his arms, palms down, trying to calm her. "Please Signora, be calm. The Germans could be all around us."

Mama became more animated. "Don't you tell me to be calm. I'll speak what I think. Mussolini is almost as mad as Hitler, and he thinks he's just as big. He's even bigger in his gut. You think I can't see what he's doing to our young men and boys? He's taking our young ones to fight in some God forsaken place called Africa. What do we care from what's going on in Africa?"

The man blanched. Shaking his head he turned and walked away.

Mama shook her fist toward the man and continued, "Don't you tell me to stop anything." She then turned to a woman who came to see why the Signora was shouting.

"Signora Capaldi, what is the problem? Your face is so red."

"Sera, Signora Moretti, il Signor Ricci thinks he's so intelligent because he's part of the village government. He reads the news. Well, I've got news for him. I remember when Signor Ricci simply ran the un vecchio mulino—an old mill. He stole part of everybody's grain. That's how he got so rich."

Signora Moretti was a Ricci supporter and tried to placate Mama. Her efforts were wasted on Mama who only intensified her outburst. "Works hard for us? I'll tell you how he works. He invited our boys to organize the so-called Fascist Youth Movement. This Balilla will ruin our youth. That's what it will do. At first it was join if you want. Now, they say it's mandatory. That how Mussolini works; pull us in, it's good for us and our country. My son will not join that stupid group."

Mama was shaking her fist so hard a can of garbanzo beans fell from the mesh bag that hung from her arm. She stooped to retrieve the can and stormed off. Signora Moretti stood and stared as the woman disappeared around the corner.

As if Mama wasn't exasperated enough, she met Signore Alessandro on his way into town. Predictably, he steered the conversation to the Youth Movement, "Signore Capaldi you have no choice, Stefano has to attend the meetings."

Mama tightened her grip on her shopping bag. "Oh, but I do have a choice. My son is too young to participate in such things. It reeks of military and I hate it. The military did nothing but take my dearly departed husband from me. When they sent him back he was just a shell of the man who had left. I won't let that happen to my son."

Listening to Signore Alessandro beg only incensed Mama more. "But if he does not go to the Saturday meetings in Market Square he will be looked down on by the other boys and he may well be punished by the party leaders."

"I think you're just trying to save your hide, Alessandro. They told you to bring him and if you don't you are afraid of what they will do to you. You are not worried about my son."

Mama continued to shake her head as Alessandro made his last push. "Okay, take your stand if you wish, but no good will come of it. I've done what I was told to do and I will report that's what I've done,"

Mama wrapped the apron more tightly around her hands as if she was preparing for a boxing match. "Signore Alessandro, I think it best that you go now and maybe sweep the floor of your house or wash the dishes."

She watched as Alessandro stormed away. He had been humiliated by a woman, and not just any woman. Signora Capaldi would protect her son with all her might.

———————◦◦◦———————

Stefano knew his mother's opinion and was proud of her stand, plus he was relieved that he would not have to go to the Youth Meetings. Although he didn't understand how the war had affected his father, Stefano saw how his father had suffered and he had no desire to follow along that line.

It wasn't that he objected so much to being part of an organization where he'd be thrown in with other boys his age, it was that it seemed to be compulsory, and anything that reeked of regimentation he hated. It reminded him too much of chores. And if he had to join a group he'd rather it be the Avanguardisti, but that was for 14-18 year olds. He thought their uniforms were nicer.

The Avanguardisti was the first youth organization created under the Opera Nazionale Balilla. Then came the Balilla and with time the Figli Della Lupa—Children of the She Wolf—for ages 6-8. Eventually the Fascist Youth Movement was the only such organization. The scouts were shut down and even the Gioventù Italiana Cattolica—Catholic Youth—were forced to have lower level activities.

<hr />

When Mama entered her home there were three young men standing rigid in the room. They were dressed in their movement dress of black shirts, long thigh-length olive green shorts and long grey stockings. They held their fez-like hats under their left arms.

They addressed Mama with utmost politeness. She was taken aback when she entered the room. She was not happy, but determined to remain calm. "And to what do I owe this call from three well-dressed gentlemen?"

Mama was pleased that the leader appeared to be caught off guard by the woman he'd been warned was a haranguing old bat. He stuttered as he said, "Signora Capaldi. We are here to make arrangements for Stefano to join us for today's rally. He will certainly enjoy it."

"I'm sure he would, but I've stated that I do not plan for him to join the Youth Movement."

Mama had to admit the leader was wise beyond his years. "But surely you do not want your son to miss out on the camaraderie of being with boys his age. He would learn so much."

"Yes, I'm sure he would learn much, some of which I do not wish him to learn. And before you go further, I've heard that Stefano should be given a choice. But, he is too young to make choices. I'm to make his choices for the next several years."

There was a long silence in the room. From his chair Stefano stood, and in his strongest voice asserted, "Mama, I'd like to join the group." He was so embarrassed by his mother's comments.

When she showed her surprise and distinct unhappiness, even when she told him to hush, it didn't faze him. "No I won't." He turned to the three older boys. "I will be joining you next Saturday. Thank you."

The three youths grinned as Stefano spoke. They turned and left the house with a gracious bow to Mama.

Stefano hardly let them out before he began pleading with his mother. "Please don't be upset with me, Mama. Don't you see, it will be easier this way? They say it's the law, and I don't want you to be in trouble. Nothing's going to happen. I'm too young to go to war."

Stefano watched with relief as Mama's anger gradually dissipated. He was inwardly laughing as she said, "You are to tell me anything they say about war. Is that understood?"

"Yes, Mama." Stefano left the house and quickly caught up with the three older boys. He was not going to join them at the moment, but he did want to know about the uniform. To his disappointment he was told that he would have to buy his own uniform and if the family could not buy it then he was just to wear his daily clothes. The Youth Movement would not provide his first pair of shoes, no new uniform.

Stefano was disgusted as the leader added an insult, "If you didn't have such a stubborn mama you could have joined when the uniforms were first issued. Now there are no more."

He let it drop. The next Saturday he joined the movement, although more physically than mentally. Recognizing it gave him a short reprieve away from the dullness of the home life, he went religiously each Saturday to the Market Square. There the boys would march around the square, which measured some 75 meters in both directions. They sang the prescribed song, "Vincere, Vincere e Vinceremo in cielo in terra e mare"-win, win, and we will win in the sky, on land and sea. There were occasionally short speeches, but really the whole thing was far less exciting than a game of football. To make them look more silly Stefano felt they should have carried wooden swords and worn hats made from newspapers. Later they were issued wooden guns, which sent Mama into another tirade.

The Saturday outings did give Stefano time to develop different relationships. He had time to be with boys his age and older. He seemed to migrate to the older boys and to one in particular, Giuseppe, who was about five years older. In spite of their age difference they enjoyed each other.

One Saturday Stefano hurried along the road to the village and Market Square. Usually Giuseppe would join him at the wall, but on this particular day the older boy didn't show. Stefano anxiously looked for him as the group made their way around and around the square, singing the song that the boys felt was stupid. His friend never showed. As soon as he heard the dismissal order Stefano ran to Giuseppe's home and he answered the door when Stefano knocked.

"Hey, Redhead, what are you doing here?"

"Don't call me that, you know I don't like it."

"I know, but it makes your face turn the same color as your hair. Anyhow, how come you're here?"

"I was worried about you. You know the leaders get upset when we don't go to the meetings."

Giuseppe attempted to appear not to care. "So what are they going to make me do, march two more silly times around the square? I don't want to go to those stupid meetings anymore."

"But why not? You're the one who encouraged me to go."

"Yeah, well come on in." They went to Giuseppe's room and both sat on his bed.

"I've got a problem. Some of the other boys were teasing me last week, and I'm not going back."

"They tease me all the time, but I still have to go. Why were they teasing you?"

It was Giuseppe's turn to blush. "You know those uniform pants they make us wear? Well, since I've grown mine are too tight and my father won't buy me a larger pair."

"At least you have a uniform, and you haven't grown that much. My pants are too tight around my middle, but I know I'm not going to get any new ones. So what's the difference?"

"Okay, okay. It's not my middle that's grown, it's my thing. When I have on those shorts it looks like I don't have anything on. One of the boys asked me if it was going to fall out the bottom. I'm afraid if it gets stiff it will pop out."

"Oh, yeah, that could be a problem which I certainly don't have. Hey, you're almost a man. Talk to your father. Ask him what to do."

"Maybe I will."

"Well, I've got to go. Mama will be wringing her hands when I get home. She's totally convinced they're going to drag me off to fight on the Russian front." Stefano got up off the bed and his friend followed him to the door.

The next Saturday, Giuseppe called to him as he was walking to the square. He ran to join Stefano. "That was a smart idea you had for me to talk with my father. He listened very seriously, and then laughed. He said he had the same problem when he was my age and I had a couple of choices. I could tie a cord around it and tie it to my leg or I could be a proud Italian."

"Ouch, a cord tied around it doesn't sound very nice. What you going to do?"

Giuseppe stuck out his chest. "I didn't think it sounded like much fun either, so I'm going to be proud like my father."

Stefano followed Giuseppe into the square and lined up right next to him. The first comment he heard was from one of the older leaders. "Giuseppe, you missed last week. Where were you?"

"You teased me about my uniform last week, so I took a week off just to watch the weed grow. Maybe if you're lucky your weed will grow."

A couple of boys snickered as the older leader mumbled something about nor letting it happen again, did an about-face and walked away.

Giuseppe mumbled, "So much for the dick patrol."

Giuseppe became not only the "gifted one" he became a leader in short order. He played the role, but Stefano knew he laughed at the whole process.

When the Germans arrived in large numbers the Fascist Youth Movement slowly waned. It was like most other things in the community. Shops closed, churches had lighter attendance, although the mothers of the village still attended, or at least prayed more. School attendance was lighter, also. Stefano was never keen on going to school and began to miss more days.

On one particular day Stefano and the other children gathered in the classroom, but the master did not show. After a short time Stefano and few of the boys decided it was a good omen and left the school. On his way home Stefano spotted the master coming down the road. Quickly Stefano took refuge behind a large oak tree. When the master passed Stefano ran down the road to his home telling his mother when he arrived that the master did not come to school.

The next day when the master had brought the class to order he turned to Stefano. "Why were you not in school yesterday?"

"Because you were not here, I went home."

"But Stefano, you saw me coming to school, granted a few minutes late, but you saw me coming to school. You hid behind a tree, thinking I had not seen you, but I did." The master went to his desk and retrieved a ruler. He returned to Stefano, "Hold out your palm."

Stefano did as he was told. The master struck the palm with the ruler three times. "Now, the other palm." Stefano obeyed. The master struck that palm three times, even harder Stefano thought, if that was possible. Stefano refused to react. "We will see you in school tomorrow, won't we?"

Stefano did not answer. His hands hurt throughout the day, and by afternoon the palms were swollen so that it was difficult for the boy to hold a pencil. He did not mention to his mother what had happened. The next morning Stefano's palms were swollen to the point he could not make a fist. The master was wrong about him being in school that day or for that matter any other day. Stefano never went to school again.

CHAPTER FIVE

· ·

ON A PARTICULARLY HOT summer day Stefano rounded the curve in the road leading to his home and stopped in his tracks. He saw that most of the beautiful oak trees were being felled. The sawing and chopping continued as he ran frantically from one man to the next, "Stop! Stop! What are you doing? Who told you that you can cut our trees?"

No one paid a moment of attention to the boy. No matter how loud he screamed, they continued to saw and chop. Stefano ran to the house, yelling for his mother. "Mama, those men are cutting our trees. Stop them!"

"I can't stop them, Stefano. I gave them permission to cut the trees. I sold them."

"But how could you? Nonno loved those trees! He even planted some of them. You can't sell his trees! If you won't stop those men I will." He started for the door.

Mama reached out and firmly took his wrist. "Come sit with me. I will tell you why I sold the trees." When they were seated at the dining table she continued, "I am sick, Stefano. I have to have an operation and treatment to kill the disease. We don't have money for the hospital and doctors. Selling Nonno's trees is the only way I know to get the money, we need."

"But what operation? What's wrong with you?"

"I have something growing here." She pointed to her abdomen. "It has to be taken out so I can be well and take care of you."

The problem was that a few months later the trees were gone and so was Mama. The virulent ovarian cancer ravaged her in a short time. Marta had known for some time that their mother was dying and she diligently reassured her brother that they would be fine. One more time, he was the last to know.

There was the usual wake for Mama, as there had been for Nonno and Ilania and Papa. Food of every description arrived at the home with friends and neighbors as they came to pay their respects. One of the neighbors arrived laden with an entire meal. She was as solemn as if the occasion was her own mother's wake. She pulled back a checkered cloth and started moving the dishes from her basket to the table.

Loud enough for all to hear, she said to Marta, "You know this is the third meal I've had to prepare for you in the past year." Pointing to Stefano she continued, "Try to see if you can keep that one from dying."

Stefano panicked, and Marta was crushed. All he could think of was that he was going to be the next to die, and all Marta could think of was how she'd like to hit the neighbor over the head with her casserole of lasagna. Instead, she smiled and said, "Signora, I will do my best."

Marta and Stefano continued to farm the land with the help of family and friends. It was the way of the community, neighbor helping neighbor, but a household of a 14-year-old girl and an 8-year-old boy would require a lot of help. However, the two children could do little to repay the kindness, so how long could the kindnesses last?

Memories are a fleeting thing for the most part. It wasn't that friends were unkind; it was that they had their own problems. Each family was working long and diligently to keep the wolves from the door, and there are only so many hours in the day. At Mama's wake many offered their assistance, but those lovely offers soon receded. It wasn't a conscious thing but simple self-survival.

Food was in short supply, as were most of the essentials of life. The Capaldis continued with their farming, but Marta's responsibilities were tremendous. Not only did she have to make the farming decisions, with the help of Uncle Sandro, she also had to care for her eight-year-old brother, and that was often taxing in and of itself. The harvest that year was not the greatest due to the lack of sufficient rain, but they stored as much food as they could, and thankfully, Alisha brought forth a calf which they were able to sell. Naturally, people tried to take advantage of the two children who were operating in an adult world. The local butcher bought the calf, and soon realized what a shrewd bargainer Marta could be. When he made her an offer for the calf, Marta scoffed as if she was truly offended.

"But, Signorina, I am but a poor man trying to make a slight living for my wife and children."

"Signore, I don't think you are so poor. Given the girth of your belly you seem to eat well. With the offer you have made to me my waist will be thinner for lack of food." She demanded double the original offer and received it.

One of the sows had two male piglets. At the proper age they were castrated and kept away from the other pigs. They received more than their share of food and grew huge. In the fall when the acorns fell from the remaining oak trees it was Stefano's job to gather them to feed to the pigs. To one side of Stefano's property a neighbor had a huge oak tree with a long branch that hung over the fence. As those acorns fell Stefano gathered them.

One day Signora Esposito, the owner of the big oak, yelled to Stefano while he was gathering acorns. "Those are my acorns. They came from my tree and you're to leave them on the ground. I will gather them."

"But the limb hangs over my property and the acorns fall on my ground. Therefore, they are mine."

"If you continue to take my acorns I will beat you. Do you understand?" She was furious that he didn't seem to fear her.

Stefano didn't respond to her threat. He continued to gather the acorns as she continued to rant. She was still shouting as he picked up his basket and started up the hill to home. He wasn't sure, but he thought the pigs enjoyed those acorns above all the others. He continued his weekly gathering while ignoring Signora Esposito, which wasn't easy. Her ranting became more intense, but his ability to tune her out became more efficient.

Although the slaughter meat was abundant, a great deal of it had to be given to the people who helped in the killing and processing. Marta decided they must sell a portion to the butcher to purchase items that could not be grown on the farm. This time the butcher didn't bother to make an offer, he gave Marta exactly what she asked.

Spring came and Stefano and Marta were down to almost nothing in the larder. Marta had cooked the last of the sausages, which had been preserved by packing them in jars and covering them with olive oil. At that point they were eating only one meal per day. Marta sadly informed Stefano one day that there was now nothing left. There was no money, and all the wheat was gone.

This was early spring and there was nothing yet from the garden. Marta and Stefano had been without food for two days when Signora Francesca came to Marta and asked if she would do a favor. All the men had gone to their respective properties, beginning to toil in their fields. "Marta, I have men working on my other property. I need a favor."

Unfortunately some of the neighbors looked to Marta as if she was just the local servant girl. Since she was not married and did not have children, she couldn't possibly be as busy as they were. Marta sighed, "What is it that you need?"

"I have men working by the river, and I don't want them to stop and come here for their lunch. I will fix a basket and would like for you to take it to them. You should get it to them by about ten o'clock, so come to my door about nine."

Marta could not believe what she was being asked to do, but being of the nature she was, she agreed. It was a long walk, between three and four miles. She retrieved the basket and placed it on her head and began the long trek. There was no food in her house and the tantalizing aromas of the food on her head were agonizing. Her mouth watered as her gut rumbled. She was passing a hedgerow when she couldn't resist any longer. She lowered the basket from her head and examined the contents. She concluded there was more than enough bread for the workers. She took a knife and cut off a large chunk of bread from one of the three loaves. She carefully folded it in a towel from the basket and hid it the bushes. On her way back she rescued the bread and brought it home.

When Marta got to the house she called to Stefano who was mucking out an animal pen. "Stefano, come into the house."

He ran up the slight hill and joined her. She took the towel from the basket and placed it on the table. Almost with reverence she uncovered the bread. "Look what I have for us." She took the knife and divided the bread. At first Stefano began to devour the loaf, but then stopped and forced himself to chew and savor each bite. He felt it was the best bread in the world.

"Think how hard I had to work for this little bread," said Marta.

Stefano wasn't sure how to take the comment. Was she implying that he didn't do any work? He resisted questioning, but the statement bothered him for a long time. He could not be angry with his sister, she did so much to keep them together.

Stefano and Marta survived from donations of some grains and a few vegetables from other local farmers. With the early harvest, their fortunes turned and they were able to exist without daily pangs of hunger. They had a couple of hens and a rooster. More than once Stefano could visualize that rooster in a pot. As if the rooster could read Stefano's mind he chased Stefano many times as if asserting his territorial rights. Marta explained why they could not kill the rooster and one could say that was Stefano's first talk on the birds and bees. The hens lay eggs, which they used and sold. They hatched a nice cluster of baby chicks, which Marta loved, and she could envision many more eggs in the future. She was overly protective and expressed to a friend she was worried the chicks were not eating enough.

The friend gave her the answer. "Put a little vino in their water bowls. It will give them an appetite."

Being the obedient girl that she was, Marta hurried to the wine cellar and drew off about a liter of white wine. She placed this in the water bowls and went about her work. A short time later she looked out and saw the chicks lying on their backs with their feet in the air. Marta became hysterical. She had killed the chicks which were so badly needed! They'd provide eggs and an occasional chicken dinner. Now there would be nothing. A short time later, still pacing in the yard Marta was shocked as she watched one chick after another get up and move about, albeit unsteadily on its feet. She was ecstatic. She and Stefano shared many laughs about the drunken chicks.

The figs seemed more abundant that year and the dark brown fruit was Stefano's favorite. The climate seemed perfect for figs: they didn't grow on bushes but on trees. The abundant Italian sun made them large, syrupy and sweet. Stefano ate figs daily as he gathered the crop for Marta to can and turn into preserves. They sold baskets of the fruit, which enabled them to buy a few staples.

One fig tree had a branch that grew out at about a forty-five degree angle to the ground. Stefano visualized the limb as a motorcycle. He would gather the succulent figs and ride the branch into fantasy land.

His favorite time in the orchard was early in the morning before the sun burned away the chill of the night. There was an old oak tree that produced a double harvest: it had a huge grapevine growing against it and it was right next to a fig tree. The vine produced rich amber yellow, delicious grapes, which became sweeter and sweeter as they ripened in the sun.

There was an age-old problem every year. High up on the tree was a hollow in which bees made a bountiful nest. Stefano had no way of retrieving the grapes. He could only throw rocks and knock down a few grapes at a time. Once, he became overly enthusiastic and threw a rock into the nest. The bees made a straight line for him! An old man had told Stefano that if he ever happened to stir up a bees' hive, he was to throw himself onto the ground and not move. Stefano hit the ground as the man had said and about peed his pants waiting to be stung. Nothing happened. "Wow, that really works."

Unfortunately, Stefano didn't learn from the episode and simply repeated the process with the rock. This time he was stung on the face several times before he could throw himself on the ground. His face was swollen for a week.

About this time Marta and Stefano received a letter from America. An aunt and uncle had sent a letter which informed them that a petition had been made to the United States government for the two of them to come to America. Although they both had great misgivings about leaving their home, they were thrilled that maybe they'd have help with daily life. They talked with Uncle Sandro about the letter and he was very happy for them. However, several weeks passed and they heard nothing more. It fell to Sandro to tell the young ones that it was unlikely they would be able to leave the country even if the U.S. provided them with a visa. With the outbreak of the war, the Italian government decreed that no one would be allowed to emigrate.

CHAPTER SIX

··

AT FIRST IT WAS just rumors. Many of the locals paid little attention since rumors had become as much a part of life in Cervaro as eating pasta. Then there was no mistaking rumor for reality. The Germans first appeared in Cervaro sporadically, but when they came it was always with pageantry. Each visit was as though an important dignitary had arrived. They'd appear in their long staff cars, six-wheel Mercedes, with four wheels to the rear. The swastikas unfurled on the front fenders amid the Heil Hitler poses. It was several weeks after the first spotting in Cervaro that they came to the Capaldi area.

Stefano Capaldi was working in the storeroom over his home when he heard the noise of a vehicle quite unlike any he was used to. He went to the window, but saw nothing at first. Then a large vehicle passed, driving much faster than the locals would. He continued to watch intently, his eyes fixed on the dirt road that passed in front of his home. He'd heard the gossip about the arrival of the Germans but could never imagine they would have any interest in his tiny community. Such a tiny place with so few residents. But Stefano was about to witness a life-changing experience.

The morning dawned bright and beautiful with only wisps of clouds against the brilliant azure sky. Stefano absorbed the beauty of the day but could feel that something bad was about to occur.

From the tiny storeroom window he first spotted the vehicle coming down the road from Cervaro. He ran down the stairs, into the house and took up an observation post at the front window.

Three German soldiers occupied the military vehicle, which stopped directly in front of Stefano's home. They were two officers and a driver. Although there were some adults in their front gardens the officers made no attempt to communicate. They walked around each of the five homes and the scattering of barns and animal shelters.

Stefano broke into a sweat when the Germans walked up the road and seemed to be concentrating on his home. "What are they looking at?" he asked aloud. Then they started toward the house. "Oh, God, what?"

A loud rap came on the door. Stefano didn't answer.

A louder rap. "Die Tür offen-Open the door." No answer.

Three more heavy raps while Stefano hid near the window. There was a lot of loud discussion and he could see the young driver run toward the house. Stefano heard him say in broken Italian, "We saw you at the window. Open the door. We wish you no harm."

Oh, God, where was Marta when he needed her? "At the market you idiot," he murmured to himself. Again he heard the same command.

Slowly, Stefano approached the door, took a deep breath and released the latch.

"Gutten tag," one of the officers said. He then placed his riding crop across Stefano's chest and moved the boy aside. Stefano looked down at the crop and his face turned scarlet. An inner voice told him to remain quiet.

The German officers walked through every inch of the house including the cellar. Then without comment they stepped outside. Stefano followed to make sure they didn't steal anything from the upstairs storeroom. But they went straight to their vehicle, and then the driver waved and said, "Auf Wiedersehen."

Stefano watched as they turned and headed back to Cervaro.

Several of the neighbors quickly huddled in Stefano's garden asking question upon question. When he told them there was nothing to tell he could sense they thought he was lying. Thank God, Marta arrived only moments after the Germans had departed. Stefano was determined he would not allow his sister to see how scared he had been.

Her first questions were to the neighbors, "I saw the three Germans coming from this direction. What did they want?"

"That's what we want to know," said two of the neighbor women in unison.

Marta could tell the neighbors were not pleased with her brother, they were all scowling at him. Then she turned and stared intently at Stefano. "Well, I'm waiting."

"Waiting for what? I didn't talk with them. They ordered me to open the door. I did, and all they did was walk through our house and then they left. They didn't ask for anything or say anything."

Marta was her usual doubting self. "Stefano, come with me." She took his hand and dragged him into the house.

Before she could start, Stefano said, "Look, I told you and everyone else what happened. What am I supposed to do, make stuff up?"

"It's hard to believe they would come in here, look around and leave without saying anything. They must have said something."

With exasperation in his voice, he replied, "Marta, I told you they said nothing. Ask the walls, maybe they heard something I didn't."

"That will be quite enough of that tone of voice."

Stefano sighed and went outside. He climbed the steps up to the storeroom and continued sorting walnuts as he had been doing before the Germans arrived.

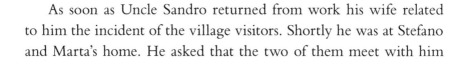

As soon as Uncle Sandro returned from work his wife related to him the incident of the village visitors. Shortly he was at Stefano and Marta's home. He asked that the two of them meet with him at his home. All Stefano could figure was that he was about to get another grilling.

Ever since the two children had been orphaned, they had continued to live alone, but Sandro assumed responsibility for them. Always a mystery was why he didn't take a more active role in making sure that Marta and Stefano had adequate provisions. Maybe with four children of his own he felt overwhelmed. Sandro was a man of few words, generally quiet but with deep feelings. He could make his point very succinctly.

When everyone was settled at his home, Sandro said, "I've been told that the Germans came today and left. I don't think it was a social call; they'll be back. I'm sure with your stubborn independence, Marta, you will not like what I'm about to say. However, I think it would be best if you and Stefano came to live with us while the Germans are here."

Marta sat in silence as if the remainder of her world was being snatched away. To Stefano, it seemed that whenever there was a problem, Marta's first reaction was silence. He wasn't about to remain silent. After all he was "the man of the house."

"That's running away! I won't let the Nazis run us out of our home."

Sandro spoke firmly, "Stefano, I understand how you feel, but it's not safe to antagonize the soldiers and I'm very concerned for your sister. I'm sure they won't be here that long."

Stefano was on his feet pacing. "What do you mean, that long? How long is long? They've been in Italy for almost three years, now. Are they going to leave tomorrow? And I know what you mean about Marta, but she's only a young girl, not a woman."

The comment from his little nephew caught Sandro off guard and he didn't want to pursue the girl-woman line. "Oh, I don't think they will leave of their own volition, but there are rumors that the Allied troops will soon be arriving. If that happens they'll drive the Germans out."

"If! How many times have I been told that if is a big word?" Stefano sulked.

Sandro knew it was pointless to argue with the little red-head. At such times Stefano was like a pit bull—tenacious. The uncle took a deep breath and attempted to hug Stefano, who immediately pulled away.

Sandro's patience was gone. "Now go home and bring what is necessary for you to stay here. Lock the house and come, no more arguing."

It wasn't much of a task for either Stefano or Marta; they had only the barest of necessities. Stefano flung his few clothes into a bed-sheet, tied it into a bundle, tossed it over his shoulder and marched the short distance to Sandro's house, not saying a word to anyone.

During the night Stefano was awakened by the noise of heavy trucks and other noises he couldn't identify. Then there was quiet and he slept. The next morning he looked out the bedroom window and was shocked to see what had happened during the night. As Sandro had said, the Germans were back and in full force. Parked on their small village road were many trucks, personnel carriers, and artillery pieces. Several of the trucks had machine guns mounted to the rear. From his vantage point Stefano could see dozens of soldiers scurrying around following the orders of the arm-waving officers.

When he came downstairs everyone was gathered in the kitchen and Aunt Antonella was going about fixing breakfast as if nothing different was taking place outside. Sandro said, "I felt they would return but not quite so quickly. I think the threesome from yesterday was a scouting party."

"Yeah, and it looks like they invited half of Germany to come to the party. Have you looked at all that stuff they brought? It looks like they intend to fight the entire war right here." Stefano spoke calmly but inside his gut was trembling.

"In that case I think we have capitulated," said Sandro. "Not a one of our neighbors is stirring outside. I think everyone has barricaded themselves in their homes."

When Sandro attempted to go outside he found a German guard at the exterior door who immediately brought his rifle across his chest, finger on the trigger. He shook his head. It was then Sandro realized that the people had not barricaded themselves in; they were not permitted out. They were prisoners in their own homes. Later they were allowed out one at a time to use the outhouse.

Early in the afternoon a sergeant, who could converse slightly in Italian, came to the door. "You can come out of the house, but you must not interfere with the military operation. No one will be hurt if you obey."

Sandro tried to be his most diplomatic self. "These two young ones live in that house." He pointed to Marta and Stefano and then to their home across the road.

The guard was friendly and smiled as he replied, "That is not possible. Officers now occupy that house. You see it is the best because of all the trees and shrubs."

Stefano could see well enough okay and with anger said, "They want it because it has the best protection, that's why they want it."

The sergeant only smiled at the boy.

The proclamation ignited a red seething within Stefano. He watched intensely as the sergeant talked with Sandro. The longer they talked, the angrier Stefano became. *I will go back to my home. They can't just come in and take over. 'All will be well, if you obey.' Well, I don't plan to obey,* he thought.

CHAPTER SEVEN

· ·

STEFANO FELT AS IF he would go crazy if he couldn't check on his home. He could easily see it across the road but it seemed so far away. He spent about three days daydreaming about how things used to be and then he snapped out of it. Though the memories continued to flow, Stefano knew it was time to deal with reality, and he had devised a plan. That evening when he went to bed he immediately drifted into a deep sleep.

Early the next morning there was a heavy fog with drizzling rain. Stefano had slept in his clothes in order to be as quiet as possible He didn't want to awaken his cousin or anyone else in the house. He had heard his uncle leave earlier. Quietly he left Sandro's and brazenly walked across and down the road to his home. Stefano had a plan on getting into the house, but he had not thought about what he would do when he got there. When he rounded the wall he was met by a German in full battle regalia, but his rifle rested against the house.

The soldier quickly grabbed his rifle, slung it over his shoulder, and shouted at Stefano, "Ach, nicht weiter." Watch out, no further.

Stefano continued walking toward the house. The soldier shook his head with an amazed look on his face that the boy would not heed the order. Instantly, he pulled his rifle from his shoulder and pointed it directly at Stefano. The boy had learned something very quickly from Sandro the day before. He raised his hands above his head and slowly backed away.

"Non c'é problema—no problem. Mi dispiace tanto—I'm very sorry." What he really meant was, "Te ne pentirai—you'll be sorry."

Stefano was determined not to retreat; he withdrew to re-group. His determination was to go back to his home. He had learned that confrontation was to be avoided, but he didn't have the patience of his uncle. The following morning the rain continued, no longer a drizzle, but a downpour. In his head Stefano was convinced that no one in his right mind would be out in that kind of weather, including the Germans. The fact that he was venturing out into a torrential rain didn't come into the calculation. He crossed the road. When he arrived at the wall that led to the house, he crouched and crawled to the end. He peered around the wall. Seeing no one he made a quick dash for the stairs to the second floor. Stefano tiptoed across the floor praying that the floor boards wouldn't creak. He could hear voices down below, but he had no idea what they were saying.

Quickly Stefano surveyed of the room, and everything appeared intact. The room was quite large, covering the great room below and part of Luigi's home next door. The rafters were bare except for the bags containing various grains, which hung from hooks attached to the rafters. It didn't appear that anyone had been in the room since he and his sister had left. It then dawned on Stefano that he had been rather stupid. He was inside, but at some point he would have to leave. Soaked from the rain and cold, he huddled next to the chimney that ran up through the floor from below.

Big shot, you're in but how do you get out? he thought. *I can't depend on the rain, it's slowing.* He sat on the floor asking himself question after question about why he was there. He concluded that he wanted to assert himself and prove that the Germans did not control him or his land. Yes, he was the property owner, but he was also a foolish boy.

After about an hour Stefano became aware of a gnawing in his stomach and realized he hadn't eaten anything since the night before. He had been too full of adrenalin that morning as he planned his adventure. Now he was wet, cold and hungry. He looked around the room and spotted a basket of dried figs. He considered cracking some walnuts but smiled at his stupidity considering how much noise that would make.

As Stefano chewed a fig, a plan developed in his mind. He took one of the dish towels that covered the figs and filled it with walnuts and figs. He opened the door and started down the steps. The rain had stopped and the garden was filled with soldiers, who were taken aback as the small boy descended the stairs. Their rifles remained on their shoulders; they just stared. Stefano walked directly to them and presented his gift of fruit and nuts. They looked at each other, smiled and one reached for the towel. He tasted a fig and shook his head up and down to indicate they were good. That soldier spoke rapidly to the others, and Stefano could tell from the animation that they were happy with his homage.

The Germans chatted among themselves and made attempts to communicate with Stefano verbally and with sign language. Then one soldier placed his hand on Stefano's shoulder and guided him around the side of the house. He was both frightened and impressed with the friendliness of the soldier. Alisha's shelter had been converted to a workshop, where a tailor and shoemaker were very busy. The soldier spoke to them and offered them some of the figs.

Stefano was fascinated by the cobbler. He couldn't believe how the man transformed the sheets of leather into a boot. He picked up a pair of boots from the ground and ran his fingers over the smooth leather. They reminded Stefano of his father's tall black boots. Stefano had not thought of Papa's boots and saber in some time. The thought of the saber now brought forth a hidden anger which had festered for years. When his father had died, the saber disappeared. "What right did Uncle Sandro have to take the saber and place it over his mantle? He didn't fight in the war." Whenever he brought it up, Marta would tell Stefano not to mention it. Mama must have given the saber to Sandro.

The Germans were amused at the way he fondled the boots. They also noted he was barefoot. After some time, in broken Italian, they told him to come back the next day.

That night Stefano thought and thought about why the Germans wanted him to come back. He hadn't told his family about his encounter with the soldiers and wasn't about to tell Marta. He could imagine her wails.

With trepidation Sandro returned to his home the following day. The same soldier who had escorted him around the house the day before greeted him with a smile and "Heil Hitler". This did not amuse Stefano in the least, as could be seen by his wrinkled nose and the shaking of his head. The soldier laughed and motioned to Stefano to follow him. They returned to the tailor and cobbler. The tailor greeted the boy and then held up a pair of shorts. The tailor had obviously taken a small-waist pair of soldiers' pants and cut them off to fit Stefano. The cobbler pointed to a log, turned on end, and indicated to Stefano to sit. He then knelt before the boy and fitted him with a pair of shoes that were a little long, but it didn't matter. At the age of ten Stefano had his first pair of shoes! Still wearing the shoes, he grabbed the shorts and ran. It was as if he was afraid the soldiers would take them back.

Stefano ran home to show Marta his new clothes. Quickly he shed his ragged shorts and put on the new pair. He recognized the fabric as that worn by the German infantrymen and his heart was divided. He hated the thought of wearing something German, but then his thoughts quickly shifted to playing football and the next day being able to walk without stones digging into his feet. Marta was not happy that Stefano was wearing German clothing, but he decided he'd ask forgiveness when he said the rosary with Uncle Sandro. Stefano would wear the shorts until the end of the war, and wore the shoes long beyond the point that they fit without squeezing his toes.

CHAPTER EIGHT

· ·

ACROSS THE WORLD RICHIE Thompson awoke from his nap at four in the afternoon. He sobbed into his pillow and then called out for his mother. He was a little old to be taking naps, but since his father had left, Richie had regressed, becoming unnaturally dependent on his mother. Anne Thompson worried for her only child. She, too, missed her husband terribly and often cried into her pillow.

Richie's father, Richard Thompson II, had left seven months earlier after enlisting in the army in late October, 1943. Previously his family's life had followed an All-American pattern. Boy meets girl early in high school, followed by an awkward period of dating. The relationship progresses and only the fear of pregnancy prevents the breaking of celibacy until the marriage. On cue, Richie arrives nine months after the honeymoon, providing an heir to both the name and the family company.

Richard took over the family business at a very early age and had been very successful. He could have run for political office. He was tall, handsome, a fair-skinned Scot, and with the perfect wife and child. The photo ops would be all as they should be. However, Adolph Hitler re-wrote the script.

Richard had been exempt at the beginning of the war because he was CEO of a significant oil company. Much of the refined oil his company produced aided the war effort. It was a shock to everyone in his life when he announced he was temporarily passing the company baton to his uncle and joining the Army Air Corps.

The young man, a first generation American, had been instilled with the meaning of right and wrong since he was a toddler. From the time America had entered the war Richard was constantly torn internally. He recognized his obligation to the company and knew he was contributing to the war effort, but he still felt he should be in the military. The Board of Thompson Oil had insisted that he apply for a deferment, which he did, but inwardly he called himself a coward. The Board reminded Richard that he was doing his part by furnishing a steady stream of oil to the military. He sensed, though, that they were more interested in the profits of Thompson Oil than in the defense of the United States.

By mid-1943 Richard couldn't live with himself. He and Anne were relaxing, coming down from the high of making love, sharing a cigarette. He was holding her hand when she broke his thoughts. "Richard, you're hurting my hand. That's not a squash ball you're holding."

"Oh, my God! I'm sorry, I didn't realize." He rolled over and took the cigarette from her lips. He took a drag and placed it in the ashtray on his bedside table. He rolled back to her and placed his hand across her waist, pulling her closer to him. "Anne, we have to talk."

Anne jumped up, grabbed her dressing gown from the foot of the bed and headed toward the bathroom. "Richard, let's don't ruin a lovely evening."

"Anne, please come back. You can't keep running away from any discussion of the war. It's not going away and I'm not going to run away from the issue any longer. Please, hear me out."

She stopped in the bathroom doorway, slipped on her dressing gown and leaned against the doorframe. "I knew where your mind was when you began to tighten your grip on my hand."

Richard stood and walked to her, pulling her into his arms. "I repeat, I'm sorry I hurt you. You know I would never intentionally hurt you in any way."

She leaned her head against his bare chest. "But you would hurt me so much if you enlisted."

He released her and ushered her to the bed. She sat on the edge of the bed and he sat cross-legged next to her. "Hear me out. I can't live with myself. I'm a pilot and a darned good one according to my instructors."

Anne interrupted, "Yes, you're a pilot and every time you go flying I'm worried sick until you walk back into the house."

"I understand that and appreciate how much you love me." Underneath he was thinking, *I wish you weren't so damn dependent on me.*

"Richard, you have your deferment. Think how many men would trade anything for that piece of paper and not have to go into this damned war."

"I don't doubt that for a moment, but I'm not one of them." He placed his arm over her shoulders and sat closer to her. "Last Saturday when Richie came home from the movies he said that he had seen newsreels of the war in Europe. He told me all about what he had seen and then asked me why I wasn't in the military like his best friend Larry's father. I could hardly look him in the eyes. I felt like such a fool and hypocrite when I attempted to explain."

"Don't use your son in that manner, Richard. It's not becoming of you."

"That's so unfair, but I understand. I wasn't making excuses. Fact is fact. Tomorrow I'm going to the recruiting station and I hope you'll go with me and support me. Now come to bed and make love to the newest soldier." He attempted to loosen her dressing gown.

"You're not the horny doughboy yet." She stood as if starting for the bathroom, stopped, loosened the sash and allowed the gown to fall from her shoulders. Richard reached for her hand and pulled her to him, burying his face between her breasts.

"Oh, God, I thought you were going to walk away again."

She pushed him back on the bed. "I've never been able to stay mad at you. I loathe what you're going to do, but I'll try to understand."

Richard's recruitment, physical and orders were all completed in less than two weeks. The company board actually tried to bully him into changing his mind. For the most part his uncle was very quiet, which didn't surprise Richard. He'd known for a long time that his uncle wanted the reins of the company. It was an older cousin who raised the most ruckus. "Richard, this is almost like treason to your country. You have a duty to produce as much oil as possible."

That comment brought Richard up short. "Franklin, I'm not sure how to respond to that comment." He paused momentarily and the remainder of the board sat aghast looking at Franklin. Then Richard continued. "I'll tell you what. I will stay if you agree to go to the recruiting center and enlist."

Franklin didn't respond but stood and left the room, red-faced.

Richard ended the board meeting with, "Gentlemen, after this little set-to, facing Hitler should be a snap." He turned to his uncle, "Arthur, this ship is yours until I come back, and I assure you, I plan to come back." Following basic training he was assigned to the 15th Strategic Air Force.

CHAPTER NINE

. . . .

AS TIME WENT ON, Stefano was allowed to come and go as he wished. He was resigned to the fact that the officers had established a headquarters in his home, and he had to admit that they seemed to be caring for the property well. They may have been the enemy, but they were a fastidious enemy. He was still resentful, but more accepting.

Stefano's unlimited freedom and reconciliation with his situation didn't set well with some of the neighbors, though. A couple of the women made snide remarks to Marta, calling Stefano a collaborator. What was worse, one was the same woman who had made the unkind remarks at Mama's wake. Marta was so completely taken aback by the woman's comments she was at first unable to reply. The second time she was more prepared and confronted the older woman with confidence.

"Signora Carini, it seems you have a difficult time saying anything nice about my brother. First you wonder if he will die soon and now you insinuate that he is Hitler's right hand man in Cervaro."

Marta's frank manner caught Signora Carini off guard. The older woman replied, "Well, I simply try to speak the obvious."

Marta added, "It's obvious that you don't like me, and for some strange reason, dislike my brother even more. Therefore, don't ever bother with us again." Marta walked away with her head held high, pleased with herself.

Later she relayed the conversation to her Uncle Sandro who congratulated her on her courage. "You did the right thing. Don't worry about it. She'll try to spread more rumors. She's an idle, evil, old woman who thinks the worst of everyone. Most of the people around here know her for what she is and will not give a second thought to her spreading of rumors."

When Nonno was alive, he had produced the best white wine in the region. Some was sold to the bartender in town, but after Marta became the head of the household she refused to sell any of the wine that had been made by her grandfather. It was as if it represented a memorial to him. She should have sold it, since the family never got to drink any of it. The German officers' cook, who worked in their home, found the wine casks in the basement. From that point on the cook had to have a daily supply, either to cook with or to get crocked. Some days he went in search of "cooking wine" and returned to the kitchen rather unsteadily. Apparently he had to sample several wines before he found the proper one for the dish he was preparing.

Stefano took it as his occupation to hassle the cook, who resented the boy's penetrating eyes. Often Grasso Gunther—fat Gunther—as Stefano called him behind his back, would find a stone to throw at Stefano, which made the boy laugh. The cook was sloshed most of the time and incapable of hitting the dodging target. He only hit Stefano once when a potato caught the boy behind his left knee.

The Germans had arrived in town with more than armament. They also brought cows, sheep and goats, which had probably been confiscated from local farmers. An officer made the decision that Stefano would have to herd the livestock, but Sandro had another plan. To the interpreter he said, "Stefano is too young to care for that many animals. I will herd the animals."

Stefano overheard the conversation and tried to argue that he was the family shepherd and most certainly could take care of three extra cows and a few goats and sheep. "Why am I no longer the shepherd?

I've been caring for Alisha and the other animals for years. What's happened?"

Sandro was fairly certain that the Germans didn't understand why Stefano was upset, but he didn't want any further discussion. He ended the conversation with his usual, no nonsense voice, and "I know you can do it, but now I will do it. It would be better if I took care of all the cows and you take care of the sheep and goats."

Stefano was frustrated but knew better than to argue with Sandro when he used that particular tone of voice.

Quietly each morning, Sandro herded the Germans' three cows and Alisha to the far back field. They only grazed there for an hour, but that's where they always started the day. During that hour all four cows were "partially" milked by Sandro. He took enough from each cow to supply his extended family. In the evening when the normal milking was done there was still plenty for the Germans, a couple of liters would never be missed.

Uncle Sandro never revealed how he brought his "stolen" milk to the house without being caught. During the occupation, necessity reared its head in many ways.

Daily, Stefano and others in the village had to peel potatoes for the cook. This was an assigned job for women, older men and children. The young men were conscripted to the lines to dig foxholes, establish artillery placements and perform other laborious tasks. The cook didn't like any of the villagers, least of all Stefano. The feelings were mutual, only Stefano got a kick out of harassing Gunther.

One day Gunther called, "Hey, Sie." Although he was called Stefano by all the soldiers, the cook refused to call him by name, just "Hey, you." Stefano pretended not to hear the call until a couple of potatoes whizzed past his head.

He turned and with a broad smile and a shrug of his shoulders, said, "Mi-me?" The boy reeked of innocence.

The cook was always complaining that he didn't think Stefano was working hard enough. Stefano made him more irate by mocking him and his speech. It was a daily battle. The cook was even more rattled that the other soldiers found the daily skirmish between the man and boy hilarious. This only served to encourage Stefano.

Cook had managed to keep Nonno's wine supply to himself until the day the Captain became irritated that he had not seen the man. He told one of the soldiers to check the basement. The soldier found the cook propped up against a wine barrel with a large glass of wine. When this was reported, the Captain made an instant decision. No longer would the cook be allowed to go to the basement alone, each man would now be allowed a daily ration of wine. It became a game; they would shoot a hole in the end of the barrel and catch the wine as it poured out. The next day a soldier would shoot another hole about one-half inch below the last hole. And so it went until the barrel looked like a honeycomb and the wine was gone.

The entire community was forced to work in the war effort. One day, to the villagers surprise, all of the artillery and tanks left. This brought on another rash of rumors, and as much as everyone hoped the Allies were moving closer, there was no evidence to substantiate that tale. The remaining German contingent was a support company whose mission was to provide food for the battle lines. The Italian women were assigned to bake bread and cook food in mass quantities, all of which was carried by truck forward to the combat lines. For the famished locals, watching food being prepared and then shipped off to others was unbearable.

Sandro's house would later be designated as the main cookhouse, since it was the largest house in the neighborhood. It had to be big in order to house Sandro, his wife and their seven children, five of whom still lived at home. The house was built in 1911. There was a large room to the left with its gigantic fireplace. Behind that room, to the right, was a set of stairs which led to the upper rooms. In the center of the house, on the front, was what appeared to be a front door, but it led to the wine cellar. The last room to the right was the cow stable. When Stefano moved in, he shared a bed with his cousin Polombo who was two years older. They shared an interest in football but had little else in common. Yet, they adapted quickly.

In the early days of the German occupation, in spite of the crowded conditions, the villagers were all determined to lead their lives as normally as possible. They were allowed to continue their farming and care-taking of their animals. However, shortages of everything, especially seeds and fertilizer, meant they couldn't keep their farms going. Gradually all activities in the community ground to a halt. First shops, then schools and finally government services closed. Life slowed to a crawl.

As the war heated up, the Germans were impacted by the shortages as much as the locals were. The townspeople monitored these developments nervously. They knew where the Germans would turn once their resources had dried up. The convoys that had arrived daily to re-supply the German troops slowed to a trickle. The livestock which had been brought in to feed the soldiers slowly disappeared. When they no longer had meat they slaughtered Alisha. To his horror, Stefano watched as the soldier struck Alisha in the head with a sledgehammer. She fell to her knees and then onto her side. The soldiers immediately cut her throat and hung her from a tree. Stefano was incensed. Inside him something died along with Alisha. At that moment he suppressed outward emotion, but hate boiled inside. He no longer cried.

As the German confiscation increased, the citizens struggled to find enough food to sustain normal life. It became obvious that the Germans would eventually take everything that was edible. The townspeople had to secure their stores in whatever way possible, and survival was the first order of every day.

Sandro was determined to care for his family. He devised a plan. "The only way to save our remaining food from the Germans is to hide it. Gather all of the empty wine jugs, they're about five liters each, and we'll fill them with whatever we have left."

Marta and Stefano were sent to their home to round up the jugs that had not been smashed by the Germans. Interestingly, they never broke anything in the house. Like dogs, the Germans didn't soil their beds. Early on, the troops invented a game using the jugs. They would set a jug about 50 meters away. Then they'd throw rocks to see who could smash the most jugs. Unfortunately, there were several accurate pitchers. As Marta and Stefano lugged the remaining jugs, the two children were amazed that the soldiers never paid any attention or asked questions about what they were going to do with the empty jugs, even after three trips. Stefano quipped to Marta, "They're bound to lose the war, they're so stupid."

"Stop it," admonished Marta. "We never know which ones understand us and which ones don't."

That night the jugs were filled with corn, wheat, flour and legumes, then they were taken to the back of the garden under a cluster of trees and were buried in deep holes. Leaves were then raked to conceal the burial grounds. Although soldiers searched Sandro's home on more than one occasion, they showed no surprise that there were no staples to be found.

A few days later a military truck arrived in front of Sandro's home, the cookhouse, and the German soldiers unloaded several sacks of flour. Through an interpreter, Aunt Antonella, Marta and a couple of other women were instructed by the cook how to mix the flour with water to make dough. The instructions were given as though the women had never baked bread in their lives. It was true they had never made bread in such a haphazard manner. Antonella quipped, "The Germans may know how to make dumplings but they know nothing about making bread."

The dough was divided into small balls and then flattened. A large pot was half filled with oil and the disks of dough were fried. The result was like pita bread with no flavor, just oily. The "pitas" were then loaded into woven baskets and taken by truck to the front. The women fried dozens and dozens of the breads.

A guard was posted with the women to assure that they didn't eat or keep any of the bread. Each evening the Germans carried away the left-over flour. However, when people are hungry they become very resourceful. Occasionally an especially thin pita would find its way between the tablecloth and the table. Marta was fairly sure the guard knew what was happening, but he never gave a hint he had seen anything. It would be kind of hard not to notice the lumpy tablecloth. After a couple of days, Antonella devised her own scheme. When they had finished for the day, she whispered to Gina and Anna, as she kissed them goodbye, "Tomorrow when you come bring a white tablecloth."

"Why do you want another cloth? If that one's unclean, let them eat dirt," said Gina with glee.

Antonella didn't want the conversation to arouse the guard's suspicion. "Hush. Just each of you bring a cloth."

The following morning, before the guard arrived, Antonella took the two new cloths and laid them over the old one with the hems slightly over lapping in the center of the table. There was a slit down the entire length of the table. It was quite easy to slide the pitas into the slit.

During this time it was obvious the fighting was becoming fiercer. Most nights the drone of bombers could be heard overhead. At other times the explosion of bombs could be heard in the distance and sometimes they were not so distant. Often there were lower passes by light bombers. It was a frightening time for everyone.

Stefano was as frightened as anyone, but only when the planes were very close would he allow himself to react, and then he did his best to hide his fear. One particular day he was certain the approaching plane was headed for his village. He ran for a German foxhole and dove in. There had been several days of rain and the hole was a quarter full with water. Stefano was drenched from top to bottom. When he could no longer hear the plane, he crawled out of the hole and ran home. It was one of the few times that Marta allowed herself to laugh. At first Stefano was shocked that his sister would laugh at him, or for that matter, laugh at all. Then he had to laugh at himself. She took him to the well and poured bucket upon bucket of water over him to wash away the mud, and gave him a towel and clean clothes. He shut out her admonishment to stay clean. He knew as well as she that he didn't have another change of clothes.

Cousin Polombo couldn't resist teasing. "Stefano, you going to become a sailor?"

At first Stefano was angry, but then saw Polombo laughing. "I always wanted a pond in my backyard. I thought I'd try that one out." They laughed and went about their work.

As the fighting got closer to Cassino, air battles became more frequent. Stefano looked up and saw a German and an Allied plane engaged in a dog fight. He was fascinated and watched from the road in front of his home. A stray projectile from one of the planes whizzed past his head. He made a beeline for the house. The two planes apparently ran out of ammunition and flew off in opposite directions. It was necessary to be aware constantly. The Allies were targeting the area daily. Late evening and very early morning became the times to work. The Germans rarely ventured out of their shelters during the day. They had been prepared for months and then waited for the fight to come to them. The German high command never talked about it with the troops, but the grunts knew it was only a matter of time before the Allies invaded.

Very early one morning a vehicle arrived with the requisite Swastikas flying. It was a Mercedes, a four-wheel type, not a high staff car. There were four men; the driver, a sergeant, a young trooper and a captain. As soon as the vehicle arrived, the young man jumped down and opened the door for the captain. He then ran to the door of Sandro's house and knocked on the door to the wine cellar. Sandro heard the knocking but ignored it. Finally the young soldier came to the door to the house. Sandro answered and walked outside, closely followed by Stefano and Polombo.

The captain raised his right arm. "Heil, Hitler." No one returned the gesture. The captain continued. He'd grown used to Italians refusing to pay homage to Hitler. "Ich bin Captain Rechstop—I am Captain Rechstop—und Ich hier lebe—and I live here." The young soldier translated with broken Italian. Without further ceremony Rechstop stuck out his riding crop across Sandro's chest as if to move the larger man aside. Sandro's face turned scarlet and his fists clenched tightly. He didn't say anything but he didn't budge.

As he walked through the house Rechstop moved items about with the crop. He made faces as if he disliked the smell of the place. That really irritated the women. They always kept the home spotless. Being as crowded as they were, rigid housing rules had to be maintained. The captain went up the steps and checked the bedrooms. He stepped into one and announced, "This will be my bedroom. Move all of your possessions out."

Sandro spoke to the young boys, "Polombo, move all of your things out of the room; you will move to the bed with Danilo. Stefano we'll clear a place for you in the storage room on the side of the house. Come with me and I'll help you clean out that room." Normally, that may not be something that the man of the house would do, but Sandro felt he had best get away from the German officer before he lost his temper, something they would surely all regret.

To Sandro's chagrin the officer followed them out of the house, and when he saw the place for Stefano in the storage room, he assigned his assistant to room with Stefano. The young soldier made a cursory reply. It was quickly apparent to Stefano that the young man had little respect for his commanding officer.

The soldier, Karl, and Stefano got along very well. Karl had a reasonable handle on Italian and Stefano had learned many words while listening to the Germans, some of which he repeated inappropriately to the delight of the Germans.

Before Karl enlightened Stefano, he didn't know that Karl was cussing. They had only been sharing quarters for a short time when Stefano tried to show off what he had learned from Karl. Stefano was in their room on his pallet when Karl came in.

Stefano calmly said, "Scheissen die tur, bitte."

Karl looked at him in astonishment and started laughing so hard he fell to the floor holding his side. Stefano was offended as he was sure he had the sentence right, and after all he had been polite and added the bitte—please. "When you try to speak Italian I don't laugh at you."

"Oh mein Gott—my God, if you merde—shit—on the door, it would get so dirty." Karl started laughing just as hard again. "The word you wanted is schliessen. That is the word for close." Then they both were laughing hysterically.

Most of their communication was still through sign language, but each learned from the other. The 19-year-old German related he had a brother back at home about the same age as Stefano. They passed their time together talking about everything. At night after they had settled in they would idly talk, with Stefano having many questions about girls. Karl related that he had a girlfriend back in Germany who he was sure would be waiting for him and they would marry. Stefano finally told of his love for a girl in Cervaro. He had never told her how he felt. Now she had gone away to stay with relatives until the fighting was over.

Karl was willing to struggle through any conversation except discussing the war. One evening, soon after they started sharing the room, Stefano questioned Karl to learn what was happening with the German troops. It was simple boyish curiosity. He had no plan to use the information. "Karl, do you know how far away the Allied troops are?"

"Don't ask me questions like that. I don't want to talk about it. I don't know anything anyway. This whole thing is so stupid. So many of my friends and family will be killed. No more talk about the war." The subject was verboten. Stefano honored Karl's wishes, and they managed to get along fine. In the early evening they would sit outside, and Stefano tried to teach Karl the card game, Briscola, but it was useless. Stefano simply didn't have the words to describe the game.

Assignments kept Karl busy most of the day. He had to polish the captain's boots, brush and press his uniforms, bring food and prepare his trays and carry messages. The captain always ate alone in his upstairs room. On more than one occasion Stefano would see Karl picking up a clump of ashes from the fireplace and sprinkling them over the captain's food. Each time the assistant did this a small smile would show at the corners of his mouth.

Stefano couldn't figure what was going on and finally asked, "Why do you put ashes in his food?"

Karl grinned, "Because he is a total arschlock—asshole—and I hate him." Karl saw the questioning look on Stefano's face. He laughed and pointed to his backside. Stefano's German vocabulary expanded again. "He's so stupid, he doesn't know the difference. He does ask why I use so much black pepper."

There was a well to the side of the property that supplied all the water for three families and now the German military, too. Giovanni, Sandro's son who was two years older than Polombo, was told by the Germans that he was "their water boy." Each day a tank truck would arrive, and Giovanni had to fill the tank from the well. It was a huge tank, and it had to be parked about 35 yards from the well.

Stefano laughed to himself as Giovanni would moan and groan about how tired he was. Yet, he never passed up a chance to show off his developing biceps.

There was a soldier guarding Giovanni to make sure he didn't put anything in the water. The soldier gave the young man a terrible time, often shouting, "Schnell, schnell laufen—run quick—schnell." Giovanni always maintained his regular pace, pretending he didn't understand. After several weeks, a routine was established. The soldier would shout and Giovanni would ignore. One day Giovanni trudged down the road, dumped the water into the tank and then stood draining the last drops over his head. The soldier was waving for Giovanni to return to the well when he sustained a direct hit from a mortar. Giovanni dropped to his knees, made a sign of the cross over his chest, and said, "Thank you, God."

Stefano ran to look at the soldier. The head was split and brain matter was hanging out of the skull. Saying nothing to anyone he walked into the house and picked up a frying pan. He started out of the house when Marta stopped him. "Where are you going with that pan?"

"I'm going to fry his brains and eat them. They killed our Alisha and ate her brains. Don't you see how much I hate them?"

Marta quickly found Sandro, who put an end to the brain fry.

Captain Rechstop paced, waved his arms and screamed at Giovanni as though he had been the one to drop the shell on the soldier. Sandro quickly intervened, and with the help of Karl, managed to get a message across to the Captain. "If you want water, don't kill the water-bearer."

After a few days Giovanni disappeared. He didn't say anything to his parents because he didn't want them to worry or to know where he had gone. The captain's plan had been for Polombo and Stefano to take over Giovanni's duties, but even he had to acknowledge the boys were not physically developed enough to handle the job. An unknown young man arrived to take over as water-bearer. He was a stranger to the community who disappeared each afternoon and arrived back with the tank truck the next morning. No one could figure out why he never spoke. He may have heard the rumors that they were collaborating with the Germans and he wanted no part of that.

Giovanni managed to hide in haystacks during the daylight hours as he gradually moved closer and closer to the forest where he joined many other young men in hiding, each wanting to become a part of the resistance movement.

Giovanni soon found that the resistance movement was basically resistant to getting anything done. He moved from one group to another, each time becoming more frustrated. Finally he found a group that seemed to be more organized than the others and he met a young man with whom he felt he could relate.

Emilio had come from a village not far from Anzio and appeared to have more experience than most of the band. One evening Giovanni approached his new friend and asked to have a quiet conversation. "Emilio, try to help me understand what we are doing here in the forest. It seems we talk and talk but don't take any action."

Emilio rose from the stump on which he had been seated, walked back and forth as if in deep contemplation. He then stopped in front of Giovanni and asked, "You are new here; how can you ask such a question? You want to run the show already. We are making many serious plans, and we will be victorious."

"I think I understand that, but what I'm asking is when am I to do something?"

Emilio gestured madly, "You want to run the show? You want to lead?"

"Hey, l'amico, calm down. I just asked a small question."

"We believe in sharing, yes, but there have to be those who direct. When we are victorious we will all share equally." Immediately Giovanni knew he had landed in the middle of a group of communists. He knew that his best move was to get out while he still could. He wasn't going to find what he was looking for with communists.

The war grew more intense with each passing day, and nothing seemed to make sense. One day, without any discussion, Colonel Rechstop came down the stairs and announced to Sandro that in a few days it would not be safe for the family to be out of doors. Soon his assistant, Karl, came down the steps with the officer's gear. Without another word the two walked out to a car, climbed in, and they were gone.

The colonel's prediction proved accurate. It was Sunday, a gray overcast day with a bone chilling wind blowing down from the mountains. Aunt Antonella could only smile when she thought of the little food left behind by the Germans. There was a piece of meat of some origin which she combined with the few vegetables and made a wonderful stew. Everyone sat down to enjoy the feast. Sandro had just finished the blessing when there was a knock on the door. Two heavily armed soldiers informed the family that they had to evacuate and had two hours to gather what they wanted to take with them.

Sandro argued, "We would prefer to stay here to care for our home." He calculated that if the Allies came they could not be worse off.

The Germans shook their heads, "That is not possible. We have highest orders and now you must obey." It was a strange manifestare—manifesto—protect the people who are your captives. Ironically the Germans seemed to feel responsible for the local people.

The family came together to plan their exodus. They knew they must prepare to live wherever they were taken. Pots and pans, utensils, blankets and the few staples that were left at that point were packed into sheets and tied into bundles. Sandro received permission to take the donkey and cart, enabling them to take a few more things. Sandro harvested a ration of grain from the jugs and replant them. Antonella went to the basement and returned with two small sacks of wheat and flour. Everything was piled in the cart, and they waited for orders and directions. As they started to move under the directions of the soldiers, Stefano grabbed Polombo by the arm and dragged him back to the house. Surprisingly, the soldiers didn't try to stop them.

Polombo was repeating, "Where are we going? We can't stay here."

Stefano beamed, "Come on, we have to get something."

They entered the house and Stefano made a quick survey. He grabbed a stack of bowls which had been left on a shelf. He handed those to Polombo and then with towels grabbed the stewpot from the fireplace. They caught up with the family and as they walked, each family member dipped a small bowl into the stew and ate directly from the bowls.

They joined a convoy of neighbors and people from surrounding villages No one had any idea where they were going. They were simply told to follow those in front. The ones in front were told to follow the military vehicles loaded with soldiers.

CHAPTER TEN

AS IT MOVED NORTHWARD, the caravan of displaced people was silent, a silence born of fear. For a time, it was as if the women's tear glands had dried up. The questions continued about where they were going or what was to happen to them, as usual, all being ignored by the Germans. That morning no fighting was evident. Even the birds had seemed to disappear. Silence dominated except for the rumble of the military vehicles.

Communication from the Germans consistently was one impatient command, schnell--hurry! Ostensibly, they were leaving for their own safety. On the other hand, the Germans rode in the leading vehicles and the Italians walked, with the riders pushing the walkers to go faster. It was about twelve kilometers to Ponte Corvo, which turned out to be a gathering area for families coming from all directions south. The scene was like the piazza of St. Peter's on a Sunday morning with hundreds saying the rosary. Eventually, the women were again crying and wailing for their loved ones, as if on command of a choir leader's baton.

The evacuation had been so sudden that family members who were away from home returned to find their villages deserted, No messages had been left because the villagers had no way of knowing where they would be.

Sandro had to make spur-of-the-moment decisions, the main one being to keep his anger inside, rather than strike out as he'd like to do. Above all he didn't want to be perceived as a trouble maker and be separated from his family.

Stefano could sense the discomfort of his uncle and made comments which Marta felt inappropriate. "They're going to wear my short legs down to my butt." He was trying to distract the others from the dreadful situation. He also felt it was safer to make jokes than to voice out loud what he was thinking. Karl had taught him significant cuss words that would have fit the moment, but it would be stupid to say them. Enjoyable but stupid.

Confusion escalated by the minute as rumors intensified. However, even the worst of rumors didn't prepare anyone for the next scene. Tractor-trailers pulled into the square where everyone had been herded, and the Germans began to divide the masses into groups which were then herded into the trailers. They were told they could only carry personal necessities due to the lack of space.

Finally, Sandro's frustration exceeded logic, and he began to argue with a young private. "You are the one who told me that we could bring the donkey cart, and we loaded it with belongings that you now say we can't take with us."

In fluent Italian, the private replied, "I'm very sorry. No one told me this was going to happen. Believe me, we're told little more than you are."

As much as Sandro believed the young man, it did little to assuage his anger. "But what will become of our things? What will happen to the donkey? We won't go. We'll return to our home."

He turned and began to tell the family about the change of plans. The private placed a hand on Sandro's shoulder, "Please, Signore, don't try to do that. In order to prevent anyone from challenging the orders, we're told to shoot the first one who resists. It's to be an example to the others. Place yourself in my position—Sie sich in meine Lager Verstzen. You must do it, please—Sie mussen es tun, bitte."

As much as Stefano hated what he saw happening, he felt sorry for the private. He had been one of the soldiers who had been the nicest to Stefano back in their village, and he didn't want the young man to be shot for disobeying orders. Without comment Stefano picked up the bed sheet containing his share of the family possessions and moved to the trailer. Numbly, the family stared and then quietly followed.

Stefano looked over his shoulder as he moved forward in the trailer. The German private caught his eye, nodded and smiled. In a short time the trailer was crowded with far too many bodies. There was no room to sit, everyone stood with their possessions wedged between their legs. It was oppressively hot with bodies pressed against bodies. The sweat of fear was palpable. Breathing was especially difficult for short people. At times Stefano felt faint, but was determined he could take anything the Germans dished out.

At around two o'clock in the morning the truck came to an abrupt halt. The rear doors opened and everyone was ordered out with the usual, "Schnell. Schnell."

About a hundred people men, women and children stood beside the road and stared into the darkness, disoriented from the journey and anxious to know what was to happen next. Other than the order to hurry, there was no comment from the Germans.

Finally, someone demanded, "Where are we?"

"This is Ferentino."

With that comment, the two soldiers got back into the truck and drove off into the night.

Sandro rounded up his brood under a canopy of trees near the roadside. "There is nothing we can do now. There is not even a moon to help us find our way, even if we knew where to go. We don't want to go into the city because that's where the Allies are most likely to bomb first. So, wrap yourselves in your blankets and huddle together. In the morning we'll make a decision on what to do."

Stefano wrapped himself snuggly in his blanket but rejected Marta's offer to cuddle. "Marta, don't you think I'm a little old to be cuddling with my sister?" She was amused later that night when she felt Stefano inch his body close to hers.

At daybreak Sandro roused Antonella. "Let the children sleep as long as they can. They were all so exhausted last night. I'll go in search of a place to stay." He kissed her on her forehead, which startled her. There had been no tenderness or affection for such a long time from Sandro. Antonella watched as he headed through the morning fog and mist into the forest.

The fog was appropriate, as it symbolized Sandro's thinking. He couldn't see a clear path forward for his family. What was wrong with his country? He had memories of the time he had spent in America and how peaceful everything had been. That's all he wanted for his loved ones. Would any of them ever see peace again?

Gradually the children arose as the morning sun filtered through the trees. At first they were disoriented but soon enough reality oriented them, not to where they were but to how they were. Marta awoke last and apologized to Antonella.

"Heaven, why did you let me sleep? I should be helping you."

"Shush, Marta, you must have needed the sleep and what's the hurry? And, what is it you're going to help me do? There's nothing to do. Sandro has gone to search for a place to stay. There are no floors to sweep, no dishes to wash, and we have nowhere to run off to right now."

Antonella had gathered twigs and small branches to build a fire. She then placed the cooking grate over the fire. The grate was one of the first things she had packed, knowing it would be needed. As each person awakened she placed a slice of bread on the grate. When it had toasted on one side she would turn it. Danilo asked, "May we have some oil on the bread?"

Antonella smiled, but it was a sad smile as she denied her child, "We have very little oil. Just eat your bread."

The boys had devoured their toast with gusto and longingly looked at Antonella. She ached for them, but calmly stated, "I'd love to give you another slice, but we have little bread, and we have no idea when we will find more."

About noon, Sandro returned with wonderful news. "I've found a nice lady with a great home. She has a large room where we can live. Everyone gather up your things; we have a distance to walk."

The home was built on three levels and the room Sandro's family was to occupy could be entered from the outside by descending a few steps. It only had a dirt floor, but the room was large enough to accommodate everyone. There were seven in the group.

The first order of business was to furnish the room. Small tree branches were cut to make bed frames. Loose hay, the residual from a harvested field, was used to make mattresses. Pieces of log were used for seating. There was a large fireplace for cooking and heat. The women created the best home they could. Polombo and Stefano shared a bed, Marta and her cousin shared, and Danilo slept at the foot of his parents' bed. Each morning the blankets were neatly folded at the foot of each bed.

Food was rationed from the beginning. The owner of the house shared as much as she could but she had little herself. Each day, Antonella formed flour and water into a ball of dough, stretched it out, and cut it into noodles. With whatever she could find, maybe just a few vegetables, she would make soup and add the noodles to it. They ate one meal a day, just after noon. Over time, Danilo complained less of hunger. His stomach had shrunk, as had everyone's.

Polombo and Stefano foraged daily and would often return with nothing more than a few dandelion greens. Antonella would dress them with a few drops of olive oil. As Stefano ate the salad, he became sad. It made him think of Alisha. Then he smiled thinking how Alisha had seemed to enjoy greens even with no olive oil.

———————⌒———————

Sandro and Antonella's two oldest children were married and off on their own. Giovanni, their third child, had found the resistance movement would never be more than talk, so he moved on and joined the Red Cross. He was able to move about the country with ease, as long as he wore his armband.

After many weeks Giovanni was able to locate his family and one day arrived at their new home with a few potatoes. The boys were very glad to see him, and more glad when they saw the potatoes. He told them where he had found the potato patch and suggested it could be a daily source of food.

That was the most intriguing idea the boys had heard in a long time. Giovanni left the next day and Stefano and Polombo decided it was time to "go hunting". The idea of potatoes was so fascinating that Stefano dreamed of gnocchi throughout the night.

The two set off early in the morning following Giovanni's specific directions. They easily found the fence surrounding the potato field, and Stefano knew from the looks of the potato plants that they were ready for harvest. Tracing the fence around the field, they finally found the gap described by Giovanni. They had brought a large basket with them and had to expand the hole under the fence, digging with their hands, in order to get the basket through. Once they were inside Stefano slapped his forehead, "Why, just tell me, why I didn't throw the basket over the fence?"

Polombo looked at his cousin and shrugged his shoulder as he said, "Could be you're not very smart."

Stefano hit Polombo over the head with the basket and then they went quietly about harvesting "their" potatoes. They were careful not to dig two plants together but scattered about trying to make it less conspicuous that they had been there. The basket was filled quickly and Stefano scampered through the hole, and Polombo managed to lift the heavy basket over the fence to him, and they joyously headed for home with enough potatoes for two large meals.

They had made two successful harvests, but when they returned to the potato field the third time, they were aghast to find that the gap in the fence had been securely patched and the dirt hole filled.

Stefano repeatedly ran his hand over the wire as if it might magically disappear. He sighed, "Okay, let's look for another place to get through the fence."

"I don't think that's such a good idea. The fact that the farmer patched the fence means he knows he has had intruders. He probably will be watching for us and I've no desire to get shot."

"But he has so many potatoes. Maybe if we ask, he will sell us some," Stefano fantasized aloud.

"And what are you going to use for money?"

"Oh, yeah, that's a point. Maybe if we ask, he'll give us some."

Polombo slapped Stefano on the arm. "Again, I don't think that's a good idea. It would be like saying, "We've been stealing your potatoes, but now that we can't steal any longer, would you give us some?"

As they headed home, Stefano wistfully said, "They sure were good potatoes. Do you suppose they were better because they were stolen?"

Polombo was taken aback by the statement until he looked at Stefano's beaming face. "Come on, I'll leave it up to you to give my mother the bad news."

"Thanks, friend."

It was hard to figure the Germans, although Stefano spent many hours trying to do so. There were the nice guys, like he had first met at the house, and generally the enlisted men were friendly and easy to get along with. For the most part, the officers displayed an air of superiority and spent a lot of their energy screaming at their men or at the locals. No one in Sandro's family had had any particular trouble with the German soldiers with the exception of the trouble Stefano had had with the cook, Gunther. And it was Stefano who had instigated most of that and had enjoyed every minute of it. Now however, the Germans were everywhere, and the family had to take care wherever they were and watch what they said.

The German attitude toward the Italians also depended on what area they were in. They occupied many areas but Ferentino was far to the north of the battle lines. The soldiers seemed much friendlier to everyone here, perhaps because they were so removed from combat. Stefano didn't notice a great deal of difference, though, because the soldiers had given him such freedom back at home.

There was one close call which was never mentioned after it had happened. One evening, as Marta, cousin Concetta, Polombo and Stefano were sitting by the fire chatting, there came a knock on the door. The door was partially open and a young German soldier stuck his head in and asked, in decent Italian, for permission to enter.

Surprisingly, Antonella invited him in. The soldier was gracious and inquired as to how the family was making out. He even offered to provide some food for them. Stefano was skeptical. He had noticed the soldier a few times when Marta had been outside. The young man had followed her with his eyes as she went about chores in the yard.

Soon the young soldier, Concetta and Marta were in a friendly conversation apart from Antonella, Polombo and Stefano, who were still by the fireplace. The girls were giggling like any 17-18 year olds. Antonella had moved away across the room but she was keenly listening to the conversation as she stirred the fire with a small shovel, and became concerned with the direction it had taken.

The German said something about his "needs". He then laughed which sent the girls into a spat of giggles. Antonella wheeled around from the fireplace and struck the soldier across the face with the hot shovel.

With pain and anger he jumped up, flipped open his holster and withdrew his Luger. "You stupid old woman!"

Everyone was stunned. They were sure the soldier would shoot Antonella. He was so angry he trembled. Marta watched his shaking hand and feared it would cause the gun to fire. He wiped his hand across his burning cheek and looked at his palm, as if he expected to see blood. There was only soot from the shovel.

"I should kill you." With those words, he placed the gun back in its holster, turned and left the house. The coals in the fireplace didn't cool nearly as fast as the burning ardor of the young German soldier.

Once the soldier was gone the family allowed themselves to relax. They were not worried that he would report what had taken place in Sandro's home. The German Command considered mingling with Italian women to be a major infraction. Back in Cervaro there had been an incident in which a German corporal was found guilty of molesting a local woman. He was taken into the piazza and shot by a firing squad with his entire company looking on. It served as a chilling warning to all the other soldiers.

CHAPTER ELEVEN

LT. RICHARD THOMPSON CIRCLED the city of Foggia from the air and was amazed at the devastation of the entire area. The Allied bombers had all but flattened the place. He made another pass over the city, imagining how it used to be. He then fell into the landing flight pattern.

The Allies had prepared the landing strip with movable pierced steel planking. It was a rather ingenious system whereby the landing strip could be placed, used and then ripped up and moved farther north as the forces conquered more territory.

Thompson had never landed on such a surface before but found it very forgiving to a novice. He followed the ground crew's direction and taxied his plane to its resting place. He deplaned and was quickly escorted with other newly arrived pilots to a rather large tent, the orderly room. There were tents upon tents lining the mud covered lanes. The only thing that didn't have a problem moving in the mud was the workhorse of army trucks, the 6x6.

Processing was rapid, after which he was greeted by the base operations commander. It had been a long flight, and Thompson was happy when all the formalities were over, and he was escorted to his quarters, a six-man tent.

He was left alone and was relieved that his bunkmates had not yet arrived. It was colder than he had anticipated, maybe enhanced by the nearly constant rainfall. The oil-barrel heater was present, but no one had made a fire. Lt. Thompson removed his boots and stretched out on one of the six cots. Within minutes he was asleep.

He had not been asleep long when he heard the Claxton sound to man his plane and prepare for combat. Fumbling with the laces on his boots, he was tempted to leave them unlaced but then castigated himself for even considering taking a shortcut.

A shortcut here, another there and soon your ass will be dead or shot down and captured, he thought. He sat back on the bunk and properly secured the laces. He sprinted toward his plane and was assisted into the cockpit by his crew boss. He felt a slap on the top of his head and the bubble canopy of the Thunderbolt closed.

Thompson taxied out following his wing leader. Within minutes the entire wing was in the air. They hadn't yet reached the prescribed cruising altitude when the Jerrys came down through the clouds. With the sun behind them they weren't seen until they were right above Thompson and the other planes.

An immediate dogfight ensued that lasted less than five minutes for Lt. Thompson. He took gun fire directly mid-ship, lost all control of his plane and plummeted into a spiral. Attempts to release the canopy were futile.

Thompson was startled awake by someone slapping the sole of his foot. He bolted upright on his cot, bug eyed. "What…where?"

Lt. Scott Martin was staring at him, "Sorry I woke you up like that. I was thinking it was cold in here but you're in a total sweat."

"No, thanks for waking me. It wasn't a good dream I was having."

"Wasn't a hot date, huh?"

"Hardly, I was in a dog fight."

Martin laughed, "Just can't wait for the real thing? Oh, by the way, I'm Scotty Martin." He extended a hand.

Thompson gripped the hand and smiled. "Oh, I think I can wait. Good to meet you. I'm Richard Thompson."

"Want to go down to the mess hall? Personally I'm starved."

"Good idea. Let me get my boots on."

The two young pilots quickly became fast friends. Within days all the pilots had fallen into a routine, flying the usual daily sorties whenever the weather allowed. Several of the men had names painted on their planes and Thompson proudly looked at "Anne" in 12 inch letters painted right under the canopy of his plane. He took great care to affix a picture of his son, Richie, to the instrument panel. The photo was in black and white, but he could easily envision in his mind's eye the freckles and red hair in vivid color.

Each time he returned from a flight he would tap the picture and say, "Well, Richie, we made it through one more time."

The Allied air raids were advancing from the south. Stefano and a boy from the next house were outside playing soccer, using a finial from a fence post as the soccer ball. They could hear the loud, high-pitched scream of dive bombers. The two planes were less than a kilometer away. One plane released its bombs, but the second must have had difficulty releasing or the pilot decided not to release. The angle of the dive and the weight of the retained bombs made controlling the plane difficult. When the pilot tried to pull out, he found he couldn't. There was an explosion from the first plane's bombs and then a much greater explosion when the plane with the bombs still onboard hit the ground.

Dog fights, bombings and artillery shelling were becoming daily occurrences. War was all around. Sandro decided to return to Cervaro with his family. They had no food and the war was simply following them. It would be as easy to starve in one place as another. They had better connections in their home area and would stand a better chance of surviving. At least they could use the stored grains left buried at home for food.

Marta and Concetta didn't want to leave Ferentino. The two of them said they had adapted to this new place, and they didn't know what would await them back in Cervaro. Stefano didn't know whether they were too lazy to make the long walk or if they enjoyed the appreciative looks from the German soldiers.

At times Sandro would take a consensus vote when the family had an important decision to make, but this wasn't one of those times. He had learned there were times when things could be up for discussion and then there were times like the present. He had to be the sole decision maker this time.

Marta was often irritated at the obvious male dominance. She had seen it initially with her father and mother, even as Mama had to take over the operation of the home and the farm when Papa was ill. He would still give orders as was the tradition of the husband, but for the most part Mama ignored them. In the present environment when there were discussions, it appeared that Sandro gave more deference to Polombo and Stefano than to the women in the house.

Antonella was the ever obedient wife and would not think of questioning her husband. However, there was one member of the family who never ceased questioning. Sometimes it was under his breath, but more often it was loud and clear.

"Uncle, you know I won't have trouble walking back or carrying my share of the load, but what's to be gained?"

Sandro rolled his eyes. *Here it comes one more time,* he thought.

Stefano picked up on the eye-roll and decided to change his tactic. Rather than challenge his uncle, he appealed on behalf of the women. "I mean the girls don't want to leave. As they said, this place has become comfortable, and at least we know what we have here. Granted its very little."

"Which is my point exactly, Stefano. We have nothing. The war is still all around us and it is getting harder and harder to find any form of food. I would think you of all people would look forward to maybe being able to eat something every day rather than spending your days searching for the plumpest insect you can find."

"And how does that make me different from everyone else?"

As he scratched his head, Sandro said, "In the food line you're no different from everyone. On the argumentative side you stand out. We leave for Cervaro as soon as we can make our plans."

Stefano brooded, "What's there to plan? We had about ten minutes to gather our stuff to bring up here, and we have less now. What's to plan?"

CHAPTER TWELVE

· ·

THE WAR HAD SHUT down the trains as it had brought to a halt just about everything else in the southern part of Italy. The family had no money to pay train fare anyway, but they searched for tracks that followed the shortest route back to Cervaro. They wanted to avoid the main roads, and because no trains were running, it was safe to walk along the tracks.

They had no way of knowing if the Germans would try to prevent them from going back south, and they had no intention to ask permission. They discussed their leaving with no one until their day of departure. After multiple "grazie mille"—thank you very much—they bid the owner of the house farewell and set off on the journey back home. Amazingly, no one questioned what they were doing or where they were going; the family was simply ignored. The Germans had more pressing concerns. The Italians were like migrating birds that had lost their sense of direction. Some trod north and some south. The Capaldis had moved north and now were headed south.

They knew they would have to take each day as it came, maybe each hour. They agreed they would simply continue south until nightfall or until they were too exhausted to go any further. The morning of their departure offered bright sunshine dappled by scattered clouds. They wore most everything they owned. The women appeared to have gained weight overnight as their layered dresses, one upon the other, filled out their slight frames. Each person was responsible for carrying his or her personal gear including a blanket, mementoes and a share of survival items. What was left of the sack of flour, which the boys had stolen from a neighbor's shed, was rationed among all, including Danilo, the youngest. He never complained and quietly carried his share.

The first day they actually made very good time, walking steadily with periodic short respites. As evening came on they found a clearing among some trees and decided to camp for the night. With the coming of night also came the chill. The family was too tired to think of gathering wood for a fire. They would not cook that night, and they would not have heat. What little they had to cook could wait another day. After a meal of bread with a few drops of oil, exhaustion took over, and everyone was ready for sleep. Sleep was often an escape from the fact that there was no food. People in the area were often reduced to scraping soft bark from trees as their only means of nourishment. Foraging for insects in the tall grasses was a way of life.

Stefano laid his blanket on the ground and rolled himself into a cocoon. The other two boys thought that was a great idea and followed suit. It was the same routine every day: walk, eat little more than a snack, walk, rest and finally sleep. For the most part, there was no talk of where they were or how much further they had to go.

On the eighth day of walking, about mid-afternoon, Sandro suddenly stopped, looked around and then craned his neck, trying to get an aerial view. He smiled and said, "I know where we are. We're about six kilometers from Pico. My cousin, Marcuso de Lucca, lives near here. I'm sure I can find his place. We'll go there. He has a very large home, and he may let us rest for a while."

Antonella looked confused. "Who's that cousin? I don't think I've ever met him or his family."

Sandro laughed, "You wouldn't have. Nonno never liked his side of the family. I hope Cousin Marcuso doesn't feel the same way about us."

When they arrived at Marcuso's home, Sandro's family was welcomed warmly. It appeared Marcuso was unaware that he had been cut from the short list of Capaldi friends. There was another family, the Constanos, sharing the home, but to an Italian family, what's another seven people? The Capaldis were relegated to one section of the basement, but the room was spacious compared to the place in Ferantino they had just left.

Antonella told the de Luccas that the fighting in the south had been so intense before, she was hoping for better. "Maybe the hard fighting has passed on."

Marcuso was very matter of fact. "I wish you were right, but the shelling has actually increased in the past few days. Our home is very sturdy, but I worry for everyone's safety. It's not safe to go out during the day."

"Nothing new there," Stefano said, mainly to himself with a shrug.

"From the looks of this house, I'd say we only have one thing to worry about," said Sandro as he looked overhead. "That's a direct hit by a bomb."

Marcuso added with a sardonic smile, "We've thought about that and we think there's a solution, but we haven't had the manpower. Now, with you here we have a lot of help. Signore Constano was struck by a piece of shrapnel in his right leg a couple of weeks ago and it isn't healing well, so he hasn't been able to help. There're many trees on our land. If we cut the trees and pile them in the upper room, we could stand a much better chance of surviving a hit."

Sandro had surveyed the area before they went into the home and estimated that 60% of all the trees in the province were on that one plot.

"Wouldn't the floor collapse under all that weight?" asked Stefano with trepidation in his voice.

"That floor is 20 centimeters of reinforced concrete. I think it will hold whatever we put on it. Tonight you rest from your long journey and tomorrow night, after dark, we'll begin harvesting logs to stack in the room."

All three families shared a common meal that night with the conversations orbiting around family news, who had heard from whom and who had had the worst time. As with all conversations in Italy, the war was discussed intermittently, but it was as if everyone knew the facts, so why keep bringing it up?

The following night the progress was rapid. The trees were felled and cut into two meter lengths. The biggest challenge was maneuvering the thickest logs up the stairs to the second floor. The wood was stacked systematically on both sides of the room with a path down the middle. Pyramids were made and then the sides were filled to make a solid structure as high as the men could reach. It was cumbersome at times working in the dark, but once the pattern was set and the men's eyes adjusted to the night, they worked efficiently. It took three nights to fill the room. They had their bomb shelter.

After the shelter was complete, their attention turned back to the main concern which was their unrelenting need of food. Although Sandro's family was eating more than they had in weeks, the reality was that they were starving just a little less. Although the cousin had been able to harvest and store much more than many families in the area, there were a lot of mouths to feed. Sandro still resented the fact they had not been allowed to stay in their own home. He felt he would have been in as good a condition as Cousin Marcuso.

All around them the land, which had been so fertile and productive, was now as barren as a desert. There was no money to purchase seed and fertilizer. Most of the small plots still under cultivation had survived by the families saving and replanting the seed from the previous year. Those seeds often yielded products like those of incestuous populations—full of defects.

After a week with Marcuso, Sandro grew restless. "I have to know what has happened to our homes. Tomorrow, war or no war, I'm going to Capaldi."

Stefano immediately jumped up, "Yes, let's do it. Why not go now?"

Sandro knew Stefano would be disappointed, but he knew also that he had to go alone. If he ran into trouble, he wanted only to have to take care of himself. A strong-headed, impulsive boy was distraction he didn't need. "If this goes well, I will have you go with me the next time."

Sandro left in the morning, with the first breaking light, to walk the twelve kilometers. The longer he walked the more amazed he was at how little he saw of Germans. Occasionally a German military vehicle would pass, but it was rare and no one harassed him. He was saddened by the destruction of the land all around him.

Sandro returned late in the evening with encouraging news. Their homes were still intact and there was no sign of the Germans in the neighborhood. They seemed to have evaporated.

The following evening Sandro, Marcuso, Stefano and Polombo returned to the home and dug up some of the jugs of wheat, corn and lentils. They returned to Marcuso's home and opened the jugs. They were pleasantly surprised to find the grains in good condition with no evidence of moisture. The jugs' contents would provide basic food for all of them for a few weeks. They discussed making a second trip to rescue the rest of the jugs, but decided they weren't immediately needed. Marcuso was still willing to share his vegetables, and they would share their grains.

For the young ones, the enemy was boredom. They had long since tired of made-up games that they played indoors. The lack of exercise was making them irritable, and Antonella finally told them to get out of the house and do something. "Just be careful where you go. Stay out of cleared areas."

That struck the boys as funny. About everything was cleared. Most of the trees that had been near the house were now in the attic of the house, the out buildings were gone, and the barren fields were like a moonscape covered with craters. The artillery shells were now increasing in numbers as well as size. The Allies were gaining ground, but very slowly. The boys soon learned that the projectiles had timed fuses. They could hear the guns fire in the distance and then hear the impact, followed ten seconds later by the explosion. It became a game: hear the fire, hear the whistle overhead, hear the impact, count to eight and hit the ground. They became so brazen a couple of times they scared themselves. The impact area was so close, dirt rained down on them from the explosion.

In addition to incoming artillery shells, there was also the threat of the Allied fighter planes that often strafed the German position. Polombo and Stefano had heard the planes diving and the rapid cannon fire, but had never seen action. In an effort to witness it firsthand, they set out for a nearby hill, which offered a vantage point from which to watch the German troop movement. It had become another game to guess in which direction the troops would be moving on any given day. Would they be retreating and re-grouping to the north, or would they be moving south as reinforcement troops?

The boys had hardly settled in when they heard a plane coming from the south. They watched it flying at low altitude, below the ridge line. Suddenly, the plane opened cannon fire, and they could see the German soldiers popping up out of the grass and then falling, caught by the rain of fire from the plane.

In the plane the pilot was smiling broadly. He had caught the Germans by surprise. He circled and prepared for another run. As he started his dive he spotted two figures running among a thicket, "Ah, two more. Bite the dirt."

The pilot started to fire just as a boy with red hair popped into the clearing. The trigger-button was half depressed when the pilot realized the figure was that of a small boy. He yanked back on the stick and the plane streaked over the boys and the ridge. The pilot could clearly see the terrified face of the young redhead. It was as if the picture on his instrument panel had jumped out of the plane. He was so shaken by what had nearly happened that the plane traced zigzag motions in the sky as his feet shook against the pedals. He'd almost killed his son or someone who looked amazingly like his son! He didn't dare attempt another pass. The event so unnerved him that he would probably botch the run, or even worse, get himself killed. He decided to return to Foggio.

CHAPTER THIRTEEN

· ·

FROM THE HOUSE IN Pico, the Capaldis had a clear view of the Abbey that sat at the crest of the Arunci Mountains. There was little that brought joy to Stefano, but when he gazed at the huge edifice the site brought warm remembrances of Nonno. From most everywhere in the Liri Valley the Abbey could be seen.

The Germans had dug in all around the mountain and had been entrenched for months, waiting for the Allies to move north. Hitler was determined to prevent the Allied forces from reaching Rome. He was sure the enemy couldn't penetrate the Gustav Line. As the Allies pushed northward it was around-the-clock cacophony, with the bombers overhead, bombs exploding, artillery fire and the constant bap, bap, bap of small arms fire.

The nights were the worst, and everyone secretly feared the log shelter wouldn't hold. Each night Sandro led the family in prayer. The voices of young and old joining Sandro brought a sense of calm to the home. Later, in bed, the boys would quietly whisper until they fell asleep. The main conversation was always around the question, "I wonder how close that one was?"

It seemed a miracle that as bombs dropped all around them, no one had been injured. The odds were bound to catch up with them. Antonella was standing in the doorway early one morning just to get a breath of fresh air when a mortar shell exploded nearby. A piece of shrapnel struck the back of her heel, ripping away a large segment of flesh. Antonella screamed at the impact but then became eerily calm. Neither of the men was at home. The boys helped her onto a bed and the children followed her instructions. "Marta, take a knife and cut a clean towel into strips. Polombo and Stefano, get hot water from the hearth, dip a strip in the water and clean the wound."

She flinched each time Polombo touched the raw gash but instructed him to continue. "Now, Stefano wrap the strips tightly over the hole and around my foot." At first Stefano was afraid the sight of Antonella's blood would bring up the contents of his weak stomach, but after the first wrap he was fine.

Rosary prayers had to work. There was no medication to prevention infection. Sandro suggested an old family remedy. "You will have to soak your foot in your urine to prevent infection."

On hearing this, again Stefano about lost his last meal. "That is so schifoso—disgusting." He ran from the house and sat next to a huge rock in the back yard. The rock had become his escape from the repetitive conversations in the house and from Polombo. "Too much closeness is just too much, and now the rock has replaced the stump." He sat there breathing deeply. Soon he was hyperventilating, feeling his lips and fingers tingling and then going numb, which only increased his anxiety to the point he was about to faint. Then came an explosion very close to the house. That broke the vicious cycle: hyperventilate, anxiety, anxiety, hyperventilate.

That evening Stefano had recovered enough from his revulsion to quip to Polombo, "I know how to cure Signor Constano's leg where the shrapnel hit it."

"What do you mean you can cure his leg? You've become a healer? You're going to start mumbling over his leg? You've seen it won't heal, just keeps draining that horrible, smelly pus."

"I know," snickered Stefano. "All he has to do is pisciare—piss— on his leg every day."

Both boys were still giggling as they fell asleep.

Something worked, either the rosary or the urine. Antonella's wound gradually healed, and she was able to walk with only slight discomfort. Signor Constano saw the healing of Antonella's heel.

Quietly he would bring his medicine in with him from the outhouse. Within days the pus no longer oozed from his leg, and in a couple of weeks the wound had healed.

Again Sandro made the decision to move. "Antonella's foot has healed, and the fighting is getting more intense. From all signs, it's going to get worse. We're only twelve kilometers from Cervaro, but Pico seems to be more on the line to Monte Cassino. When we've been home we see no signs of fighting. In a few days we're going home."

Stefano had asked himself on more than one occasion why they had stayed with the cousin when they were so close to home. He could see his uncle enjoyed the company of another adult male and understood it was helpful to have someone else assist with decisions.

Each day brought more news of what was happening with the war. There were word-of-mouth messages, some reliable, but most simply speculation or wishful thinking. Sandro and Marcuso ventured out in the early mornings to talk with neighbors. These neighbors had talked to other neighbors, and from this human chain, information was shared.

The main message was not encouraging. As hard as the Allies were fighting they were making little progress. The Germans had had to pull back to just north of where the Capaldis were staying, but they were determined to hold the Gustav Line. As the fighting intensified, there were more locals who felt as Sandro did; they had to get out of the area. The entire countryside seemed to have turned into the main military route.

On the morning of February 12, 1944, a neighbor came to the house and talked with everyone. His name was Adamo, and though he was several years older than Sandro, they had known each other for many years.

"We're going to leave our home tomorrow. As we talked right after Antonella was injured, it's not safe here any longer," said Adamo.

"I agree," said Sandro. "We're going back to our village outside Cervaro. According to the gossip tree, I think there is little to no fighting there now. Where will you go? You know you can come to our home. It will be crowded, but we're used to crowds. We'll manage."

Adamo smiled. "Thank you, my good friend, but my family and I are going with several other families to the Abbey. We feel that it's the safest place to be. Even after all the shelling and bombing, there's no evidence of any harm to the Abbey. There we will be safe. Would you be better off there than in Cervaro? You can see the fighting is spreading."

"Perhaps, but we feel as if we've been running for months and want to be in our place. Marta and Stefano are anxious to return to their home. Good luck to you, my friend."

Adamo rose, and at the door he turned back and waved. "May we all survive this Hell."

The following morning a column of people strung out along the road leading up the mountain to the Abbey. Polombo and Stefano had gone down the road to watch the procession. Stefano asked, "Will they make it up the mountain? There's been so much shelling between here and there."

Polombo had mixed feelings, "You're right, but maybe they're doing the right thing. The Abbey is like a fortress. They should be okay. I hope."

That afternoon an Allied jeep carrying a driver and a junior officer of the New Zealand army arrived at Marcuso's house. As soon as the jeep came to a stop, the young officer jumped out and approached the house. Marcuso opened the door before the man could knock.

In perfect Italian the officer asked, "Is there a man here called Sandro?"

Marcuso nodded, stepped back and invited the soldier in. "Sandro will return shortly. He is just outside."

Stefano came over. "I'm Stefano, Sandro's nephew. Why do you want him? How did you know he was here?" The boy didn't believe in beating around the bush. His arms were folded across his chest.

Marcuso took Stefano's arm, "Don't be impolite."

"No, it's fine," the officer said with a smile. He extended his hand. "I'm glad to meet you, Stefano. As a matter of fact we heard about your uncle from…"

Before he could complete his sentence Sandro came in and asked, "Who is our visitor?"

The officer crossed the room. "I'm Lieutenant O'Brien of the New Zealanders. And you're Sandro?"

"That's correct," Sandro replied in English.

O'Brien grinned, "You speak English fluently?"

"It has gotten rusty, but I can get by."

"I detect an American accent."

"That's where I learned. I lived in America for a bit."

"That's wonderful. We're so glad to find you. Would you be willing to help the Allies?"

"Of course, but I don't know what I can do."

"We think you can be of great help to us, if you're willing. You're Italian, you've lived here a long time, and you know the terrain. We need all the help we can get."

Sandro pointed to Stefano and smiled, "Well, a good while ago it was rumored that my nephew here was collaborating with the Germans. I suppose we could even it up."

O'Brien went rigid. Before he could speak, Sandro laughed and continued, "Relax, it was a stupid rumor started by a neighbor. No one hates the Germans more than Stefano."

Sandro turned to his family and spoke in Italian to tell them what was being said.

"Excuse me, sir," said O'Brien. "We should go now."

"Go now?" questioned Sandro. "Where are we going?"

"To our headquarters, and it's a good ways. Grab your personal belongings—your toothbrush and such--and let's be off."

"Lieutenant, would you mind waiting outside?"

"No sir." The officer turned and left the room.

Sandro told everyone where he was going and then added, "I don't think we should talk about this outside. Some folks may believe in the Germans or are suspicious of the Allies. I assume I won't be back tonight since he said to bring a toothbrush. He doesn't realize our toothbrushes wore out months ago. I can find a twig anywhere."

He hugged Antonella and his children. He spoke to Polombo and Stefano, "Take care of the women. Stefano, I can see you chomping at the bit, but you weren't invited."

Stefano was furious when his uncle patted him on the head, "I probably could tell them more about the Germans than you know," mumbled Stefano.

Sandro heard enough to glean what the redhead had said. It was difficult not to laugh. Instead he grabbed his ragged jacket and stepped out the door.

By the time they reached the New Zealander's headquarters, it was dark. The driver navigated the roads and paths as if he was on native soil. The jeep came to a halt as a perimeter sentry stepped from behind a large bush. He held his rifle at the ready and shouted, "Sheep."

The driver replied, "Only the best wool."

The guard stepped back and the jeep moved forward. Again, they stopped in front of an area which was camouflage covered. The fishnet enmeshed with branches and leaves extended about ten by ten meters.

O'Brien jumped out of the jeep and said to Sandro, "Please wait here, sir."

He was gone about five minutes. As he approached the jeep he said, "Come with me, Signore."

The men took three steps down into the bunker and stopped in front of a double flap tarpaulin area. They passed through the first flap and when O'Brien had secured it, he opened the second. The lantern light blinded Sandro momentarily.

O'Brien saluted the three men seated at a small table covered with maps. The officer in the middle looked up, then stood and extended his hand. "Signore Capaldi, I'm Lt. General Freyberg. Thank you for coming."

"I'm not sure why I'm here. I don't know what I can do, but I'm willing to help."

"That's wonderful. Have a seat and I'll explain what we need."

O'Brien brought a canvas chair from the corner, and Sandro sat.

"This is the situation," Freyburg began. "The exercise to take Monte Cassino has proved far more difficult than our intelligence led us to believe. Far, far more difficult by the day."

"We've had mixed signals about the Abbey, whether it's occupied by the Germans or not. There have been reports both ways from higher up and our intelligence is no better. In one of our flyovers, two pilots reported completely opposite sightings. One said he observed German uniforms hanging on hooks in the courtyard and saw an antenna atop the Abbey. The other pilot said he saw nothing to indicate there were Germans in the place."

"Up the line our officers have been assured by the Vatican that they were told by the German commander, General Kesserling, that he would never place any men in the Abbey. We don't exactly trust the wolf to guard the henhouse."

"At any rate, the Germans have waited a long time for us to come to them, and we know they haven't been sitting around with their thumbs up their arses. They've proved they are hunkered in tight."

Sandro interrupted, "But General, I have no idea what's going on in the Abbey. I haven't been up there in years, well before the Germans came."

"That's too bad. My main reason for asking you to come here was to ask questions about the terrain up there."

"Ahh, that I can tell you, but you're not going to like what I have to say. It's hard to get up to the Abbey, even by walking up the road, and I don't think your enemy is going to invite you to do that."

"You're right about that. Our intelligence tells us that there are gun placements all around the crest of the mountain. We've had them firing down on us daily."

Sandro leaned forward over the desk. "What are all these numbers? Orient me as to where the big landmarks are."

A colonel sitting next to Freyburg stood and with a short pointer indicated the position of the Abbey on the map. "The various numbers are what we see as strategic hills or placements."

Sandro said, "I understand. So, this is the Rapido River. This will be a very hard obstacle to cross. So much of the forestation has been destroyed, and from what I understand they have rechanneled parts of the river, which has increased the current tremendously. Your men will have little cover. They'll be like ducks in a shooting gallery."

"Getting up the mountain is next to impossible. In most places the rock faces are practically straight up. There are areas that are worse than others, but none are good one."

Sandro pointed to the map, "If I can have your stick." The Colonel handed over the pointer. "This area and this are impossible. The faces are absolutely vertical and tall. If I remember correctly you may have a better chance in this area."

The colonel marked the two impossible areas with a black grease pencil and the more possible area in red. He asked, "Can you tell us anything about the German troop movement? Generally, we know they have been pulling back in recent weeks. But, we encounter groups going both ways. Today our troops have had to fight in the Cervaro region. From your reaction, do you know that area?"

Sandro reeled when he heard the news of Cervaro. "That is my home! We live just outside of Cervaro in our tiny village of Capaldi. In fact, we were making plans to return home very soon."

"I certainly would advise against that, at least in the foreseeable future."

For the next two hours the military men questioned and Sandro answered them as best he could. They were interrupted by a series of radio exchanges. One heated exchange was between the general and someone Sandro never was able to identify. General Freyburg spoke to his aide. "Get Clark's group. Tell them I want the Abbey taken out. They've heard that before, but tell them again. We're helpless with the krauts sitting over our heads."

The aide left and returned in about a half-hour. "Sir, we got the same response which I'm afraid you won't like again. General Clark has bumped it up the line. He won't decide. His men said, and I quote, 'Tell Freyburg he'll get his answer when there is a decision.'"

Freyburg slapped the table. The plastic overlay jumped, and the grease pencils appeared to hang in mid-air. "That fucking, lily-livered son-of-a-bitch! He's up there at Anzio putting armored plates over his arse while I watch my men and those of the other Allied units drop off like deer on opening day of hunting season."

He turned to his aide again. "Find a bunk for Signore Capaldi." The general stood and spoke to Sandro, "Thank you for coming. We'll talk more in the morning. Try to get some sleep."

"I hope I've helped. I have so little knowledge of these things. How long will I be here?"

"We'll get you back home tomorrow."

Sandro stayed on for another day which was spent going over the same details again and again. When he finally said, "I know nothing more," he was graciously thanked and O'Brien drove him back to his family.

The family ate well that night. Freyburg had ordered O'Brian to procure a box of food from the mess hall. What was meant for one meal was stretched out over three days.

CHAPTER FOURTEEN

· ·

TWO DAYS AFTER SANDRO had been summoned by the Allied Command, Stefano left the house with a cursory goodbye to Marta. It was cold and his thin jacket offered little in the way of protection from the winds whipping down from the mountains. He didn't invite Polombo along, as his cousin would have cramped the plan. Stefano had told the lieutenant that he knew more about the Germans than his uncle did, and the boy refused to be brushed aside. He would show them all. He managed to find two small sheets of paper and a pencil nub the night before and had secreted them away in his pants pocket. He wasn't deterred.

Immediately he tried to determine which was needed most, gun placements or the location of the German soldiers. He concluded the Allies would need to know both. He headed directly north and over the second ridge he observed activity in the distance. There were many personnel moving about, and in his estimation there were at least fifty men in the group. He held the paper on his thigh and made notes.

His next argument with himself was whether he should scout around to the east or the west. As he was about to move, he heard the drone of a plane or planes. Then he heard the unmistakable screech of a diving plane. He fell to the ground with his head raised enough over the ridge to see where the plane was headed. He noted two machine gun placements and one artillery piece firing at the two planes. This information he scribbled on his piece of paper. The planes retreated out of range, and finally there was quiet. From Stefano's vantage point it didn't seem that the planes had made much of an impact on their target.

The cold was getting to him, and Stefano knew he had to move. He could either go back home to warm up, or he could do what he came to do. Slowly he backed down the hill and then around to his right. About 500 hundred meters beyond, he came to a clearing. The wide open area looked enormous, and if he started across the area there would be no cover. Stefano reasoned that if he could no longer see the Germans, they couldn't see him.

He stood and strolled casually along a path as if looking for something on the ground. He tried to whistle quietly in a nonchalant way, but either it was the cold or his fear hindered his ability to pucker his lips. No whistle would come. He made his way to the opposite side of the clearing and around another hill. In the distance Stefano could hear the Germans talking but couldn't make out anything that was being said.

Slowly he skirted around the hill to where trees ran along a ridge. He reached the trees and then began silently creeping forward, tree to tree. Stefano was about 50 meters from the German encampment when he paused and strained to hear the conversation taking place. Again nothing discernible. Stefano was about to move higher when he felt a firm hand on his shoulder. He turned and was looking up at a German soldier.

Stefano fell to the ground on his back, petrified.

"Was ist los—what's going on?" demanded the soldier

"Niente."

The soldier reached down and pulled Stefano by the arm with as much ease as if he was lifting a dried leaf. He half carried and half dragged the boy up the hill to the camp, where he deposited him amidst three bewildered German officers.

The older officer gazed down at the shivering boy and asked, "What do we have here? Where did you find him?"

"He was down the hill, hiding behind a tree."

"I see." Then it was obvious to Stefano that the man was directing his questions to him, although he could only understand an occasional word. "Why were you hiding behind a tree? The other side must be getting desperate if they're now using children as spies."

All the soldiers laughed, and Stefano knew it was at his expense. He raised his palms upward and shook his head. "Non capisco."

The officer then called for a soldier by name. Moments later a young man came running up to the group. After the obligatory, "Heil Hitler" he asked, "You wished to see me, Sir?"

"Yes. We have here a waif who claims he doesn't speak German. Talk with him and find out what he's doing here, hiding behind a tree."

The young soldier knelt next to Stefano and spoke in Italian, "Why are you here?"

"I was out looking for something to eat and got lost. I was going to climb to the top of this hill to see if I could get my direction."

The man looked up at the officer and relayed what Stefano had said. The officer looked neither dismayed or skeptical, and said, "That doesn't surprise me from the looks of him. All the same, put him in that tent and give him something to eat. Perhaps if he has a full stomach he will want to be our friend, and we can ask him about the enemy he may have seen."

The soldier motioned for Stefano to follow and led him to the nearest tent. When they were inside, the man pointed to a stool and Stefano sat. He told Stefano that he was going to get food for him. The boy nodded his head up and down and smiled broadly.

After the soldier left Stefano quickly removed the two sheets of paper from his pocket, tore them into tiny pieces and ate them. It was difficult to get them down he was so scared, he didn't have much saliva, yet he knew it would not be good for his drawings to be found.

When the soldier returned with a tray the first thing Stefano grabbed was the metal cup of water to wash down the lingering scraps of paper in his throat. Then he started to eat. He forced himself to take small bites and not gobble the food on the tray. The food certainly didn't taste like a cannoli, but it was good. The young soldier simply stood over Stefano and watched. Between bites Stefano looked up and smiled.

Minutes later Stefano's guard was called outside and the boy was left alone in the tent. He finished his food and began to look around the tent. There was nothing of interest lying out in the open, but his eyes landed on two backpacks in the corner of the tent. Stefano knew trying to look inside the pack was risky and knew he would regret the risk if he got caught

He sat back on the stool and concentrated on listening. When the soldiers spoke slowly, Stefano was surprised at how much he understood. At one point he could make out they were talking about the recent plane attack.

After about an hour the soldier returned to the tent and motioned for Stefano to follow. The soldier told him not to be scared. When they again faced the older officer the man stared at Stefano.

Addressing the translator, the officer said, "Ask him questions about the enemy forces, how far away they are, anything he has seen."

Stefano did his best to play stupid. He wasn't about to say, "Well my uncle is with the command people on the other side." Repeatedly he insisted that that he hardly left his home, and that was the reason he was lost in the woods today. He did not know the area beyond his village

Eventually the officer seemed to grow weary. "He's obviously not going to tell us anything, even with a full belly. Put him in one of the trucks and take away all of his clothing except his underwear. Maybe the cold will loosen his tongue. He is bound to have seen something."

The translator told Stefano to take off his clothes. Obediently he stood, removed his threadbare jacket and then his shirt. When he unfastened his pants the men could see he had on nothing underneath. The officer was stunned. "If that's all this boy is wearing in this weather he is already cold. A little decrease in the temperature won't affect him. Get him dressed and place him in the guard's tent. If he tries to run, shoot him."

The translator was stunned by the order but obviously knew better than question his superior. He explained to Stefano what the officer had said and escorted him to the tent located on the perimeter of the camp.

Stefano ducked into the tent, and the translator closed the flap and secured it.

Looking around, Stefano was amazed. They were holding him in a tent which served as an armory for an assortment of arms. Boxes of various types of ammunition, as well as a partially assembled rifle, two rifles that appeared ready for action and a bayonet lay in open view. For Stefano, however, the main items of interest at the moment were the heavy wool blanket and canvas cot. He wrapped himself in the blanket and fell exhausted on the cot, really warm for the first time that day.

After sleeping for about an hour, Stefano awakened, disoriented, until he heard the soldiers speaking outside the tent. He sat on the side of the cot, once more taking an inventory of what was in there. He cautiously picked up one of the rifles but knew immediately that it was of no use to him. It was very heavy. His eyes locked onto the bayonet and immediately he had a plan.

He pulled the blanket tightly about his shoulders and sat plotting in his mind. His thoughts ranged from fear to excitement, excitement that he may learn something that could be of use to the Allies. Fear when he considered the idea of escape.

The rumble of a passing truck brought Stefano's thoughts together. He pulled the flap of the tent apart slightly and saw that dusk was setting. He thought of Marta and imagined her pacing the floor. He envisioned Antonella shouting that she was going to beat him to a pulp when he arrived home. Maybe being a prisoner was safer.

"I've got to get out of here but not tonight. I'd never find my way home."

The guard noticed the gap in the tent flap and Stefano's head protruding He pointed his rifle toward the young boy's head. Stefano conveyed in his broken German that he was lonely and just wanted to talk with someone. He realized too late that he pretended, up to this point, that he spoke no German. As an adult spy, he would have lasted less than an hour. The guard glanced about, and seeing no officers, replied with the few words of Italian he had learned since being in the country.

Much to Stefano's frustration, the guard seemed to know little about what was happening in the camp. About all he knew was that the Germans were waiting for re-enforcements and then they would be moving north.

Later on Stefano was fed well and then slept several hours. He was awake well before dawn. At first light he crept out the slit he had cut in the rear of the tent. "Thanks for the knife, mein freund."

Very slowly Stefano crab-crawled all the way to the densely wooded ridge. Just as he was about to take off, he heard loud yelling from the area of the guard tent. He was certain the Germans had discovered his escape, so he ran as fast as he could and for as long as he could without looking back.

Stefano assumed the officer in charge probably figured he wasn't worth trying to catch. He listened, but he heard no sound of a party in pursuit. Nonetheless, he ran until he felt he would black out. Falling to his knees he fought to regulate his breathing, and once the feeling of nausea passed, he began to run again. Stefano reached home a few minutes before Sandro returned with Lt. O'Brien.

As the jeep pulled up to the house, He leaped up and ran to his uncle. He began talking so fast that his uncle stepped out of the jeep and placed two firm hands on the boy's shoulders.

"Slow down, I can't understand what you're saying."

O'Brien looked at the excited boy and assumed he was relieved to see his uncle. When he started to pull away, Stefano jumped, and ran in front of the jeep. O'Brien had to slam on the brakes to avoid hitting the boy.

O'Brien shouted at Sandro, "What's he want?"

"I don' know! Stefano, don't be crazy! You could have been seriously hurt or killed."

Pointing to Lt. O'Brien, Stefano answered, "But this guy wanted to know about the Germans and I have some stuff for him."

Sandro was almost afraid to ask, but was intrigued by what his nephew may have gotten himself into now. "Okay, young man, settle down and tell us what it is that you know."

"Is il Senore O'Brien interested?"

"You bet I am, little guy."

Stefano looked the officer straight in the eye. "If you're interested, don't call me little guy."

"Stefano, mind how you speak."

"Sie, mi dispiace—I'm sorry, but I don't like to be called little." Then drawing a deep breath, he was off and running. He described to the officer exactly where the company of Germans was located and how they were dug in. He had counted 47 soldiers and six officers in the encampment which was in the same area that had been strafed by planes early yesterday. Stefano saved the most important piece of information for last. "A very large gun is to be brought to the area very soon."

"How in the world do you know that?" asked Sandro.

"I heard the Germans saying something about Cannone di grandi dimensioni. Karl taught me the word for gun."

At this point O'Brien was out of the jeep taking notes as fast he could. "Tell me again, Stefano. How far away from here would you say that was?"

"Uncle, how far is it from our home to Cervaro?"

"I'd say a little less than 12 kilometers."

"Then I'd say at least six kilometers from here, and it's straight in that direction." He pointed to the northwest.

O'Brien was practically jumping with excitement. He could hardly believe what the kid had relayed to him. "Stefano, you have been more than helpful. We had been told that the Germans were bringing in heavy artillery in anticipation of the Allied move toward the Abbey. They were hoping to use it on our back side. If you'll excuse me, I have to get back. Thank you both for the service and the valuable information you have provided us." He hopped back in the jeep and sped off leaving Sandro and Stefano standing in the road.

Stefano started for the house. As soon as he heard Sandro speak he knew it wasn't going to be good.

"Stefano, come back here."

The boy turned slowly walked sheepishly back and stood before his uncle.

"What in the name of God were you doing some six kilometers from here, and how did you get close enough to hear what the Germans were saying?"

"I was out for some exercise..."

"Wait, hold it right there. You were out for exercise. Do you expect me to believe that?"

Stefano stared at the ground. Sandro continued, "Don't look down Look at me and tell me the truth."

Stefano shuffled his feet but raised his head to address his uncle. "I was angry that that soldier wouldn't let me go with you to talk to the Allied people. I've seen what the Germans have been doing, and I could have told them but you wouldn't let me. So, I went looking for something special. I came upon a lot of German soldiers in a wooded area and I moved in close to hear them and they found me."

"You mean they captured you?"

"I guess, sort of. They gave me food to eat and kept me in a tent during the night. At first I couldn't find out anything, but during the night I heard them talking and that's when I learned about the big gun."

"Is your German that good?"

"Karl taught me a lot of words and if I listen real close, I can understand some. I can't say much."

"Now, tell me again. You were caught by the Germans, they gave you food, and released you?"

"Not exactly." He then relayed how he had used the bayonet to escape. Sandro's eyes grew bigger, and he shook his head in utter disbelief.

"I'm just sorry I wasn't able to give O'Brien the drawing I made, but I knew if the Germans had found the drawings of their camp

I don't think they would have believed my story. I told them I was lost."

"You made drawings of their encampment? What did you do with them?"

"I ate them."

"Oh, Stefano, what are we going to do with you?" Sandro wanted to be angry but was so thankful his headstrong little nephew was safe, he said nothing more, except, "Young man, I don't think we talk any more about this. Marta will have a fit."

Stefano smiled, "That's fine with me."

They entered the house and before Marta and Antonella could begin questioning or berating Stefano for going missing for over twenty-four hours, Sandro stopped them. Later Sandro thought, *Not for a minute do I think the women believed our tales, but nobody questioned. So, I'm not bringing it up again.*

CHAPTER FIFTEEN

THE WEATHER WAS ATROCIOUS. One snowstorm followed closely on the heels of the last, and high winds made any flights impossible. Finally, after several days of howling wind and snow, the weather eased. Stefano had ventured outside when he heard a barrage of shelling from the Allies. He looked up the mountain and observed that the artillery was different from any he had seen before. The shells were exploding in air rather than upon impact. Debris appeared to spew from each shell. Two shells exploded fairly close overhead and Stefano could see papers floating down to earth. Against his better judgment he raced to where the leaflets were falling. He knew Marta would be furious, but if truth were told, he did something on a daily basis to make her furious, so he figured, "what's one more?"

He scooped up a leaflet off the ground. On it was written a warning for all occupants to leave the Abbey immediately.

Adamo was standing outside the Abbey when one of the leaflet shells exploded overhead. He caught one of the messages and ran inside to share the information with the Abbot. The Abbot didn't believe for one moment that his God would allow the monastery to be destroyed.

Adamo hovered with his family in a hallway listening to the argument among the monks. The Abbot said, "This is getting us nowhere. We must decide on a common plan in order to advise the refugees of what is best for them. I will talk with the German Command."

When the German hierarchy arrived at the Abbey the next morning, it was their concerted opinion that the leaflets were a desperation move on the part of the Allied Commanders. "They are simply at the end of their rope and hope their tactics cause panic among you good people."

A few hours later, Adamo gathered his family and friends together and announced, "We are now safe. Let's settle here and support each other through this horrible time in our lives until we can return to our homes."

As Adamo spoke, he could hear the familiar drone of the B-17 Flying Fortresses. On that day there were 142 of the mighty bombers in the air surrounded by 87 smaller planes. Moments later the Abbey occupants felt the percussion of the first explosion. Soon the Abbey and courtyard were filled with smoke. The bombs continued to rain down on the monastery. As mighty as the building was with its walls 3 meters thick at the base, it and the whole mountain shook.

By the time it was over, 450 tons of bombs and incendiary devices had been unleashed on the Abbey. Fire spread to the trees around the building and burned on through the next day and night. The Abbey was reduced to rubble and only a few occupants survived the attack. Adamo and his family were not among the few.

Many of the planes involved in the monastery attack were from the 15th Strategic Air Force, and one of the pilots in the raid was Captain Richard Thompson. When the crews had been given their orders, Thompson was relieved to see the coordinates were nowhere near the area where he had seen the young boy who looked so much like his son, Richie. Since that day of strafing, Thompson had thought many times of how close he had come to killing the boy.

When the bombing started, it was as though the rest of the war in the area took a holiday. The Allied troops took shelter wherever they could find it, not bothering to engage the enemy. Unfortunately, the inaccuracy of bomb delivery meant there were many Allied casualties from friendly fire.

From their vantage point in the valley, Stefano and his family could see the planes flying overhead and watched as the mountain lit up like an erupting volcano. Sandro dropped to his knees and began praying the rosary. The family joined him, and even though Stefano's lips said the words, his mind was a hodge-podge of pictures as he imagined what fate had come to Adamo and his family.

The entire family was paralyzed with fear during the bombing and too distraught over what they feared had happened to friends to begin their evacuation. There was no way they could leave anyway as the fighting all around them intensified.

As the bombing ceased, the artillery fire seemed to increase. It was as if the entire world around them was going to be engulfed in fire and smoke. Stefano caught a heavy whiff of smoke blowing down the hill. He coughed violently, and when the spasm had passed, he remembered the times he had tried to make fake cigarettes. He smiled quietly to himself; the acrid gun powder smoke was worse than rabbit tobacco.

Four days after the bombing, Lt. O'Brien appeared at the family's house. When Sandro saw the jeep come to a stop in front of the house he thought his services might be requested by Freyburg again. Instead O'Brien had been dispatched to thank Sandro and Stefano for their help.

"Signor Capaldi, everything you told us proved correct. You've seen the destruction of the Abbey and for that we're extremely sorry. The crossing of the Rapido was a military disaster. We lost many men. This whole area has become a hellhole. I think Hitler is determined to hold his Gustav Line."

Stefano listened as O'Brien spoke, and then offered, "It's probably going to get worse. It looked like thousands of parachutes dropped down where the Abbey was. I watched them when I was outside yesterday."

O'Brien shook his head, "I'm afraid you're right, young man, and we did find that big gun you talked about. Our air forces were able to take it out before it could reach its destination. Those paratroopers you saw, we believe, are Hitler's best. It's going to be rough all the way."

O'Brien continued, "I have to be going. I was on my way to the Polish army headquarters and was so close to here I felt I had to stop and give you this." He handed Sandro a fistful of lire. "You deserve that. Good luck when you travel back to your home."

The battle continued for weeks. It wasn't until May 16th that the Polish troops finally secured Monte Cassino. Word rapidly spread throughout the region and everyone was prepared to move back to Cervaro. When they set out on the road a couple days later they immediately met a family they knew from very near their home. The father of the family begged Sandro to go no further. Cervaro was in chaos, he said, and the Germans were in a counter offensive. It was quite heavy hand-to-hand combat all around. The other family didn't know exactly where they were going, but they proposed skirting around the mountain and moving north. That plan appeared to be counterproductive from Sandro's perspective. The fighting was headed north.

Stefano's family elected to remain in Pico for the time being. They decided the men and boys would make another trip to Capaldi to dig up more grains and to scavenge anything they could find in the way of food. If things were as bad as this guy said, then they would return north where they had been weeks before.

The Capaldis' foray back to Cervaro had to be aborted a kilometer short of their goal. It wasn't a surprise; they knew almost immediately upon setting out that the trek was going to be tough. Incoming flak intensified when they were no more than two kilometers from Pico, and there was little available in the way of shelter, so many areas had suffered complete deforestation. Rather than the straight route which had been taken before, they were forced to hug the edges of the barren open areas as best they could.

Sandro wanted to send the two boys back to the safety of Pico, but he was hesitant to let them go off on their own. Then he laughed at himself when he realized the boys were making much more headway than the two adults. Stefano and Polombo easily scampered from tree to tree.

The foursome had been literally running for the past half hour. There was no way they could run this way carrying five-liter jugs of grain. Sandro called the group together and expressed his doubts about continuing further. Marcuso was in total agreement. Both boys held out for continuing. Cervaro was where the food was.

"It's not practical to continue," said Sandro.

"But Uncle, we're so close. I'll bet if it was daylight we'd be able to see our house from here," exclaimed Stefano.

"You're probably right. But look around you, there's plenty of light from the exploding shells and they're not just in front of us. The explosions are picking up behind us, too. We have to go back while we can."

Stefano was about to argue for continuing on when they heard the unquestionable rattle of an incoming mortar. Without comment or thought, the four hit the dirt. The mortar hit so close that they could hear the shrapnel hitting the trees next to them.

"I'm with you," joined Polombo.

"Wait," Sandro said. "From the pattern of the explosions I think either one side or the other has spotted us as the enemy. Let me think."

The four scrambled around on their bellies until they came face to face. Each was breathing hard and each one could smell the sweat of fear. Without warning, another shell hit a little closer than the last.

Sandro knew they had to move out. "This might be crazy thinking on my part, but I believe if we stay together we're going to take a big hit. Obviously an observer has us spotted and he's homing in on us. "Boys, can you find your way home?"

They both spoke at once, "Sure."

Polombo added, "We've explored almost this far several times. If they'll keep lighting the place up we'll be fine."

"Now that's a great thought," said Stefano in a strained voice.

"Polombo, I don't want to face your mother if you get lost, and Stefano, I hate to think what Marta will do to me. You're in more danger being with adult figures right now. We're going to leave one at a time, you men will go first, then Marcuso and I will follow."

Stefano caught the loose use of the word, "men". *So, I've just grown up. Hope I live to enjoy it,* he thought. "Who goes first, Uncle?"

He was afraid he knew the answer, but knew he had to react as soon as he got the word. "You're first."

Sandro had hardly gotten the words out before Stefano pulled himself into a sprinting position and took off. He hadn't gone twenty meters when the ear-splitting sound of a machine gun opened up. He instinctively hit the ground. Bursts of gun fire continued but he heard nothing that made him believe the bullets were aimed at him. He got up and began running with all his might.

He leaped over the last bluff they had crossed and headed straight for a cluster of trees he could see in the distance. He abandoned their previous route of tree-to-tree, feeling that in the open he could be seen to be a child. That was his gamble.

When Stefano was deep within the tree cluster he knelt beside a large trunk to take a breather. For a few minutes everything was quiet. He thought he heard German voices to his left and was reassured that he was heading in the right direction.

He crept to the edge of the tree cluster and again prepared to run full out. He'd only gone a short distance, though, when he plunged face first into a hole. At first he thought he'd fallen into a shell crater. Before he could right himself an explosion lit up the sky as well as the area all around him.

Stefano, sitting on his haunches, found himself face to face with a dead German soldier whose eyes glowed in the reflection of the illumination. Stefano lost control and let out a blood curdling scream. On pure impulse, born of terror, he quickly stuck his wrist in his mouth and bit down. The pain brought him back to his senses. He scrambled out of the hole and didn't stop running until he reached the farm house. He ran past it at first but recognized a nearby house, turned to his right and saw his home.

With the house just meters away Stefano dropped to the ground gasping for breath. As he waited to regain strength in his legs he began to worry about where the others were.

The next to arrive was Sandro. When Stefano saw him coming up the hill he called, "Uncle, over this way."

Sandro looked around and spotted Stefano on his knees, waving. He ran over to his nephew and sat down beside him. "Have you seen the others?"

"No, I'm here alone, but I didn't want to go in the house by myself. There's no way I could explain what's happened," said Stefano.

"How long have you been here?"

"At least 15 or 20 minutes. I was so scared for everyone."

"I'm worried too. You certainly made good time. You okay?"

"Yeah, something happened that scared me into running faster."

As Stefano was about to explain, he and Sandro saw Marcuso walking in the direction of the house. They went to greet the cousin.

When they were close enough to talk, Stefano asked, with trepidation, "Have you seen Polombo?"

"No, he isn't here?"

"He's not come yet?" Sandro choked out the words. "Oh, God, let him be safe. I've got to go find him."

"No," Marcuso said. "Don't try that. You have no idea where to look in the dark. It will only be a short time before dawn and then we'll all go look for him."

Sandro dropped to his knees and began to pray. The other two joined him in quiet pleading and petition.

Before long a familiar voice broke the silence. "Is this a private prayer time, or can I join in? I definitely want to pray."

Sandro jumped up and grabbed Polombo wrapping him in his arms. Polombo laughed and said, "Sorry I'm late, but I twisted my ankle."

The man hugged his son so tightly the boy couldn't breathe. He managed to wriggle free, "Take it easy. I traveled all this way and now you're going to smother me!"

The four "men" stood hugging each other for several minutes before they went into the house. The uncle confessed it had been a mistake to attempt such a dangerous journey for the grain. Grain was of little use to a dead man.

After the risky night-time excursion, Marcuso decided he would move his family also; they would go to his wife's family to the northeast. Before leaving they generously shared flour, vegetables and other staples with the Capaldis.

On the second evening of preparation, Stefano noticed a German jeep pass by their house, heading north. The same thing happened the following evening, and Stefano told his uncle what he had observed. On the fourth evening Sandro and Stefano were waiting by the road and waved down the driver.

Stefano was the interpreter, "Is it possible for you to take our family up north? There's just you and the other soldier."

After a long discussion, mainly due to their language barrier, it was decided the Germans would transport two people and some supplies each evening. The bribe was small, and there was little use for the lira the New Zealanders had given Sandro. They wouldn't need money because there was nothing to buy.

Sandro and Danilo were the first to go. Everyone was anxious watching them leave, not knowing where the Germans planned to take them. When the jeep returned the following night it was explained what had happened. Stefano had a lot of difficulty understanding where Sandro was, but the Germans assured him that Sandro was safe and there was a place for the family to live.

Antonella and Concetta left on the second night and on the third Marta, Polombo and Stefano crowded into the rear seat of the jeep-like vehicle. Using his broken German, the ever-inquisitive Stefano asked the soldiers questions during the entire trip. He determined the soldiers were serving as messengers, which explained why the soldiers made the round trip each day. Much to everyone's surprise, they found themselves very near to where they had started, close to Ferentino.

The house to which the Germans took the family was very old and spacious. Germans occupied the first and second floors, and the family was allowed to use the basement. Stefano commented that he was beginning to feel like a mole, they had lived in so many basements over the past several months. The house sat on the top of a hill and was surrounded by many hectares of rolling farmland. Essentially everything was undisturbed and intact, unlike their home area.

The first night Stefano was in his new bed he had difficulty falling asleep. He soon realized it was the quiet that was keeping him awake, no bombings or sounds of artillery fire. He heard only the comforting night sounds of a peaceful countryside.

Even though they had brought a great deal of supplies with them when they came north, those would not last. Two weeks passed without incident. The days were calm and quiet, but the old, haunting ghost of low rations was once again upon them.

Sandro continuously asked the Germans if there was some work he could do in exchange for food. Eventually he was given a job some distance away from where they lived. Somehow the Germans learned he could speak English and they used him to interpret intercepted messages. He did his job faithfully, fearing to do otherwise, Occasionally he would leave out an important detail.

He departed in the early morning and didn't return until after dark. When he came home at night, he always brought a container of soup and a loaf of bread. Antonella rationed the food, a portion would be eaten immediately and a portion was kept in reserve. The following day Antonella added some noodles and a couple of vegetables to the soup, which became the morning meal for the children. More than once Stefano noticed that his aunt and uncle served themselves last and ate very little. Everyone lost a great deal of weight, including Stefano. Pants that used to be snug were now difficult to keep up.

Each day Stefano watched to see what scraps the German cook discarded. Fearful of being caught, he carefully collected the discards, washed them and turned them over to Antonella. Cook was not like Fat Gunther, the cook back home. He had watched Stefano and was soon saving the food scraps and handing them out to the refugees each day.

There appeared to be a great deal of hustling back and forth by the Germans. At times the place was a complete hubbub with soldiers running in and out of the house. One day a small car pulled up to the house. The military men talked in the front garden while Stefano pretended to be sleeping, propped up against a tree stump. He was able to decipher parts of the conversation, learning that the Allies were making ground and advancing north. But the Allies had advanced before. The Allies and Germans were like two sword fighters, lunging and retreating.

Quietly Stefano stood, made a show of stretching and walked into the basement. "Aunt Antonella, I just overheard the soldiers out front talking and the Allies are pushing further north. We'll be liberated!"

Antonella was elated at the news, but was cautious. "Shush, quiet. You mustn't let them know you're listening or that you understand anything." Her heart was beating rapidly as she clasped her hands and softly said, "Thank you Jesus, that's such wonderful news."

That evening the family consumed every last bite of the soup and bread. They enjoyed a subdued celebration, but Marta confessed, "I don't think we're going to be rescued tomorrow, or the next day, or maybe ever. We still have to be careful and not trust anything the Germans say."

With Marta's words everyone was sober. Stefano looked at her with disgust. "Marta, do you always have to be so down?" Almost immediately he watched the hurt cloud his sister's face. But he couldn't bring himself to say he was sorry, because he wasn't. He stood up and went outside. He attempted to listen to the soldier's conversations, but didn't gain any more information as to the location of the Allies.

CHAPTER SIXTEEN

OVER THE NEXT TWO weeks the Allied forces moved throughout the area around Ferentino pretty much at will. Rumors abounded that American troops had moved up about two kilometers away. The boys rounded up a couple of friends and ran to see if they could watch the Americans.

On the way Stefano stopped so abruptly that Polombo ran full force into his cousin's back, sending both sprawling on the ground. Stefano was having second thoughts about meeting the Americans face to face. Suppose they noticed his German shorts and shoes, maybe taking him for German. Sitting on the ground he realized how stupid he was, after all he had red hair and everybody knew that Germans all had white hair. He felt so silly he wasn't about to share his thoughts with Polombo.

He jumped up, grabbed Polombo's arm and said, "Don't sit there, let's catch the others." Polombo looked at him not sure it was safe to follow his weird cousin.

When the four boys reached the main road they stood staring in amazement at the GIs making camp. There was none of the rigidity they had observed when the Germans had arrived. Some of the Americans were bare to their waist as they worked to set up the encampment. Others laughed as they worked, like they enjoyed what they were doing. They paid little attention to the four boys hovering at the perimeter.

Finally, a very young-looking soldier spotted them and walked over to where they were standing. Their first impulse was to run, but it was hard to run from someone who sported a gigantic smile. The soldier said something and then waved for them to follow as he led them to a large military vehicle. He spoke rapidly to another soldier who jumped up into the back of the truck. In a couple of minutes he leaned over the tailgate and offered them bread. It was different from any bread they had ever eaten. It was white and gave off a wonderful aroma. They handled it and then each boy took a bite. The slices were quickly ingested by four happy mouths.

The soldier offered them second slices, and they, too, disappeared. The young soldier told them to slow down, but they had no idea what he was saying and it probably wouldn't have made a difference. The first soldier then opened four cans of some sort of meat, which Stefano thought tasted very salty, but he gladly ate it.

The two soldiers were packing boxes of food for the boys to take with them, when gunfire erupted. Soldiers began running in every direction. The young soldier shoved the boys under the truck bed and crawled in beside them. With an index finger he drew a swastika in the sand and pointed to the wooded area. They heard a couple more burst of a rifle, then nothing.

The young soldier crawled out from under the truck and surveyed the camp. When he was satisfied it was safe he motioned for the boys to come out too. He handed the four boys boxes of C-rations, and with a laugh and a shooing motion with the back of his hand, told them to leave. They traveled down the path and the other split off carrying boxes of the food with them.

The setting sun painted a lavender and pink glow across the western sky. There was total quiet, which was wonderful. Stefano and Polombo had not heard another shot after they left the Allied camp. Then as they approached the bottom of a gulley two hundred meters from home, they heard machine gun fire, followed by rifle retort, then machine gun fire from two different directions. The cousins could see their house at the top of the hill. They paused and then cautiously resumed their way home. They were used to the sounds. Then bullets began to zoom over their heads. They both hit the dirt among tall grasses. They had learned earlier from the German soldiers what to do when you come under attack. Crawl on your belly as flat as possible! Stefano and Polombo pushed the food boxes under a pile of brush and began to crawl.

Their elbows and knees were raw, but they paid little attention. They just wanted to get home, but there was no way they could reach the house through the crossfire. Polombo raised his head enough to see the top of the hill and quickly sat down again in the grass next to Stefano.

"The Germans have set up a machine gun placement right next to our house. Really accommodating of them to put it right there." He looked over at Stefano and asked, "You okay?"

"No, I'm not okay," Stefano answered with a shaky voice. "With the Germans up there on the left and the Americans on the right, it's possible to get shot by either one or both at the same time. Yeah, I'm scared."

"I'm scared too," replied Polombo. "But we've got to get out of here. It's almost dark. When the firing slows I'm going to make a break for it. You follow right behind me."

Suddenly the firing stopped on both sides. Polombo said, "Let's go." He took off running in a half crouched position. He looked behind him and realized Stefano hadn't moved. Polombo ran into the house and waved for Stefano to follow.

It was decision time for Stefano. He argued with himself. "I don't really have to go up to the house. I have all that food down at the foot of the hill. I can sleep out here okay." When you're starving it's hard to leave food behind.

Looking up at the house Stefano saw that the front door was now closed. That did it. He took off like a bat, not even bothering to crouch as he had seen Polombo do. When he was almost at the house the front door flew open and Sandro yanked him inside.

The firing commenced immediately. It was as if both armies had ceased fighting, knowing that the two boys were down the hill. Uncle told everyone to keep away from the windows and to stay down on the floor. Stefano didn't really care what anyone did. He was so tired he collapsed on his bunk and was instantly asleep. The gun fire continued for another thirty minutes, but Stefano didn't flicker an eyelid.

CHAPTER SEVENTEEN

· ·

STEFANO WAS VERY HAPPY that the past week had been pretty much routine. He had retrieved the boxes of food that the Americans had given them from the bottom of the hill, but the C-rations would last only a given number of days. The family decided to use the canned goods during their travel home.

Stefano had had enough adventure for a while. He awoke one morning and heard the Germans above and outside the basement. Everyone in the house, including the Germans, wondered where the Allied troops had gone. They were so close a week ago and now they seem to have disappeared.

Stefano sat on the side of his bed and thought, *Another day.*

He was right. The day started out much as the many days before, with boredom and hunger. A heavy rain the night before had awakened Stefano with a blast of noise. He was startled to hear war activity at that time of night. Usually the Allies didn't bomb during total darkness. With the second clap of thunder and the accompanying lightning, Stefano realized a heavy storm had moved in during the night. When he ventured out the next morning, he was met by the smell of the new day. The rain had washed away the ever-present odor of gun powder, and Stefano had the feeling that it may truly be a new day. However, it wasn't long before he became aware that it may be a new day outside, but inside it was the same.

Uncle Sandro had long since gone to work and Gabriella and Marta were cleaning the house, as they had done every day for weeks. House cleaning was the women's therapy. It gave their life purpose. Their main therapy, cooking, had long since been taken away from them. They spent much time wishing and thinking about cooking, but it didn't take long to plan a meal when there was nothing to cook.

The daily routine for Polombo and Stefano included rising early, making trips to the outhouse, brushing teeth with sapling twigs, and then deciding where they should make attempt to forage for food. Some days there may be a small amount to eat before they took off, but there was nothing on this morning.

After waiting for Polombo to rise on his own, Stefano went to their bed and kneed Polombo in the backside. "What's with the laziness? Let's get going before the sun gets too hot."

"Get out of here," groaned Polombo. "I don't feel good, I've had the trots all night. I'm surprised you didn't hear me running in and out the house. My gut feels like I'm dying."

Stefano told Gabriella about Polombo's comment. Gabriella responded, "I know he must have picked up something bad last night from what we at for supper. Marta and Danilo are sick, too, but not like Polombo. You know they ate the escarole and we ate the cabbage. I have to admit the escarole didn't smell just right, but I didn't want to throw out food."

Stefano could only think, *So, instead we toss out your son's guts.* He didn't say a word as he headed out the door. He met Marta coming back in the house, apparently returning from the outhouse. She looked as pale as pasta made without eggs. He felt sorry for his sister, but definitely didn't want to discuss the delicate subject.

As he made his way across the area in front of the house, Stefano paid little attention to the activities of the Germans. He didn't relish another day of foraging, but it was better than sitting in the house. Maybe the American encampment was still set up. The American food was salty but it was better than nothing. It was strange to him that the two opposing armies were about four kilometers from each other and existed as if they didn't know the others were there.

Instead Stefano decided to try the area where they had stolen the potatoes. There was the possibility of a new crop. All he would need was a way into the field. His conscience had long since given him permission to steal as long as it was food.

The field was quite a distance away from where the family lived alongside the Germans. It didn't matter; he had nothing better to do with his day. He knew he'd be able to find a few crickets or other insects to eat along the way. He and Polombo had learned that it's always advisable to pull the legs off crickets before placing them in their mouths. Sometimes the legs seemed to catch in the throat. The legs had to be eaten separately. Those little creatures had a way of somewhat satisfying hunger, which defied logic since they were so small. Maybe it was the idea of eating bugs cut the appetite.

The day was peaceful, as only occasional gun fire broke the silence. The sky was mostly clear with gathering dark clouds on the horizon. Stefano periodically checked the clouds. They did appear to be slowly drifting in his direction, and he hoped there would be another storm. It had been so dry recently and the wild field greens were not growing. A storm was needed.

As Stefano neared the potato farm he stopped short, not believing what was directly in his path. It was the most beautiful sight he had seen in weeks. There in all their glory was a mass of blackberry bushes laden with large plump berries. He gobbled down six or eight berries, swallowing without even chewing. Without hesitation he slipped off his shirt and began gathering the bounty. It was like dealing cards, one for the shirt and one for the mouth. By the time Stefano had stripped the three bushes of the ripe berries plus a few that were not truly ripe, he could hardly close the corners of his shirt together. As he started for home he noticed the berries were staining his shirt. He shrugged his shoulders and kept on walking.

From the position of the sun Stefano knew that it was well into the afternoon. Artillery gunfire had picked up during the last hour, but he paid little attention. Nothing could dampen his spirits. He would provide fresh fruit for the family which they had not had in months. Now that he had discovered the berries, he and Polombo could return for renewed harvest every other day as more berries ripened.

Stefano picked up the familiar drone of planes. Though not the heavy rumble of bombers, the sound grew louder and he knew the planes were headed in his direction. Since he hadn't seen any sign of Germans over the past couple of kilometers he didn't feel that the planes were headed anywhere close by.

Within minutes, though, the planes appeared over the horizon and within seconds German anti-aircraft fire could be heard. Bursts of black smoke filled the sky. The planes were strafing the countryside in the distance. One Allied plane was hit as it pulled up from a run. Five or six additional planes joined in, and Stefano thought it would be impossible for the Germans to miss, there were so many planes in the air.

Stefano took cover in a shell crater. Stray bullets and shells could appear out of nowhere. Finally, a few of the planes peeled away and headed south. Only two planes remained and they went in for a final run. The lead plane made a successful run while the second plane took a direct hit and exploded into a ball of flames. The first plane pulled out and began a near vertical ascent when it took a hit to its tail section. The plane rolled twice and was about to nose dive when Stefano was startled to see the pilot bail out. He gasped with horror as he watched the plane and pilot fall from the sky. He couldn't believe the pilot survived the hit. The pilot fell toward earth with Stefano's eyes locked on the scene.

Suddenly a white billow appeared in the sky and with the pilot swinging beneath it. Stefano was aware of a wet feeling in his clothes and thought he had peed his pants. Looking down he realized he had been squeezing his shirt and blackberry juice was running down his legs.

The parachute was still high in the air, and he watched as it drifted almost directly overhead. It soon disappeared over a ridge near where he had gathered the berries. Instinctively, Stefano dropped the berries and started running toward where he had seen the pilot disappear. As he came over the ridge he could see the parachute on the ground. He didn't think about any danger; he simply wanted to reach the pilot. As he neared the still partially inflated parachute, but couldn't see the pilot. He circled around the chute and saw the pilot hobbling in the opposite direction. Hearing the boy approach, the pilot turned and dropped to his knee with pistol drawn.

Stefano stopped dead in his tracks and threw his hands in the air. As he did so, the pilot smiled, lowered the pistol and placed it back in its holster. Stefano could see that the pilot was limping and approached to help gather the parachute. When all the silk was rolled into a ball the pilot looked as if he was searching for a place to hide it.

Without asking, Stefano pulled the ball of silk from the pilot's hands and ran to a nearby crater. He tossed the chute into the hole and began scraping dirt from the rim over the silk. The pilot limped to the crater, knelt down and began scraping dirt along with the boy. In very short order the white parachute was totally covered, and Stefano and the pilot sat looking at each other.

The man reached out and shook Stefano's hand, and then pulled the startled boy toward him and hugged him tightly. Stefano didn't feel threatened, just bewildered. The pilot seemed to apologize although Stefano couldn't understand a word. He was relieved when the man released him. He then reached out and rustled the red hair. When Stefano looked up he saw tears in the man's eyes, which he made no effort to hide.

The pilot stood and began to survey the surrounding area. He tried to take a step, but a grimace of pain clouded his face. He pointed to his right ankle. Stefano glanced at a wooded area and set out to find a sturdy limb which could be used as a crutch. Soon Stefano had found what was needed. He brought it to the pilot and stuck it under his arm.

Stefano started back toward where he had gathered the berries and waved for the pilot to follow. The man took one last look around, felt they were momentarily safe and limped after Stefano. When they had reached the blackberry brambles, Stefano motioned for the man to slide in between the berry bushes and the farm fence. It didn't look like much of a shelter from the Germans but it was certainly better than standing in the open. Once the pilot was in hiding, Stefano ran off in search for a more substantial hiding place. Around the corner of the fence a short distance away, there was a small shed. He returned to the pilot, led him to the shed and had him sit on a burlap sack filled with something reasonably soft.

Again the pilot's eyes filled with tears as he began speaking to Stefano with such a soft voice, the boy was taken aback. He couldn't understand a word the man was saying but realized he was in pain. He knelt before the pilot and began to unlace his boot. When the boot was off it was as if a balloon had been inflated beneath the skin. They could watch the ankle swell. The pilot picked up a small twig from the floor and snapped it. He pointed to the break and then to his ankle, smiled at Stefano and shook his head. Then he reinserted his foot into his boot and through gritted teeth began to lace it tightly. Stefano began to shake his head and said, "No, no."

The pilot understood, but replied, "Si, si."

The pilot's injury and pain overshadowed the greater danger, the Germans. They certainly would not take kindly to Stefano helping an American. He tried several times to make the situation known to the pilot, but he got nowhere.

Finally, in frustration, Stefano asked, "Parli Italiano? Un po'?"

The pilot understood and simply shook his head.

Stefano sat and tried again. "Sie sprecht Deutsch?"

The pilot beamed, "Ja. Sie?"

Stefano's hopes rose when he thought the two could now communicate. Before he knew what was happening the pilot was off and running in German. Stefano held up his hand and shook his head. He momentarily thought and then said, "Gross problema."

The pilot smiled, "Ja, gross problema." He realized that his college German was not much better than Stefano's "on the job training".

Stefano waved his hands about. "Deutsch. Deutsch."

The pilot frowned and thought, *That's what I was afraid of. Wonder how far to the Allied lines?* He sighed and a melancholy look came over his face. "Ich ein kind habe, ein sohn—I have a child, a son..." He stopped when he saw the blank look on the Stefano's face.

He tried again, "Ich heiße Richard, Richard Thompson."

The boy beamed, "Ja, Ja, il mi nome e' Stefano, Stefano Capaldi."

They shook hands once again.

Richard stood up and took a step, grimaced with pain and held onto a shed stud. "Ich gehen—I go."

"Nein, nein—no, no." Stefano reached for Richard's hand and helped him back to the sack. He pointed a finger toward Richard and then to the floor of the shed. He placed his hands on Richard's shoulder and gently pressed down. "Ich…" In his limited German he couldn't begin to tell the man that he was going for help. He simply pointed to his chest and then with two fingers made a walking, running gesture. Pointing in the distance he held up two, then three fingers and motioned that he would return.

Richard was amazed that the young boy could use such understandable sign language. The inbred Italian gesturing had its place. Richard wasn't sure about staying in the shed, but nodded his head and Stefano took off. He was over the ridge and running as fast as he could toward home when he came to an abrupt stop and retraced his tracks about fifty meters. He retrieved his shirt with the half-squashed dripping blackberries and resumed his race to home.

He was about 100 meters from the house when two Germans stepped in front of him. His first thought was that they were going to take his harvest. They started speaking so rapidly he could understand nothing. "Non capisco—I don't understand."

The soldiers rattled off questions and Stefano could sense irritation in their voices. Again Stefano replied, "Non capisco." However, this time he caught enough to know they were looking for the pilot. Inner fear reared its head, but Stefano fought to maintain his composure, although he was sure they could see his heart rate pick up. His heart could easily be seen thumping behind his rib cage.

Giving up on words, the soldiers used sign language too. They made gestures of planes flying, planes crashing and then one soldier made his hands like a canopy and swayed back and forth toward the ground. He pointed to Stefano, then to his own eyes, and then out toward the distance.

Stefano assumed the "stupid look" that he had used so many times with Gunther, the German cook, and shook his head. He held up his shirt with the blackberries and pointed to an area far from the place where he found the berry bushes, the shed and the American.

One of the soldiers eyed him with suspicion, but the other waved him on toward his house. Stefano was well aware the Germans knew where he lived, he had seen them both about the house, which didn't give the boy relief of mind. He continued on toward the house but at a more measured, leisurely pace.

Upon entering the house he closed the door and placed his back against it. Marta looked up from scrubbing the floor and immediately knew something was wrong. "What is it? What've you done now?"

Stefano resented the insinuation that he had done something wrong. He banged the back of his head against the door, took several deep breaths and calmly answered, "What I've done is walk several thousand meters and found these wonderful blackberries. That's what I've done."

He walked over and placed his harvest on the table. With no further comment he plopped two berries in his mouth, turned and walked back out the door. He knew he couldn't discuss what had happened with anyone except Sandro and maybe Polombo, definitely not Marta. He knew the longer he waited to act the more likely it was that the Germans would find the American, and he didn't want to think what would happen if the Germans did find him.

CHAPTER EIGHTEEN

IT WAS NIGHTFALL BEFORE Sandro made his way home. Stefano had been waiting for hours, sitting on a boulder in front of the house. The moment he spotted Sandro, he jumped up and ran to meet his Uncle. In his excitement he started talking very fast and then realized that there were Germans all around. Forcing himself to calm down he said, "Uncle, we have to talk, but not here. Let's walk away from the house."

At first Sandro laughed and said, "Stefano, I've worked all day and walked a long way. The last thing I want to do is go for a walk." Then he saw the seriousness on his nephew's face. "Okay, we walk."

Once they were a good distance from the house Stefano quietly related what had happened and where the pilot was. Sandro sat on a boulder and rubbed his head. After a few moments, he looked at Stefano and smiled. "When you get yourself into something, it's really something! Now, what are we going to do?"

Stefano glanced over his shoulder toward the house. "We can't tell them. The women will go pazze—crazy."

Sandro nodded his head and laughed lightly, "You're probably right on that. So, we wait until it's totally dark, and we go to your new friend. If we're lucky it will be as dark as it was last night. Can you find the way in the dark?"

Stefano shook his head, "I could find my way with my eyes closed. I'll follow the scent of the blackberries. Let's go see if they've saved any for you."

Marta hardly looked at Stefano, and he was just as glad she didn't. Polombo felt much better and was upset that his mother didn't think he should even try a berry. Once more Sandro had to intervene and said that his son could have two. Antonella carried on at great length about how so many berries had been mashed, to the point that Stefano wanted to smash the remainder over her head.

After they had finished the bread and stew Sandro had brought in with him, he said, "Boys, let's go out and mingle with our German friends. We may learn something." Fortunately Danilo wasn't interested. Polombo looked as if he was about to protest when Stefano nudged him in the back and pushed him up the steps to the outside.

There were only a few soldiers around, but the three Italians were still very guarded about their walk. Polombo kept asking where the heck they were going only to be told to keep quiet. When they were a good distance away from the house, Sandro said, "Polombo, don't speak, let Stefano tell you about his day."

Stefano gave an abbreviated version of what he had told his uncle. Polombo uttered repeatedly, "Il mio dio—my God."

Darkness settled around them to the point it was hard to even see the person in front. Stefano led the way without a hiccup. As they approached the shed he stopped and listened for any voices. He heard nothing and moved on.

He reached the shed door and whispered, "Richard, it's Stefano." He then pulled the door back. Richard was scrambling to his feet. He'd been asleep.

"Richard, dies ist Sandro und Polombo."

Richard struggled to answer in German. Sandro said, "It's okay. I speak English."

"Oh, thank God. Maybe I do have a guardian angel! Thank you so much for coming back to help me. I don't think I would've survived without my little friend here." He reached out and placed his hand on Stefano's head. He then asked Sandro to relay to Stefano that he had a son back in the States who looked so much like him.

When Sandro did so, Stefano thought, "Well, that explains the hugging."

Sandro brought the pleasantries to a close and spoke with Richard, "We've got to get you out of here. How bad is the ankle?"

"I don't think it's broken, but it hurts like a bitch. I can hobble, but if we have to run, there's no way I can do it."

"We'll help you with the walking. If we're where I think we are, the Allied lines should not be too far away. It's going to be challenging in the dark, we can get confused easily. The moon has come out which is good, but it would be our only direction indicator."

"I can help with that," said Richard. He felt around in his flight suit pocket. "Look what I've got." He held out a compass with a face that glowed.

Sandro smiled. "That should do it. We want to head south and bear slightly to the west. Our German friends are all around the house where we stay. We should be fairly safe until we get you home to an Allied unit. Stefano, you and Polombo are going to be the scouts. Stay about 100 meters in front of the lieutenant and me. We'll use our bird calls to communicate. The owl means okay and the whippoorwill danger. And you boys thought our evening games of bird calls were silly!"

He then translated for Richard.

"Stefano, you got us into this, so you take the compass and lead the way. Polombo, stay back about 25 meters. And everybody remember we're in no hurry. We've got until the sun rises to get this done. Now let me show our point on the compass."

After the quick compass lesson, Sandro asked, "Do you understand, Stefano?"

"Si, let's go."

Stefano instinctively knew to choose the darkest path. He walked slowly through tall grass wherever he could find it. Many areas were denuded of any cover. His biggest concern then was falling into one of many blast craters. They had been going about an hour when

Stefano heard a whippoorwill call. He dropped to the ground and listened. Again he heard the call, this time answered by a more near call. He was confused as to what he should do, and decided to drop back and confer with Polombo.

When they were together, Polombo whispered, "The first call was Papa." Then they heard the call again.

"Let's go back and see what's going on," said Stefano.

When the boys reached Sandro and Richard, the two men were sitting quietly. Sandro looked up and explained, "We neglected to make a signal to tell you we had to stop. I hoped you'd get the message. Good going. Richard is having a hard time with his pain."

Richard spoke through a strained voice, "Tell them to keep going, I won't hold them back again. I think my fear of capture just eclipsed my pain."

Sandro told the boys what Richard had said, and without comment, they turned and set off again.

Another hour passed, and Stefano was about to send out an owl hoot to signal they were doing fine when he heard distinct German voices. He dropped to his knees and attempted the whippoorwill call, but his throat constricted and only air passed his lips. He took a few deep breaths and tried again. The call was loud and clear. He made three calls and then paused to listen, he could hear Polombo relay the call. He could still hear the voices but they seemed to be moving away to the east. He decided to wait rather than retreat to the others.

During the wait he had a lot of different thoughts, mainly what am I doing here? Then resolve won out when Stefano saw himself in charge. When he could no longer hear the voices, he waited several more minutes before he gave a good owl hoot.

The sound had hardly left his lips when he heard crunching of grass, close. Too darn close. Instinct took over and out came a mild whippoorwill call that he hoped was loud enough for Polombo to hear. He was relieved to hear Polombo repeat the call.

Total silence completely surrounded him. Then he heard the Germans speaking quietly. They couldn't have been more than five meters away. Stefano thought about another call, but would not have been able, fear had overtaken his body. He was completely covered in sweat, and the harder he tried to keep his body still the more it was determined to shake.

Then he heard movement and quickly brought himself up into a sprint position. Was the patrol coming closer? The harder he tried to listen, the less he seemed to know. Then it was obvious, they were moving away to his left. He quietly moved out of grass area and onto bare soil. He followed along the grass back to Polombo and without comment pulled his cousin along. They retreated to Sandro and Richard. Without a word he placed his forefinger over each of their lips. Then he pulled everyone's hair, bringing their heads together.

In a very low whisper, "There's a German patrol out here somewhere. I think they are heading east, but I can't be sure. I think I almost stepped on them."

Sandro patted Stefano on the back, "Good man. Let's just stay here for a while and hope they continue to move away." He then interpreted for the pilot.

Eventually, Richard spoke to Sandro, "It's been thirty minutes. Should we move out?"

"Yes," replied Sandro. Okay, boys, move out."

They took off, moving quickly back to their previous positions. As Stefano neared where he thought he had been, he stopped and listened. Satisfied with his observations, he gave an owl hoot and moved forward.

Slowly he crept, following the direction dictated by the compass. His anxiety rose the more time passed. He figured his luck was bound to run out. "Just keep moving. Just keep moving."

After another hour he heard an order directed at him. "Halt."

Stefano could detect an accent, but it wasn't German. Then, "Heir kommen, langsam—come here, slowly."

The boy had no idea what was being said, but it sounded more like German. Then, "Kommen."

The shaking quickly returned to Stefano's knees. He finally found his voice, "It's only me," which in Italian meant nothing to the Allied soldier.

There was a lot of conversation and Stefano realized it was Allied troops. He started to run forward, but quickly heard, "Stop."

That he understood and immediately, English or Italian, he understood. He stopped. He tried to tell the soldiers that he was not German. He took a chance and moved out from the grass. One of the soldiers spoke to the others, "It's okay. It's just an Italian kid."

Stefano took another chance and let out several loud owl hoots. Polombo, emerged from the grass. Stefano went forward and when he was within reach of a soldier, he motioned for the soldier to follow him. That was met with a vigorously shake of the man's head. He wasn't about to follow the kid into the grass.

Soon Sandro and Richard arrived. Richard hobbled forward and fell against a soldier. "Oh, thank God."

It was music to Richard's ears when he heard the soldier exclaim, "Damn, it's a Yank."

Rapid conversation ensued, and Sandro tried to keep the boys informed of what was being said.

On the horizon broke the first signs of light. Sandro announced that they had to start for home immediately. Richard thanked the four for saving his life. He then told Sandro that he would like to hug Stefano. When Stefano heard the interpretation he smiled and went to Richard and hugged him. Before they parted, Richard kissed him on the top of his head and then slowly released the boy.

Stefano handed the compass to Richard. He shook his head and folded Stefano's hands around the compass. Stefano looked up into Richard's eyes and whispered, "Grazie, mia Amico." Then the three headed back into the grass for their long trek home.

CHAPTER NINETEEN

OVER THE NEXT FEW weeks it became obvious that the Germans were losing ground at an accelerating rate. All of the Germans around the house left within 24 hours. More and more the Capaldis could see that the Allies were advancing. No longer was there the seesaw of the Allies advancing and then dropping back, it was more a steady stream of troops advancing northward to Rome. Sporadic skirmishes could be heard in the distance or an occasional sortie of planes flying over, but even those were flying at very high altitude. It was as though peace settled over the region.

Stefano had to adjust to the difference when the shooting ceased. It was as if the silence was tentative. At night he found himself waiting for the shelling to begin, but there was no bap-bap-bap, no bombs, no artillery fire, just eerie quiet. Hard to imagine that he missed the fighting, but it had become a known quantity.

The fighting had stopped, but the perpetual problem of starvation continued. Again it was time for the family to face the trek back to Cervaro. Antonella used the last of the flour to make two loaves of bread and this was packed along with other essentials. The whole family agonized much less about what they should pack and what they left behind. The one thing the family never considered leaving was the cooking grate. It symbolized food even if there was nothing to cook. This time they planned a seven day road trip with a known destination and some assurance that they would not be shot. Stefano had reached the point he didn't worry about being shot. Individually each member of the family had silently thought to be shot would be a relief from the starvation.

The first four days of the trip were filled with the relief of knowing they were going home. Stefano was oblivious to how tired he was, it wasn't a topic of conversation. Though it was summer, the nights could still be very chilly. Stefano wrapped his blanket around him like a cocoon and slept deeply.

At about noon on the fourth day the family shared the last of the American food gift. While the food was in the bushes, animals had carried off everything that wasn't in a can. Those supplies along with a few things tossed from passing Allied troops made up their pantry. They had rationed themselves to one can of meat for each day. Even at that, there weren't that many cans. The last of the bread was consumed on the fourth night. A U.S. soldier commented later that as they came up through Italy it was one wasted area after another, filled with filthy, starving people. The soldier didn't see Stefano's family. They may have been starving but they took great effort to be clean. Antonella ran a tight ship, even in roughest seas.

By the end of their sixth day they had gone for two days without food. Danilo was stumbling from weakness. Polombo and Stefano took turns trying to support him as he walked, which only made two people stumble.

Danilo simply couldn't keep up, so Stefano called for everyone to halt and while they rested, he and Polombo fashioned a sled from tree branches. They took turns pulling Danilo.

Sometimes it's the little guy who seems to have the wisdom. Stefano pleaded, "Hold up, Polombo and I can't pull Danilo this way. It's killing our arms. Let's make a carrier."

Antonella, Marta and Sandro were too exhausted to think or worry about what the boys had in mind. They ventured into a thicket of brush and gathered two small but sturdy branches. They then folded two blankets over the poles and soon had a perfect litter for Danilo.

Danilo rejected the idea of being carried on a litter, but Polombo had had his fill and snapped, "Shut up, and lie down. We have to carry you, but we don't have to listen to you complain."

When Antonella started to reprimand Polombo, Sandro nudged her with his elbow and shook his head. No more spoiling the baby.

When it appeared everyone was about to collapse from exhaustion and starvation, Antonella spotted a farmhouse which looked as though it had been untouched by the war. It was like an oasis in the desert, too good to be true. It sat on a small rise and a vegetable garden could be seen beside the house and there was a well in front. As they had traveled, whenever they found a stream they washed themselves and filled their water jugs. The image of cool water without sand was fantastic.

When they reached the house, Sandro appealed to the family for anything in the way of food. The owner said they would willingly share what they had. The woman of the house prepared a green salad and placed homemade bread on the table. It called for restraint to not gulp down the food.

The family invited the Capaldi family to spend the night and that evening they were treated to a wonderful lamb stew. Marta and Antonella repeatedly admonished the boys to slow down their eating, but they were given assurances that there was plenty of stew and to help themselves. Those were the most wonderful words heard in months. Stefano had the propensity to ignore Marta and one of those times was upon him. After Stefano finished his second bowl of stew, he had onset of gripping abdominal pains. He quickly excused himself and ran outside. His gut simply was not used to the richness of the meal and in such vast quantity. Even so as he headed back to the house, he wondered if it would be impolite to ask for another bowl. The boys had lost so much weight they teased each other that they could pluck their ribs like mandolin strings.

During dinner the farm family related how fortunate they had been that the war had not touched them. They were reluctant to tell the visitors of their good luck when it was obvious others had suffered so much. At no time had the Germans occupied a significant presence in their area. Even their sheep and goats hadn't been confiscated. The farmer shared they had been accused by some of collaborating with the Germans, which he declared was totally untrue. Their home simply wasn't in the path of the Germans or the Allies.

The following morning the farmer's wife made more of that wonderful bread and poured warm milk over it. Stefano thought he had died and gone to heaven. He knew he was among angels. With his belly full Danilo made a quick recovery.

When the Capaldis left, the family packed vegetables for them and gave them a small bag of unground wheat. The next day Sandro gave the boys a lesson in cooking. When they had stopped for rest, Sandro found a rock with a concave surface. He took another rock, ground the wheat and mixed it with water, making a dough. He stretched the dough like a pizza and used the grate to cook the bread. Stefano thought it should have come off the fire sooner. "It's all burned," he complained.

Antonella cut up tomatoes and sprigs of basil provided by the farmer, drizzled on a few drops of oil and folded the bread like a calzone. There had been no cheese in years, so it wasn't missed.

Although they were not sure where they were, they sensed they couldn't be far from home. Stefano wondered why they hadn't taken the route by the railroad as they'd done before. He wondered but was not about to say anything. He would never grumble about anything, except maybe that the bread had been burned. If they'd stuck to the rail route they would have missed the "house of plenty".

They were fortunate that the weather held for them. It was early summer and yet there was little rain. The days were growing very warm and they had to be sure they had an ample supply of water. The nights were still cool and each morning they awakened with a coat of heavy dew on their blankets.

On the eighth day they found another oasis. It was a very rapid stream and Antonella told everyone it was total bath day. Shy Stefano went upstream to find a private place to strip and bathe. He did allow Polombo to go with him. Antonella gave them a small sliver of soap that had been contributed by their most recent hostess. "Don't waste it."

A hundred meters upstream the boys found a waterfall that cascaded into a small pool. They quickly started to strip and then Stefano said, "Polombo, if we bathe and put these dirty clothes back on we're going to stink the same way."

Polombo was already naked and just stood looking at his cousin. "And where are we going to get clean clothes, bright one?"

Stefano laughed. "Let's wear our clothes in the water and wash them, then us."

"Sounds good to me," said Polombo as he quickly redonned his shorts and shirt.

They had a wonderful time romping in the icy water, paying the temperature no mind. As Stefano soaped the back of Polombo's shirt he said, "Whew, I didn't know you were so stinky."

Polombo bragged of his older age. "That's because I'm more of a man than you. Don't worry, in about another year you will stink as bad as me."

"Oh, I can't wait," retorted Stefano with distain, but inwardly he couldn't wait. They shed their clothes, carefully rinsed them and laid them on the bank and then scrubbed themselves.

As they were getting out of the stream, Stefano got the last laugh. "After that cold water you're not as big a man as you were when you got in."

Polombo swatted Stefano with his wet shirt. "We'd better get back." They put on their wet clothes and started downstream.

"Yuk, I didn't know these German pants would be so stiff and uncomfortable when they're wet."

"But you're so clean. Don't worry, in this sun you'll be dry in no time."

When they rejoined the others Antonella shook her head. "Did you fool around and fall into the stream?"

"No, Mama," said Polombo. "We washed our clothes. Want to smell us?"

"No, I don't want to smell you. I've smelled you men quite enough for the past few days. We need to fill our water containers and move on."

Stefano jumped up from the rock where he had been sitting. "Don't fill them here! Come back up the stream where we were. There's a waterfall and the water is very clear. Nonno taught me a long time ago that you never drink from a still pool, but fast rushing water will be fresh and clean."

When they reached the waterfall, Marta asked, "Now where did you two bathe. We don't want water from there!"

Stefano turned to make a snap reply, but saw the wry smile on his sister's face. He laughed and said, "Polombo and I will fill the jugs, we're wet anyway."

They gathered their belongings and continued their journey. Late in the afternoon they came upon a U.S. encampment. The family approached the soldiers and expected to be warmly greeted, but it was just the contrary. Sandro made gestures to tell them they were very hungry. There was discussion among the soldiers, and one corporal made it obvious he didn't want to be near the family.

They were instructed to have a seat together and were brought containers of soup and bread. The soup was good but didn't compare to the recent lamb stew.

The corporal mumbled in the distance. Finally, as he walked by the family, and commented to his sergeant, "We should have killed them all."

Sandro's face dropped. The corporal's words wounded him to the core.

As soon as everyone had finished their soup Uncle said, "Let's move on. They don't want us here." He told them what the corporal had said.

When they returned the soup containers, Sandro spoke to the sergeant. "Thank you very much for the soup and bread, Sir. We also thank you for giving our land back to us."

The sergeant was startled that Sandro spoke such perfect English, and started to say something, but Sandro cut him off. "I lived in the United States for several years. Thank you again."

As the family passed by the corporal, Sandro stopped and looked the man in the eye and said, "And we thank you too, corporal."

The corporal attempted to reply but the family turned and walked away and didn't look back as they continued down the dirt road heads held high. They didn't have food, but they had their dignity.

The closer they came to Cervaro, the more devastation they observed. Not a tree was left standing anywhere. Ninety percent of the homes were damaged in some way or totally destroyed. By nightfall they were back at Sandro's cousin's house. The log barrier had proved its usefulness. Sandro was shocked to see that the house had taken a near direct hit which had taken away a corner of the roof and multiple chunks had been taken out of the outer walls by shrapnel. Thankfully no one in Macurio's family had been harmed. They had remained in the house throughout, except for the couple of weeks they had spent with Macurio's in-laws. The cousin was able to provide good news for Sandro's family. Their home was still standing, but he was not sure about Marta and Stefano's place.

Stefano was frustrated. "How do you know about Uncle Sandro's house and not know about ours? It's right across the road."

"I'm sorry Stefano. I know about Sandro's house because a friend told me he had seen the house. He didn't mention yours. I'm sorry."

Stefano wanted to go immediately to check on their home, but Marta prevailed upon him to wait until morning. Sandro added, "I know the trek has taken us longer than we expected but Marta is right, wait until morning.

Stefano had a restless night, with his mind swinging between anger and frustration. He and his sister never seemed to receive a bit of good luck in life.

No one in the family was prepared for what greeted them. Sandro's house was intact, as the cousin had reported. Marta and Stefano's house was basically destroyed. Only the second story room survived. It resembled a cabin on stilts.

CHAPTER TWENTY

· ·

THE WHOLE AREA HAD the stench of war. There were decaying bodies scattered around. One German soldier's body was hanging out of what was left of an upstairs window in Stefano's house. In back lay two more bodies, or rather, partial bodies. In a neighbor's front yard was a soldier's body mostly covered with dirt, unnoticeable except for two feet sticking out. It was impossible to tell if someone had done a poor job of burying him or if he had been covered by an explosion. As Marta and Stefano sat in the road in front of their home, Marta cried as Stefano held her, Sandro tried to comfort them. He knelt beside them, wrapped his big arms around them and quietly said, "Come back to the house. It's still your home. We'll be all right there."

Stefano was haunted by nightmares for weeks. Frequently in his nightmares he saw the American pilot and relived the night they helped him back to the Allied lines. Often he dreamed of being captured and imprisoned by the Germans. He had trouble remembering the details of the dreams but the fear lingered. Almost daily he found himself wondering if the pilot was still in Italy or if he had been sent back to the States to be with his family.

Stefano's mental state wasn't helped by watching the removal of the German bodies. The day after everyone arrived back in the village, men in uniform came and began removing the remains. After so long a time there was massive decay, and when the men tried to move the bodies, they mostly fell apart. At first Stefano watched with satisfaction that he was witnessing the rottenness of the Germans, but then he remembered Karl and several other German soldiers who had been kind to him. The longer he watched, the more revolting the scene became. The horrible odors closed in on him. He ran to where his grandfather had fallen from the ladder, and vomited until nothing was left. Once his gut settled, he propped up against the tree stump and talked to his grandfather.

"Oh, God, Nonno, I wish you were here. No, no, I don't. I wouldn't want you to see what a mess your beautiful farm is. All of your trees are gone, even the fruit trees are twisted and broken. I'll make it right, though. It won't stay this way." He rocked but couldn't bring himself to cry.

Over the next couple of weeks, crews from the township came and removed all of the rubble. Truck upon truck hauled away the devastation. Stefano watched from a window and one part of him longed to explore more of his property, but another side froze him to the point that he couldn't go out of the house except to go to the toilet.

Stefano's family left him alone and gave him room to sort out his feelings. What finally brought him out of his depression was that Antonella told him he would have to start doing his portion of the chores. As much as he hated her demands, he came to see she was trying to help him.

Life changed when they returned to the village. Stefano and Polombo continued to be friends, but soon it became apparent that Polombo had developed broader interests, especially in girls. Sandro's other children seemed to feel that Marta and Stefano, who were not really a part of the family, should do all the chores in the household. When Antonella would say she needed wood or water, the other children ignored their mother, knowing that Marta or Stefano would pick up the slack and do whatever was needed. They felt obligated since they were living there for free.

Marta and Stefano talked about the way their cousins had changed. The suffering the family had all shared had been a binding force, but now that there was some sense of security, the bonds loosened. Marta, in her saintly way, continually reminded Stefano to be grateful. He was grateful but frustration mounted, and that, mixed with anger, seemed to overwhelm the boy.

Stefano gradually slipped into a phase that would be properly termed "Shell Shock". He had seen so much killing and maiming that to avoid those memories, he closed out the world. Days went by when he refused to eat. It was as if his stomach was locked into a state of perpetual starvation. The days became weeks and he lost weight at an alarming rate. It wasn't as though he had excess flesh to start with, and Marta became extremely concerned watching the last member of her family fade away. She did everything she could imagine, from cajoling to berating, but all to no avail. Eventually he reached the point that he would only consumed small amounts of water, and looked no more than a skeleton.

Sandro placed Stefano on a small single cot in the room he had shared with Karl, the German. Marta was certain her brother had contracted some horrible disease from the many decaying body parts that had been strewn about the area or had malaria from the army of mosquitoes which seemed to have replaced the German army. Stefano's deteriorating condition was the talk of the neighborhood. Even the neighbor who had complained of having to cook to contribute to the Capaldi wakes, planned what she would fix for Stefano's.

The medicine woman was called but she had no more idea what the diagnosis was than did Marta, but that didn't stop her from going through her incantations and prescribing a potion. He took a few doses but finally refused to take the vile tasting stuff. After all, it only made him vomit which certainly didn't help his nutrition. Before the war, the closest doctor was in Cassino, and now there was no Cassino. There was no doctor and they had no money to pay him, if one had been available.

Sleep was Stefano's escape from the world that seemed to have imploded around him. He slept through the nights and most of the days. Marta spent hours by his bedside, praying and fingering her rosary. That probably accounted for his recurring nightmare of someone or something being sacrificed on an altar.

Finally Stefano ceased all communication and there was no indication he recognized his family, not even Marta. As distressed as she was, she continued to have words of encouragement for him. Although he appeared to be semi-conscious, he had a level of cognition where he wished Marta would stay quiet or at least give the rosary a rest.

It reached the point where Stefano was more or less just another piece of antique furniture. It didn't move and had lost its purpose, but it was still there. Marta continued her vigil, but the rest of the family avoided him. They were concerned, but whatever he had they didn't want to catch it.

Stefano remained in a semi-comatose condition for weeks. One day, Luciano, a cobbler who made and repaired shoes came to the house. He had looked around the neighborhood and asked Sandro if he could work in Stefano's room. "It has the best light and is the coolest place I've been able to find. I've heard about the boy and I don't think I'll disturb him." Nothing seemed to disturb the boy, so why not.

While he worked, the cobbler loved to tell stories of his travels and what he had seen. As he was measuring Sandro for a pair of boots, he related a story he had heard of a woman who would not eat. "She stopped eating all together and if she did eat she would throw it back up."

"Did they give her any medicine?" asked Sandro.

"I understand they did, several kinds, but she refused to take any of them. By Mary and Joseph, when she stopped drinking water, she was dead in three days."

Though no one was aware of it, Stefano was absorbing everything the cobbler said. He didn't want to be the next Capaldi to die. As if he had been visited by the Archangel himself, Stefano suddenly sat up in bed and asked, "Where is Marta? I want something to eat."

It was a good thing Stefano wasn't on the verge of death. Marta and Antonella had to recite ten prayers of thankfulness before they brought him a bowl of broth, which he managed to swallow and keep down. That evening when dinner was ready, Stefano came to the table. He was so weak, Sandro had to help him walk. He wasn't hungry and felt that if he ate he would vomit, but he forced himself to eat a few bites of what he knew was a wonderfully prepared meal.

I've got to eat, or I'm going to die, thought Stefano. In reality he feared he'd gone too long without eating and he would die.

It was a daily ordeal to ingest anything, but he was determined and after a few days he began to gain strength and appetite. On the tenth day he challenged his cousin, Polombo, to a game of Briscola.

Stefano continued to make progress and soon was back to his determined, strong-willed self. After a month he announced to Marta, "We are going to move back home. I can't stand this any longer. Except for Uncle Sandro I think everyone will be glad we're gone. I know I may have pushed their patience too far when I was sick, but that's gone, and I want to be gone too."

CHAPTER TWENTY-ONE

· ·

MARTA WAS ANXIOUS, AS usual, but the idea of being back in their home was irresistible. Within a short time she was eagerly helping to make plans for what needed to be done. With the help of Sandro and other neighbors, they made the one room their home. The first thing that had to be rebuilt was the outside stairway that had been blown away. The chimney and fireplace on the second story created a construction nightmare. That problem was solved by a mason who was a relative of Sandro's. The room was partitioned, providing a private bedroom for Marta. For Stefano a bed would be in the common room.

They gradually added some modest furniture and a few small decorations. To the two children of 12 and 18 years, it was paradise. It seemed like an eternity since they had been evicted from their home by the Germans. They wanted a new start and leave behind all the horror they had seen.

Stefano wanted to begin the dangerous job of reclaiming the property. Remnants of artillery shells as well as undetonated bombs lay strewn about in the fields. The Germans had left a cache of ammunition beside the road near Stefano's house which contained everything from hand grenades to bullets and artillery shells. Some of the artillery shells were filled with explosive that was in strings that carried the name macaroni powder. When lit, it would pop like a firecracker and reignite again and again. In the night it looked like shooting stars.

In one of his moments of non-thinking, Stefano decided to tease one of the younger neighbors by igniting a string of macaroni powder. Quickly the string became uncontrolled, bounced around and landed on the munitions pile, setting off other pieces of the string powder. Both children turned and ran for home. Fortunately a quick-thinking neighbor walked by at that moment, took off his jacket and smothered the fire.

The neighbor then called for Stefano. "Do you realize you could have blown up the entire village? If you want to be the man of this house, it's time you acted like it."

Stefano expressed his regrets and registered one more lesson in his memory bank. It seemed his memory bank was overloaded with lessons learned the hard way. He figured he had made far too many deposits in that bank.

The Germans had literally created a mine field on the Capaldi property, with plenty of booby traps. The area was covered with weeds about two feet tall. The mines were often planted where one would least expect them. The first day Stefano set out to clear the weeds he met a man from a neighboring town. When Stefano told him what he was about to do the man implored him to be very careful.

"Please, watch every step you take. I just lost my brother-in-law. He was at the back of our property gathering figs with his cousin. They climbed a very tall fig tree and when their baskets were full, they jumped down. His cousin was unharmed, but my brother-in-law jumped directly on a mine and was killed instantly."

With those words of warning the man continued on toward Cervaro, shaking his head as he went. Stefano gazed out across the field of weeds and thought long and hard. *There has to be a safer way of doing this.*

He decided not to start that day, but thought about his problem overnight. The next morning he had a solution. It was a perfect day, warm and calm. Stefano stuck his forefinger in his mouth and held it up to check the wind direction as he had seen Nonno do many times. On that particular day he felt no breeze. Stefano's plan was to burn the weeds in the field and save a lot of work. In fact it might possibly detonate any explosives within the area. He retrieved a box of matches from the house and decided to start the fire on the high side of the irrigation trench. That would act as a backfire for when he burned the larger section. A plan well thought out, like the man of the house would do.

The weeds ignited easily, and Stefano was proud of his ingenious work. It was only a short time, though, before the wind began to pick up. Very rapidly the wind-pushed flames shot 10 meters in the air and raced toward a neighbor's house. It all happened so fast Stefano stood in shock, not knowing what to do. As the flames spread they did ignite ordinance. Shrapnel began flying everywhere and a large piece whistled so close to Stefano that he hit the ground and crawled around a stone wall. Fortunately his neighbor had recently plowed a wide swath between his home and the irrigation trench. With nothing left to fuel the fire the flames died quickly. Stefano had not been injured nor had anyone else. Another lesson learned about planning ahead. Another deposit in the overflowing bank.

Stefano's world was infested with ordinance. Most everyone had a pistol, rifle and even a few mortar launchers. Why anyone would want to own a mortar or launcher was a mystery. At times it was almost as dangerous to leave the house as it had been during the war, only difference then, it was most dangerous during the daylight hours. People, Stefano included, did stupid things like exploding ammunition or shooting into the air, mainly at night.

Stefano found a bolt action rifle with a broken stock. At night he tied the rifle to a tree stump and shot tracer bullets into the air. It was great fun as he watched the tracers in the dark sky. On the far side of a hill it was as though someone answered his message firing after each time Stefano fired.

After a few weeks the frequency of the night shootings lessened, either from boredom or people running out of ammunition, but they continued sporadically for several months. Fortunately there were no reports of anyone being hit by the rifle or pistol fire. However, almost weekly people were killed by accidental explosions of unspent shells or land mines.

CHAPTER TWENTY-TWO

. . . .

MARTA AND STEFANO KNEW their top priority had to be to grow something in a garden as quickly as possible. They had shelter, but they had little to eat. In a small section where the weeds had been burned they prepared the soil by hand for l'orto—a vegetable garden. Each shovel-full of dirt had to be turned by hand before it could be raked. It took days, but strong backs and determination carried them through the task. They planted escarole, cabbage, potatoes and a few other vegetables for which they could get seeds. They planted, but then there was no rain, so each plant had to be watered by hand. Stefano watered the plants one bucket at a time, which required many trips to the well.

After a few weeks they were able to harvest the first of the escarole. They had planted several rows of the green vegetable, and day after day Marta cooked, sautéed, boiled and even baked escarole. It seemed to go on forever. Finally Stefano had had enough.

"Marta, please stop the escarole. My stomach is full of escarole, my brain is full of escarole. I close my eyes and escarole is all I can see."

Marta smiled that saintly smile that sometimes made Stefano feel like he was living with a nun. "Stefano, you know it's all we have to eat. Now hush and eat your dinner."

Of course he did, but he didn't do it willingly. Each day he checked the garden to see if there wasn't something that could substitute for the escarole. Finally there were a few cabbages that were ready for harvest.

Then it became escarole six days a week and cabbage on Sunday. No matter how much he wanted to complain, Stefano was determined not to mention food again. Marta was working as hard as he was and she went about her day in her angelic state.

One of the things that made the vegetables more palatable was an item left behind by the Allied forces. As they passed through they had left behind many items that proved useful. Stefano found a five gallon tin of what appeared to be lard next to a downed tree on the backside of their property. Marta tasted the white goo and exclaimed, "Oh, it is lard! Oh, Stefano what a find."

They shared the lard with Antonella, and they finally were able to show some small token of appreciation to their "other family".

Everything left behind by the Allied Forces was utilized in some way. Old tires were cut into pieces and fashioned into sandals. Ammunition boxes, which were scattered over the terrain by the thousands, were cut, flattened and used to patch a roof or used for siding on a shed.

Also left behind was a huge pile of cigarettes, so tall that Stefano could sit behind the pile and no one could see him. Mainly Canadian brands, Stefano was determined to try each one. Daily he would sneak behind the pile and try a different cigarette. After a few days of enjoying his new-found pastime a huge rain came, and he could stop the hand watering.

The following morning Stefano dug into the pile, determined to find ones that were dry. He did but for some reason, they did not taste the same. He had failed to enjoy rabbit tobacco and real cigarettes weren't much better. He gave up cigarette smoking as a lost cause. The rain may have prevented an addiction.

Once the garden began producing string beans, potatoes and tomatoes, Stefano and Marta ate well, though they lacked protein in the diet. They had hoped to sell some of their vegetables to the merchants who were reopening their stores, but in reality they had little more than they needed. Still they dreamed.

The two young people attempted to live life like all their friends and neighbors. On a Sunday a festival was held in Cervaro with a feast and parade. They went into the town and followed the procession. Unless it was a military extravaganza, most parades marked a religious celebration and there were many, even in the small village of Cervaro, the most elaborate being at Easter and at the feast of Corpus Christi. Miraculously, the small church had escaped any direct damage during the war.

On that particular Sunday, the procession was led by the priest and altar boys. The small statue of the Virgin Mary and the Christ Child statues were carried from the church, held aloft through the village's few winding streets, around the piazza and back to the church.

Vendors set up booths along the parade route hawking their wares, from hand-embroidered linens to delicious gelato. Several children enjoyed the rich, cold treat, while Marta and Stefano stared.

One of the neighbors, Francesca, who also happened to be sister of Luciano, the shoemaker, noticed the two and approached Stefano. "Do you have money to buy gelato?"

Stefano was embarrassed, but answered honestly, "No, we're just looking."

"This is a feast day. You should have gelato. Take this money."

Stefano flushed with embarrassment. He looked down at the street and softly replied, "We couldn't do that, just take money."

The woman quickly covered for the boy. "Who said I was giving you money? You must bring walnuts to me tomorrow. Now take the money and be off with you."

"Thank you very much. I'll bring the walnuts tomorrow."

Stefano and Marta treated themselves to gelato and also bought some chocolate. Back at home, Marta inquired, "Why did she give you money? I watched, but couldn't hear what you said."

"It's okay. I told her I'd bring her walnuts tomorrow."

"Stefano, we no longer have walnut trees, they were destroyed. Where are you going to get walnuts?"

"Uh, that's a problem. Don't worry, I'll find them somewhere."

"Stefano, I don't want you getting into trouble. People no longer are so willing to share. Be careful."

"Marta, you need to relax. You say people aren't willing to share, but Francesca gave me money didn't she?"

Marta shook her head, picked up a broom and began to sweep the floor. Stefano took off for the back of their property. He knew there was a small walnut tree just across the fence. Quickly, he scaled the fence and in a short time had tossed enough walnuts over to his side of the fence. He then re-crossed the fence, picked up the nuts from the ground, and filled his straw-hat.

He placed the hat full of nuts under the stairway leading up to their home. He slept well that night and the next morning awakened much later than usual. He leaned against the cool wall and looked out the window at the beautiful morning. The sun was shining and only a few scattered clouds drifted across the sky. He ate some bread with milk and started out the door.

Marta questioned what he was up to. "And where are you headed in such a hurry?"

"I have to deliver the walnuts to Francesca."

"And where did you get the nuts, may I ask?"

Stefano smiled broadly. "I picked them up off the ground on the back of our property."

"Stefano, look at me."

He looked her straight in the eye and said, "Honestly, I picked them up off our property."

Marta was skeptical. "I don't understand how you could have done that since we don't have any walnut trees."

"Marta, be more positive." With those words Stefano dashed out the door. He called back to Marta. "Do you want to go into town with me? I still have some money and you can buy a few things."

"I have the washing to do. Just buy bread, we'll make do with that."

"Suit yourself." He picked up the walnuts and headed for Francesca's.

The kind lady took the opportunity to pass on a few more liras. "You have brought me such a nice supply of beautiful walnuts, I feel I owe you a little more money. Wait here." She soon returned and pressed the extra money into Stefano's hand.

He felt flush. It was the easiest money he had ever earned. "Do you think you would want some more walnuts tomorrow?"

"No, dear. I think I have all that I'll be able to use for a while. I'll let you know."

That was a disappointment and Stefano continually thought about how he could make money.

***

The next real money Stefano was to earn would carry a heavier price. After the war repatriation meant money flowed into Italy for reconstruction of the towns and cities. It seemed to flow everywhere, except into the Capaldi household. The town of Cervaro received financial aid and also CARE packages. These packages were intended for those who most needed them and Marta and Stefano certainly qualified as needy orphans.

Barefoot, Stefano walked into the town office and asked for shoes and CARE packages for him and Marta. The people distributing the packages looked him over and didn't question that he qualified to receive a package. He was taken aback however, when received nothing for Marta.

He started to leave, but turned back and asked, "Please, may I have a package for my sister?"

The stern man at the counter, annoyed that Stefano was not satisfied with what he received, replied, "Sorry, but there are none left."

Stefano wouldn't let that ride. "But I can see other packages in that room." He pointed behind the distributor.

"I said there are no more. Those are for other needy souls."

Stefano turned and mumbled, "Sure, other needy souls like your friends."

The man heard Stefano and quickly came around the counter. "What did you say?"

Stefano didn't reply but stared at the man without any sign of fear. After a moment, he turned and left the office and walked home. Everyone in the town had talked of how the politicians got the top layer of cream and then most of what was left went to their friends, but they had little power to do anything about it.

Stefano took a long time walking home because he didn't want to tell his sister that there was only one package, and it was for a boy. He was happy to have a pair of shoes, and Marta was happy for him, but disappointment showed in her face and pulled at Stefano's heart. He felt he had failed her one more time.

This was an uncertain time in the life of the orphans. All of their neighbors' homes were headed by adults. The men and women worked the farms or the men went off to the cities, like Cassino, for employment. It was impossible for the two young people to farm their land alone. They would have to hire people to do the plowing and seeding, and they had no money to hire anyone to do anything. A Catch 22, they needed money to get the farming done in order to have money to hire the people to get the farming done. They couldn't even start the cycle. The neighbors wanted to help, but they were too busy trying to survive themselves.

CHAPTER TWENTY-THREE

ON A CLOUDY MORNING, a morning that matched his mood, Stefano was doing busy work around the outside of their home. He was bored stiff and frustrated. Around mid-morning a man with a donkey cart ambled by and greeted Stefano with all the gusto of a happy Italian.

"Buon giorno, amico."

"Buon giorno," answered Stefano. "Come sta?"—How are you? He smiled when the man's donkey gave an extra bleat of welcome.

"Molto bene—very well. I've had a successful morning collecting copper and brass. Do you have any that you would like to sell?"

Dejected, Stefano replied, "I'm afraid we don't have anything that you would want to buy. I wish we did." As they talked Stefano surveyed the metal objects in the man's cart. "Did that metal come from artillery shells?"

"Yes it did, amico mio. I will come around again in two weeks. If you find any metal, I will pay a very good price for it. Now I must go. Ciao."

Stefano's mind began to race and he envisioned bringing in money so they could buy food. Another vision entered his mind too, as he remembered a close call he had with his cousin Giovanni. They, along with another friend, were walking down the road toward Cassino when they came upon an Allied Forces hand grenade lying beside the road. The friend and Giovanni began playing a game of football with the grenade. They could see that the pin and spoon were missing from the grenade, so they assumed it to be a dud. Giovanni put extra boot into a kick, and the grenade flew up into the air and landed in a ditch. As soon as the grenade hit the ground it exploded. If it had landed on the road, they would be dead. The shrapnel blew upward and into the sides of the ditch. The three boys found several large pieces embedded into the ditch bank. That episode underscored the danger of handling explosive devices.

In Stefano's head there was a running debate, the pros of money and the cons of death. In the end, he felt he had no choice. The money, which they so desperately needed, won the debate. He walked around their property and searched for unexploded ordinance and found several. It wasn't as though there was a shortage in the area.

Back at the house, Stefano looked but couldn't find anything he could use to remove the brass and copper from the shells. He went to Sandro's and in a tool shed found a hammer and a heavy chisel. As he examined the first shell, the two-inch-wide band of copper gleamed in the sun. He circled the shell several times and then squatted next to it. He began talking to himself and realized that wasn't a good idea. It made him more nervous.

"Just get the darn thing off. Don't think." He tapped the shell with the hammer and then wedged the chisel next to the band and began lightly tapping. The band didn't budge. He increased the force of the hammer and in about 15 minutes he was holding the trophy in his hand.

"I did it! I did it, and I'm still here," was all he continued to say to himself.

By the end of the day he had the bands from four shells. He congratulated himself and figured he had pushed his luck far enough for one day.

Day after day Stefano searched the fields for the unspent shells. There was no plan or pattern, he went wherever his feet led him. Some days he walked two or three kilometers looking for shells that he felt were safe. He was never quite sure what made him decide to work or not work on a particular shell, but instinct hadn't failed him so far.

When the scrap man came around again, Stefano brought out his cache. The man weighed the metal and made an offer. "Amico, I will give you fifteen hundred lira for the lot."

Stefano shook his head. "That isn't enough."

"But amico, I am a poor man."

"That isn't enough. What I'm doing is very dangerous. You don't risk your life. If I'm your friend you won't try to cheat me."

The man went through the process of weighing the metal again. "You are a tough business man. I will add another 800 lira."

"That is closer. Add another 200 and we have a deal."

"I'm paying you too much, but I need the metal. It's a deal, and I'll be back in another two weeks. I hope you'll have more for me then."

Stefano couldn't help adding a little smart comment. "You must not be paying me too much if you want to come back. Thank you."

He carried the money out in front of him like a chalice, and gleefully showed the handful of lira to Marta. "Look, we can now go to town and buy what we need. We have lira."

"Stefano, I worry about what you're doing, but I'm grateful." She pulled him to her for a big hug. "I love you, my little man."

"Let's go into town now."

"I have so much to do here. You made the money, you go, and I'll tell you what we need. You deserve to spend the money. Thank you."

Stefano went into town and shopped for eggs, milk, soap, olive oil and then he splurged on bread. Marta baked bread every four or five days, but today Stefano wanted fresh bread. He wasn't sure he wanted to eat the bread so much as he wanted to feel the warmth against his chest and inhale the wonderful aroma of the yeast as he walked back home.

Marta started to tell him he had wasted money buying bread, but caught herself as she saw her brother caressing the bread as though it was his first girlfriend. That evening she made pasta e fagioli with fresh tomatoes from their little garden. Stefano beamed as he drizzled fresh olive oil over the dish. They both ate with gusto.

Stefano gushed, "This is the best thing I've had to eat in such a long time!" Oil dripped down his chin as he added, "Thank you, thank you."

Marta smiled, "I should be thanking you. You're taking such risk. I'm not sure this wonderful meal is worth that risk."

"I'm fine," said Stefano, but he wasn't sure he believed himself.

The next morning he was back in the fields looking for shells. He pushed thoughts of danger out of his mind; it was an automatic process without thought. More and more Marta worried about the risk and asked him to stop, but he was on a roll and visualized more lira. The money was like an addiction. It had been so long since he had had money, now he wanted more.

It had been eight days since his transaction with the scrap man and Stefano had accumulated much more in those eight days than he had during the previous two weeks. He was a good distance from home when he came upon the largest shell he had ever seen. It was just off the road and he would have missed it except he had become very good at spotting the copper glowing in the sun.

The copper band was about five inches wide. He walked around the shell and tried to imagine the best way to remove the huge piece of copper. He couldn't figure why it hadn't landed nose first in the ground. If it had, there would be no way he could have moved the shell to get to the nose. It was lying flat on the ground, and there was something about the situation that didn't look right. He sat by the shell trying to decide what he was going to do. A big part of him told him to walk away.

After about a half-hour Stefano got to his feet, picked up his hammer and chisel and sat astride the shell. Several times he drew the hammer back, but he couldn't bring himself to strike the chisel. He sat on the shell, trembling and sweating. He recalled the German soldier who was hit by the shell as he was guarding Giovanni at the well. He also recalled Karl telling him about a friend who had been hit by a shell and all they found of his body afterwards were four fingers. He thought, *If the shell exploded between my legs I know darn well what they wouldn't find, that or any other whole piece of my body.*

His hands were sweating so badly he had trouble holding onto the chisel and hammer. "Do it now or walk away." Wiping his hands on his shorts and then holding the hammer, he made the sign of the cross over his chest. He looked up at the sky and prayed, "Please God, don't let this thing explode." He then brought the hammer down, hit the chisel squarely and then waited. Nothing happened. It took an intense 30 minutes of pounding before the ring of metal slipped over the nose and onto the ground. He picked up the copper, hammer and chisel and walked away, frankly expecting the shell to explode at any time. When he was 100 meters away he sat down on the road and shook.

Openly he talked to God. "Thank you God for delivering me through that. I will never go near another bomb."

The next week when the scrap man came around, Stefano demanded one thousand lira for the trophy find and another three thousand for the rest of the metal. When the transaction was completed, Stefano stuffed the lira into his pocket.

The man said, "This was a big haul of copper. I'll look forward to seeing you in two weeks."

Stefano shook his head and said, "Don't bother to come again. I'm through. I'm lucky I'm not dead, and I won't do the collecting anymore."

The man smiled and said, "Oh yes you will, amico. You enjoy having the money."

"You're wrong. No, you're right, I do enjoy the money, but I made a promise to God and I won't break that promise."

Stefano kept his promise and sometime later the government sent men to find and collect unexploded ordinance. Stefano earned a few hundred liras by helping the government men find the shells. He recalled the location of every shell he had rejected for his personal adventure. He had been right on some of his rejections, as a few exploded while they were being moved.

Prior to the harvesting of shells, farmers plowing their fields would often strike a mine and be wounded or killed. Over time those accidents became fewer and fewer.

Stefano had made enough money in those four weeks to provide very well the things they needed for sustenance and to get a very small area plowed. It was an investment in the future, not for immediate food. As their food supply began to dwindle, he and Marta again faced a near crisis. There simply had to be something he could do that would provide a more reliable income, but what? Stefano knew that it couldn't involve unexploded shells. Marta had said, "We," but it was obvious it had to be him. The only work for women was in a knitting guild, and that paid little.

CHAPTER TWENTY-FOUR

· ·

IN CERVARO MANY OF the destroyed buildings were being repaired and rebuilt. The buildings were constructed of stone and mortar and many men were needed for such heavy work. Stefano walked from one construction site to another asking for work, but invariably he was told that at the age of twelve he was much too young and too small for what they needed. No matter how he begged and he literally did beg, he was met with the same answer, "Come back when you are older and we will give you a job. We like that you're eager, but we can't use a boy for a man's work." The phrase, "royally pissed" best described his frustration. He was convinced he could do anything that any man could do.

No matter how hard Stefano sought work he was rejected because of his size or age and sometimes because of both. Nico, Sandro's son-in-law and Stefano's cousin by marriage, came to the rescue. They often saw each other as Nico came by frequently to see his wife's family, and he had rebuilt the fireplace in Stefano's home.

Stefano's desperation was surfacing as anger. He was trying so hard to find work and was being rejected on a regular basis. All he wanted was a way to provide for Marta and himself. One day he was particularly angry as Nico walked by.

"Hi, young Stefano, Why so glum?" asked Nico.

"Hi, Nico. I'm in no mood to talk," replied Stefano. Even though he had a short fuse, he was usually very courteous.

Nico was taken aback by his cousin's reply. "I've been meaning to talk to you, but if you don't want to talk, it's okay. So, just listen. I heard you're collecting metal from artillery shells. It's not my business, but I'm telling you to stop. I know, I got no right to tell you anything, but I'm telling you. I..."

Stefano looked up at Nico from the boulder on which he was sitting. "Don't worry, I stopped doing that. I admit I was too scared to keep at it."

"That's good."

"No, that's bad. At least we were paid for the copper. Now we have nothing, and I can't find work."

"What kind of work do you want to do?"

"I don't care. Believe me, I'll do anything. I went into town and tried everywhere to find work, but everybody turned me down. I went to the construction sites and thought there must be something I could do, but everywhere it was the same story. 'You're too young or you're too small.' Right now I hate me."

"That's no good. Tell you what, you can work with me. Yeah, you're small but I know you got guts. To do that shit with the shells, you got guts. You can be my helper."

Stefano was hopeful, but skeptical. He got up from the rock and walked closer to Nico. "Thanks, that would be great, but do you think they'll let me on the job?"

"Come with me tomorrow morning and we'll see." He held out his hand to shake with Stefano.

"I know you pass here at seven. I'll be waiting! Thanks, Nico."

Stefano ran to share the news with Marta. He looked over his shoulder and shouted to Nico, "Ciao."

He could hardly sleep, frequently waking during the night, imagining what it would be like to actually have a job. He had seen the masons at the construction sites and knew the work would not be easy. But he was determined.

A few minutes before six Stefano was outside waiting for Nico at the roadside. He watched the morning's emerging sunrise. Slowly, the orange ball broke over the mountain top, surrounded by a clear lemon circle. As bright and clear as the morning was, Stefano could feel it could be a good day. Reality made him understand that the work foreman could still turn him away, but he had to hope.

Nico arrived on time, and the two of them proceeded into Cervaro. As they approached the site where Nico worked, he turned to Stefano and directed, "Say nothing unless the boss directly asks you a question and then tell the truth."

"Okay, whatever you say, and again, thank you for doing this."

"Don't thank me too soon. You're going to work your little ass off if you're with me!"

As they approached the foreman, the two exchanged greetings. "Ciao, Nico."

"Ciao. I need to talk with you. My cousin here needs a job."

The foreman turned to Stefano. "Didn't I talk to you a couple of days ago?"

"Yes, Sir," replied Stefano.

"And didn't I tell you that you were too young?"

Nico interrupted, "He will be a good worker. I've seen him work on his property. It's just him and his sister. He needs this job real bad."

"Sorry, he's just too young. I'm looking out for him. I don't want him getting hurt."

Nico showed slight agitation. "So what's going to hurt him more, lifting mortar or starving?"

"I understand, Nico, but there's nothing I can do."

"There is something you can do, but you're saying you won't. If you don't hire him as my helper, I'm leaving."

The foreman was incredulous. "What do you mean, you're leaving? You can't leave. You're my best mason."

Nico frowned and then smiled. His chess opponent had just exposed his queen. "If I'm your best mason then you know I can find another job where they will also hire Stefano. He don't work, I don't work. Come on, Stefano."

The foreman trailed after the two. "Okay, but when you can't take it, or when you ache from head to toe, don't say I didn't warn you, young man. The work is hard and there will be no slack given just because you're Nico's cousin. Understand?"

"Yes, Sir," smiled Stefano.

The foreman turned and walked away. Stefano couldn't contain himself. He jumped up and down, hugged his cousin with all his strength and kissed him on both cheeks.

"Hey, save that manpower. You're going to need it."

Over the next couple of hours Nico showed Stefano how to mix mortar to the proper consistency. He then showed him where to take the concrete mixture, the amounts that would be needed and all the other details of his job description.

Within three hours Stefano was hauling the large bucket of concrete over the obstacle course of the construction site. He was thankful he had been able to get a pair of shoes through the CARE program. His feet wouldn't be able to stand it otherwise. He made several trips with the mortar and when he was sure Nico wouldn't run out, he put the bucket down and proceeded to move pieces of lumber and other objects out of his path.

He tossed a rather large piece of board to the side, almost hitting the foreman.

"What're you doing? You're supposed to be toting mortar, not trying to kill me," yelled the foreman.

Stefano thought, *If I'd wanted to hit you, I would have.* Instead he quietly said, "I wasn't trying to hit you. I'm just trying to clean this place up a bit."

"You're not being paid to be a housewife, you're being paid to carry mortar. Get back to the job you were hired to do."

Stefano could think of several things to say, but he didn't want to get fired on his first day. He simply replied, "I'm not wasting time. I'm saving time. After I get all this stuff out of the way, I'll be able to make the trip from here to there much faster."

The foreman paused for a moment and seemed to want to say, "Good thinking." However, he couldn't bring himself to say that. Instead, in a calm voice, said, "Then hurry and clean it up. Don't stand here talking to me." With that he turned and walked away.

On the next mortar trip, Nico asked, "What's with you and the foreman? I saw him talking to you. Don't create a problem."

Stefano smiled, "He was thanking me for being such a good worker."

Nico didn't buy the answer for a second, but decided to let it go. "Remember, in a place like this, sometimes the less said the better."

"It will be my motto," said Stefano as he picked up the bucket and headed for his mixing box.

Sure it will, thought Nico.

For the first few days they worked on the first floor of the building. It was hot, sweaty, exhausting work, but Stefano didn't think of complaining. Daily he was so tired after his walk home, he had difficulty staying awake long enough to bathe and eat. In fact, the first day he had fallen on his bed to rest slightly and awoke early the next morning, starved.

When construction moved on to the second story it was a whole new ball of wax. Ladders were set up and everything had to be carried up the ladders. Stefano had a system of shoveling the concrete into the bucket, hoisted the bucket to his right shoulder and walking to where the concrete was needed. The first time he attempted to ascend the ladder with the bucket on his shoulder, he fell backward after just a few steps. Unfortunately, the foreman happened to be walking by.

"It's a good thing you didn't spill that. That stuff is expensive," said the foreman. He never asked if Stefano was hurt.

Stefano didn't answer, but he was again pissed. The fiery red-head was so angry he felt he could throw the bucket to the second story. He decided to cool it and changed his strategy. He carried the bucket in one hand and held the ladder with the other. Within a day he had his balance and was again carrying the concrete bucket on his shoulder. He joked with Nico that he was going to become a knuckle-dragging monkey. He felt his arms stretched longer with each bucketful.

Stefano wished he had a partner at the top of the ladder who could pull the bucket up by hand. "No, no, no! That would be too sensible," he murmured to himself. "Don't think, just do your job and shut up."

The days were long, they usually worked from sun up to sun down. There were no rest breaks, except if you absolutely had to take a pee break, and then it had better be a short one. Lunch time was 15 minutes. A long, long day.

After a year, the work in Cervaro slowed. The last building was the police station, and the progress was fairly rapid. Most of the workers grew increasingly anxious about where they would find employment next.

About two weeks before the station was finished, Nico took a day off, and Stefano worked with Pablo, Nico's brother. It was like night and day the difference between the personalities of the two brothers. Not only were the personalities different, they had little resemblance physically. Nico was tall, wiry and carried a ready smile. Pablo was much shorter and stowed excess baggage around his waist. Food shortage didn't appear to affect him. He possessed a short temper, spoke little, and the words he did say were negative. It was as if he was angry with the world.

The day Stefano worked with Pablo was the longest he could remember. As evening came on Stefano felt he would collapse if he had to haul another bucket of cement to the third floor of the building. The sun edged below the horizon. When Stefano reached the top floor with the next haul, he spoke with his boss, "Pablo, are we about finished? The sun has set and I'd like to go home. My sister is going to be upset that I haven't come in yet."

Pablo paused with a trowel of mortar in his hand. At first Stefano was afraid the man was going to strike him with the trowel. "Your sister will be upset that her baby brother is not home for his supper? You'll stay here until I've finished. Do you understand that, you little weakling?" His eyes burned holes into Stefano.

The redhead was about to fire back but was afraid for his well-being. He turned and rapidly climbed down the ladder. He returned with another bucket in half the time of a usual trip. "That bastardo will have mortar up to his ass," mumbled Stefano.

It had become very dark. Without saying a word, Pablo climbed down the ladder, leaving a small amount of mortar on the slab of wood. Stefano waited for about 15 minutes, thinking Pablo had taken a pee break. He hadn't taken a break, he had gone home.

Stefano stood on the top floor of the police station and stared into the dark. He was the only person still on the site. He was so pissed it was he who needed a pee break. He picked up Pablo's trowel and threw mortar in every direction. "That bastardo. If I have to starve, I'll never work for him again!" He flung the trowel down into what was left of the mortar and walked off, not bothering to clean anything.

When he reached home Marta was not only worried that something had happened to Stefano, she was also angry. "Where have you been? I've been worried that you were hurt. Here I've worked to fix a good meal for you, and now everything is cold. Why do I even bother?"

"Whoa, why are you angry with me? It wasn't my idea to stay at work 'til the owls came out. It was that Pablo. He made me stay and then left without telling me that we were through. I've worked over twelve hours and then I come home and you come at me like a donna pazza —crazy woman."

"Stefano, don't you speak to me like that!"

Stefano didn't reply. He went to the hearth and grabbed a half loaf of bread and stormed out of the house. The anger from dealing with Pablo and then Marta was too much. He walked directly to the spot where his grandfather had died, sat by the broken tree stump, and tried to eat the bread. It seemed to swell in his throat and he couldn't swallow. As tears streamed down his face he stood and threw the bread with all his might. He looked up at the sky which seemed to be covered with a million stars and said, "Sorry, Nonno, I don't know which of those stars is you. I get so tired. I bring home a lot of money and we're eating very well. We even have meat sometime." He paused, smiled and then said, "That sounds kind of silly, doesn't it?

"So, I've got a little money now, and maybe it has made me very stupid. I just threw away half a loaf of bread. A couple of years ago I'd have given my left nut for that loaf of bread."

He got up and walked to where he had thrown the bread. Fortunately, it had landed on a large clump of grass. He picked it up, brushed it off with his hand and ate as he walked back to the house.

When he entered the house, Marta started to speak. Stefano looked at her and held up his hand to stop her. "I'm sorry I spoke the way that I did. I do appreciate all that you do for me, but I get very tired too. I don't want dinner, and I don't want to talk. I just want to go to bed."

That was the first time he had ever defended himself with Marta. As he was lying in bed he wasn't happy that he had spoken the way he did to her, but he felt good deep inside. With those thoughts he fell asleep. When Marta called him to come to breakfast he was in the same position in which he had fallen asleep.

Neither Marta nor Stefano mentioned the argument from the night before. Frankly he didn't think about the incident until he went out the door. He stopped and started to apologize, but instead took a deep breath and continued out to meet Nico who was almost in front of the house.

"Ciao, Stefano, how did work go yesterday?"

"Molto bene—very good—just don't take another day off."

"That bad, huh? Pablo can be difficult. What happened?"

"I don't want to talk about it. I think his wife cut him off. Just so you know, I won't work for him again."

"I can't make it right if you won't tell me what happened."

"I said I don't want to talk about it."

Nico was taken aback by Stefano's assertive tone. "Okay, I won't mention it again." Nico had to turn his head to prevent Stefano from seeing his big smile on his cousin's face. "The kid's growing up," thought Nico.

As they continued to work, Nico steered the conversation to better topics. "You know we'll be finished with the police station within the next few days. I'm going to look for work in Cassino, and you're welcome to come with me. You're a good worker and I don't want to lose you. What do you say?"

"When are you going?"

"I had to take yesterday off to be with my family, so I can't take any more time off here. The first day after we finish this building, I'm going over. I'll have to go through the same routine with the foreman to get you in, but you've got a proven record now. It shouldn't be a problem."

"What did you do with the family?"

"Oh, we had to take the boy to his doctor. He has an ear infection. To make him forget we packed a picnic, walked up into the hill, ate, drank some wine, slept a bit and them came home. It was very nice."

"It sounds like a great time," said Stefano wistfully.

Nico caught the tone of voice and quickly changed the subject back to work.

The day they finished the police station Stefano was relieved. He felt like he hadn't rested in a year. Man, could he ever use a picnic in the hills! He hoped it would be a while before they moved on to Cassino, but in only three days Nico was knocking on the door. Stefano hoped for a few more days rest, but he couldn't complain.

"Here is the name of the foreman and directions to the site." Nico handed Stefano a slip of paper. "He wants to see you before he'll say you're hired. After you've talked to him he'll tell you where to find me. I'll be taking a shortcut from my house to Cassino, so I won't be passing this way each morning. If you have any problem I'll come and talk with the foreman again. You should be fine."

"Thanks, I'll see you tomorrow." Stefano went into the house and looked at the paper, took a deep breath and said, "Oh, merda—shit."

Marta was turned from the fireplace. "What did you say?"

Stefano's face flushed. "Io voglio la merenda—I want a snack. Why?"

Marta shook her head. "I don't think that's what you said. I hate to think what you're learning from those men you work with."

Stefano rolled his eyes and descended the steps to the road. He picked up several rocks and threw them at blackbirds squawking from the rooftop. He laughed and ran down the road shouting, "Merda, merda, merda."

The following morning Stefano walked to Cassino, some 13 kilometers away. He had to pass through Cervaro on the way. As he passed the local bar, the owner, Rodolpho, stepped out to greet him.

"Hey, young Stefano, I haven't seen you in a long time. How are you?"

"I'm good. You know I've been working with Nico as a mason's helper here in Cervaro. Now the work is gone and I'm on my way to Cassino to see if they'll hire me to work with Nico again."

"That's good, my friend. If you wait a few minutes I'll give you a ride. I'm going to a warehouse just outside Cassino for some supplies for my store. We haven't talked in too long a time."

Stefano said, "That'll be great. I'll wait."

Momentarily Rodolpho's small pickup chugged down the alley. Stefano ran around the front of the truck and climbed into the passenger side. After a few hiccups from the engine they were off in a billow of diesel smoke.

"So tell me about yourself, you've really grown."

"Yeah, I guess I have. Not much in the height though. I think I'm doomed to be a runt."

"You're not a runt, my friend. Besides, girls don't care how tall you are. They just want you long in the right place," Rodolpho said with a hearty laugh.

Stefano laughed along. He had known Rodolpho a long time and they had always laughed and joked together. Stefano thought back to the many times he had accompanied Rodolpho when he went into town to the bar to play cards.

"I guess I'm going to be okay there. I'm getting muscles everywhere."

Rodolpho laughed so hard he almost ran into a ditch. As the little truck huffed along they talked about many things, including the girl Stefano had had a crush on for a long time. He only saw her at church and waited for her afterwards to say hello. Her father never allowed them to be alone for any period of time.

"Lucia's father is very strict. He doesn't even want me to talk with her."

As they pulled up to the construction site office, Rodolpho said, "Maybe her father is afraid you'll exercise your muscle." He clustered the fingers of his right hand to his pursed lips.

Stefano, still laughing as he hopped out of the truck, said, "Thanks for the lift. I'll try to get by to see you. You've given me laughs and I need as many as I can get."

As Stefano walked up the steps to enter the office, he saw a sign nailed to the wall beside the door. "ONLY JOBS ARE FOR PICK AND SHOVEL"

He was in such a good mood he didn't even hesitate. He told the site supervisor that Nico had sent him. The man hardly looked at Stefano.

"Didn't you see the sign outside? Or maybe you can't read."

"I can read, but I told you Nico wants me to be his helper."

The man rose up off his stool and stood before Stefano, towering over the boy. The foreman gestured with both hands beside his head, palms up, "What don't you understand? I told you there are no jobs except pick and shovel and you're too damn little for that. So, what's not to understand?"

Stefano remembered Nico's admonishment when he applied for the job in Cervaro, "Say little."

He turned, left the office, and went in search of Nico, but he was nowhere on the site. Disheartened, Stefano started for home. He took a much smaller road than he and Rodolpho had taken on their way to Cassino. It was more like a dirt path, but a much shorter distance.

He was about halfway home when an awful smell enveloped him. The further along he went the stronger the odor. He rounded a bend in the road, and there directly before him, were the decomposing remains of a military motorcycle rider. The mangled motorcycle was wedged against the tree trunk and the soldier's leg with a boot on it was stuck at the top of the stump about ten feet up. The helmet still covered the head, which was on the ground along with scattered pieces of the soldier's uniform.

Stefano began running to escape the scene but also to get away from the odor. He ran all the way home, attempting to escape the urge to vomit. He ran directly to the well, pulled up a bucket of water and poured it over his head. He couldn't shake the image of what he had seen. He sat beside the well taking deep breaths until he hyperventilated. Then he felt as though he couldn't breathe fast enough. It was a vicious cycle. He felt as if he was about to pass out when he saw Nico walking toward his in-law's home. This snapped him out of his panic attack.

He called to his cousin, "Nico, wait up. I went to Cassino as you told me to and they turned me away. Same stuff as when I went to Cervaro."

"What's wrong with you? You're soaked and your eyes are as big as if you'd seen a ghost."

"I did. I saw a body, in uniform, or at least parts of a body in uniform. I didn't stick around long enough to study it."

"Oh, I know where you're talking about. It's the body of an Italian soldier, not from the war, but it's been there for weeks. I know it was reported. God, it must be awful by now. I saw it at least two weeks ago. I'll report it again."

"Trust me, it's worse than awful. Let's change the subject before I toss my guts. Where were you today?"

"They sent me to inspect a couple of buildings, partially destroyed, to see if I felt we could save them rather than demolish. We can't." Nico shook his head. "I can't believe they sent you away, I talked to the guy. I go back to work on Monday and you come with me."

"I'll see you there. Thanks. Ciao."

"Ciao."

On Monday Stefano arrived at Nico's house well before daybreak, but didn't knock. He waited until his cousin came out of the house."

"You are anxious, aren't you? Come on, it's a long walk."

At the employment office, the manager asked what he could do for Nico. He recounted the events of the previous week and what Stefano had been told. It was the same story all over again. Again,

Nico had to threaten to go home himself before they allowed Stefano to go to work.

Cassino was a mess. The city sits at the base of the mountain and the bombs rained down on the city as well as on the mountain during the battle of Monte Cassino. People had been clearing the rubble for months and it still looked like a disaster area.

As Nico and Stefano stood on what had previously been a street lined with prosperous shops, there was not a building standing. There was a corner of a shop next to where they stood and there was a partial tree with one horizontal limb about fifty meters down the street. The rest was totally flattened and piles of debris dotted the landscape.

"See this place here, Stefano?" Nico walked over and placed his hand against the remaining corner of a building. "This was a three story structure. It was a very high-priced ladies dress shop with apartments on the upper floors. Dear Jesus, what these people have gone through. We had it bad in the country, but nothing like this here."

Stefano didn't want to think, even for a moment, about the war, "Where do we go? Where do we start?"

Before Nico could answer, a man came up and said, "Follow me."

Pointing to a huge pile of rubble, the man said, "Behind all this crap is a wheelbarrow and some shovels. Start clearing. We have to move everything to that pile over there." With that he walked off.

Stefano stared at the wheelbarrow and then at Nico. "You're a great mason. Are you going to have to shovel this stuff?"

"Big lesson for you here, young man. Look around you. Do you see anyone building anything? They're moving little piles of shit to a big pile of shit. You've got to get rid of the shit before you have land to build an estate. Start shoveling."

Stefano had thought carrying mortar was hard work, but shoveling building rubble was twice as hard. He thought his back would break during the first morning. By the third day he had acclimated and worked right along with the men, doing his share.

After a month his friends back in Cervaro commented on how big his chest was getting.

Stefano stopped in to see Rodolpho one Sunday after church and related what had happened the day they drove to Cassino and how Nico had again saved the day. He explained about the rubble clearing and the fact that Nico had been doing the same work for the first two weeks and then was pulled to start making plans for the first building. Stefano continued clearing the site. He simply took it in stride.

Rodolpho stocked his shelves while they visited. As Stefano was leaving, he turned back to Rodolpho and winked. "I'm getting bigger muscles on this job. Do you think I ought to talk to Lucia's father?"

"What amazes me is that you young guys can work as hard as you do and still have your mind on the girls. If I did what you do, I'd be no good for a woman. See you soon."

The work at the site was all by hand, and when he went home at night he felt as if his arms wanted to stick out in front of him after using the wheelbarrow all day. Once the site was cleared, men dug for the foundation. It would be constructed of reinforced concrete and the walls would be of stone and mortar. Once the trenches were dug, Nico instructed Stefano on the placement of the rebar before they began to pour the concrete. The new task was most welcome.

Stefano had heard that there were several men from Cervaro working in Cassino, but he hadn't seen anyone he knew, and even if he had, there was no time for socializing. He exchanged pleasantries with the men on his site once they realized he was one of the workers like them.

During his first day on the job, one of the men working on the next site over called, "Boy, come here."

Stefano looked around and didn't see anyone so he kept on walking toward his site. The man called again, louder, "Boy, I said come here."

"You talking to me?" asked Stefano.

"Yes, I'm talking to you!" The man raised his arms in disbelief. "You see another boy anywhere around? Bring me some water."

Stefano laughed and replied, "Sorry, you'll have to get your own water."

"What kind of water boy are you? I said I need some water. So bring me some water." The man was indignant.

"That's not my job. I'm a mason's helper. Can't help you."

The man scratched his head, but didn't comment further. As he walked away, Stefano heard the other men harassing their co-worker. "Careful Renzo, that "water-boy" will take you on."

Everybody laughed, including Nico. He had known Renzo for a long time and worked with him many times. "Renzo, this buck will show you up when it comes to work. He's the best helper I've ever had."

The comments gave Stefano a great feeling of pride. He was more determined than ever to do a good job and to keep up with the grown men.

CHAPTER TWENTY-FIVE

EVENTUALLY STEFANO DID MEET another guy from Cervaro. Rocco was the son of the barber who cut Stefano's hair, not that a haircut occurred very often. It was cut when it fell into his face and bothered him at work. The last time he was at the barber's he commented that he had to have a haircut because he was tired of looking through a red forest.

Rocco was about five years older than Stefano and his friendship came at a time when Stefano felt he was the only person in the world in his circumstance. The first day they talked, Rocco proposed that they could walk back and forth to work together, so the journey would seem shorter and less lonely.

They agreed to take the shorter route, against Stefano's better judgement. "Rocco, have you see the body of that Italian soldier?"

Rocco waved his hands across his face. "God, yes, it's impossible to miss the stench. I still can't figure out why it's still there after all this time. "The first time I saw it I thought I'd lose my breakfast. I can't figure why the animals haven't dragged the pieces away. When we get in range let's pull our shirts up over our noses. That might help."

Their shirts may have helped slightly, but the odor seemed to permeate everything. Stefano swore he could detect the stench in his clothes even after he took them off at home. Fortunately he now had a change of clothes and had clean ones to wear to work.

Apparently the clean-up squad had finally gotten the word because the body was removed the next day, but for several days afterwards, the odor hung in the air. It didn't disappear until the surrounding area was sprayed with some sort of chemical. The next day it was worse, if that was possible, with the mixture of decay and chemicals. By the second day the odor began to dissipate.

As it turned out, Rocco needed a friend as badly as did Stefano. As they walked from work their second day, Rocco brought his father in the conversation. "My life is not easy."

Stefano thought it curious that Rocco's comment floated in out of the blue, but answered with a wry smile, "And that makes you different?"

"It's my father. You probably know he's a communist and thinks that everybody should have equal shares of everything."

"No, I didn't know he was a communist, but if he can arrange for me to have the same money as the village mayor, I wouldn't mind. I don't think the mayor is going to give me half. How's that make your father different?

"But my father doesn't practice what he preaches. He takes all the money I earn and doesn't share back," said Rocco as he kicked at a rock in the road.

"Was that your father you just kicked?" asked Stefano.

Rocco laughed and then kicked the rock even harder. "Maybe so. He makes me very mad at times. He really does demand that I give him every lira I make. We were paid yesterday, and I hardly got in the door last night when he had his hand out. I gave most of my pay to him, knowing that I had to, but I put 100 lira in another pocket. I work all week and I have 100 lira. I have to beg if I need to buy something."

"Then you'd better stop kicking that rock, or you'll need new shoes."

"You're right, but you know my father. He cuts your hair."

"Sure I know him, but he doesn't get much from me. I usually give him a 100 lira note and claim that's all I have. I'm sure he doesn't make much cutting hair."

"That's why he says he needs my money. I've always given him my pay envelope."

"You going to keep doing that? You're kind of old for him to treat you that way."

"Of course. I have no choice. He is my father, and I must respect him, but I don't have to like him. He's so unfair. I only have the vegetables from the garden for my meals and he has those along with pasta. Last night, after he was asleep, I got up and ate the pasta that was left over from his supper. I'll probably catch hell tonight."

"Wait a minute, you give him all your money, there is pasta on the table, and you're not allowed to eat it? What does your mother say? Won't she defend you?"

Rocco didn't answer immediately. When he did his voice cracked "My mother is dead. She was visiting her mother in Cassino the night the bombing started. I think my grandmother's house took a direct hit."

"Oh, my God, Rocco. I didn't know. I'm sorry."

Rocco shrugged. "It's okay. It gets easier. I wish she was here when I want to kick his ass."

"Does he hit you?"

"Not any more. The last time was about a year ago. I told him that he'd better not beat me again, because I'm now much bigger than he is. I won't let it happen again. I'd leave home, but you and I both know that's not easy for a son to do."

"Rocco, I'm really sorry you have to live like that, but I do know what it's like to not have a mother. Mine died when I was eight. I wish we had room so you could move in with us."

Rocco smiled, and said, "I'm sure Marta would love that. I can hear her now."

"I don't know, she might like having a man her age living in the house." Stefano reached out and punched Rocco on the shoulder.

"Hey, what you doing, trying to sell your sister?"

"No, I'm not trying to sell my sister, bastardo. I was being funny. You know, I heard that happened when the Americans were here. Some guy tried to sell his sister."

"Yeah, and I know who he was. The U.S. MPs threatened to throw him in jail with the soldier who took him up on the deal."

"Wow, who was it?" Stefano was wide-eyed.

"You probably don't know him. A guy by the name of Canalleto who lives over in Pico."

"Nah, I don't know him, but I spent a lot of time in Pico. I've been hungry, but never thought about something like that."

They were at home. Stefano said, "Ciao, see you tomorrow."

"Ciao."

———

The next day seemed lighter after Stefano shared some history with Rocco. Stefano looked forward to their daily exchanges, and he felt he could talk with Rocco about anything, even Lucia. Rocco never missed an opportunity to harass his younger friend.

They were nearing home one evening when Stefano asked, "Do you think I should try to talk with Lucia more, even if her father doesn't like me?"

"Probably her father doesn't want her talking to any man. She's very pretty, and I can see why you like her."

"I wouldn't know what to do."

Rocco chuckled. "Oh, I think you'd know what to do from the way your pants are poking out in front."

Stefano turned scarlet, and he quickly thrust his hand in his pocket, which only made Rocco laugh harder. Stefano jumped him from behind and tried to bring Rocco down by locking his legs. It was no contest, Rocco simply lifted Stefano off his back and tossed him in the ditch. Then he reached down and helped his friend back to his feet.

"Obviously you really like Lucia. What harm is there in talking with her? I'll go with you to church on Sunday and afterwards we both will talk with her. Maybe her father won't be so upset if it's the two of us."

"You'd do that?"

"What's a friend for? Enjoy your day off tomorrow and I'll see you at church on Sunday."

"Thanks, Rocco. You're the best."

On Sunday Rocco was true to his word. He was waiting for Stefano on the church steps. They entered the sanctuary, and Stefano waited for his eyes to adjust to the darker room. He started to sit with Marta, but Rocco tapped him on the shoulder and pointed to where Lucia was seated with her family. Rocco led the way and took the pew right behind Lucia. Stefano could hardly keep still and definitely couldn't pay attention to the priest's sermon.

Lucia turned to see what the rustling noise was and saw Stefano. She smiled broadly. His eyes met hers and he turned scarlet. Her father nudged her with an elbow. When the service ended, everyone stood to leave. Rocco took the lead.

"Lucia, how nice to see you." Rocco then spoke to each of her family members by name. The mother smiled and acknowledged the greeting, the signore stoically stared at Stefano.

Rocco nudged Stefano, who once again turned red, but managed to speak, "It's good to see everyone. The day is so beautiful and clear."

Rocco rolled his eyes. "Then why don't we all step outside to see such a beautiful day?"

Stefano moved to the aisle, but Rocco pulled him back and nodded to Lucia to go first. After she had passed, Rocco pushed Stefano out behind her. It was obvious that didn't sit well with Lucia's father, but he didn't say anything.

Outside the church, Rocco followed Lucia while Stefano tagged along. They moved a little way down the street, and with hints from Rocco, Stefano finally found his tongue. Once he started talking he was a chatterbox. Rocco kept an eye on the father, who stood watching. After a few minutes he joined to the group.

"Lucia, we will expect you home for dinner."

Lucia waved and responded, "I'll be along very shortly. Thank you, Papa."

Once the family had left, Rocco quietly eased away, leaving Stefano alone with Lucia. From a distance it appeared they laughed and talked easily. After about ten minutes Lucia turned, left, and waved to Rocco.

Rocco approached his friend. "Now was that so hard? Yeah, well, yes, I can see it was."

Stefano didn't try to cover himself. He laughed and said, "I was so afraid it was going to happen while she was in front of me."

"Uh huh, I'm surprised that didn't make it happen."

"Rocco, would you come and have dinner with us?"

Rocco smiled, "Still trying to fix your sister up, huh? Sure, I'd be glad to eat with you."

"I don't know what there is, but you'd be welcome."

"I guarantee it will be better than what will be on our table at home, and I won't have to hear about the wonderful world of Communism."

Marta was taken aback when Stefano arrived with Rocco in tow, but she quickly set another place at the table and seemed to enjoy talking with their guest. After the meal, Stefano took a cue from what Rocco had done and left the house. He was not sure how long Rocco actually stayed, but after about an hour, Marta called to Stefano to bring her water from the well.

The following morning dawned bright and sunny without a cloud in the sky. Rocco's mood matched the morning, and he was even more effusive than usual. "I had a wonderful time yesterday, thank you. Your sister is very nice, and we had a good talk. It was a good day."

Stefano hoped that maybe Rocco would show further signs of interest but it didn't happen. Stefano wondered if Marta had let Rocco know that she had no interest in any male. Neither of them talked of Marta again, however, Rocco continued to encourage Stefano to be more assertive with Lucia, "Stop being so shy. Think of yourself as a man."

As the weeks went by, construction in Cassino gained momentum. Many more buildings were going up and more and more workers employed. Electricians and plumbers came from neighboring towns and took part in the expanding economy.

The carpenters had framed out the building that Nico was working on. The rafters, joists and sub-roof were in place. It was time for the masons to install the roof tiles—tegolo—which meant more weight for Stefano to carry. The red clay tiles were usually red and were shaped like sections of bisected pipe. They interlocked, one up, one down, and once they were in place the masons sealed them with mortar.

Nico told Stephano, "It's time you learned to interlock the tegolo. When I have enough mortar, we'll go up and you can learn to set. It's not as easy as it looks. It'll give you a break from just lifting and carrying, but I don't want to have to tell you when I need more mortar."

Nico then took Stefano up on the rafters and showed him how to lay the tegolo. Stefano was proud that his mason would trust him to do this "finish" work. He worked slowly at first but quickly became very proficient. He always kept one eye on the mortar tray to make sure Nico never ran out. "He trusts me and I won't let him down."

On a Monday of the following week, Nico and Stefano came down from the roof and walked across the piazza just as a small pickup truck careened into the area. Screams came from the truck bed where Stefano saw two men, one badly injured. He was lying on his back with his belly wide open and his intestines oozing out, the truck bed was covered with blood. The other man held his friend's head in his lap. He screamed for someone to help, "We were working to clear the German mines." Seeing the injured man and all the blood set off horrible memories in Stefano's head. The bombings, the killings, the bodies, the smells of gunpowder and death had traumatized Stefano more than he knew. Gripped by the flashbacks of war, Stefano stared at the scene, unable to move.

Nico placed a sympathetic arm over Stefano's shoulder with understanding of what raced through the boy's mind. Nico spoke to the driver of the truck, "There's an infirmary at the end of this street. It's been set up as a first aid station for people injured here. Take him there."

Nico squeezed Stefano's shoulder. "Go gather your lunch pail. I'll take you home on my bicycle." Neither of them spoke on the way home, for which Stefano was grateful.

The next morning he met Rocco at their usual rendezvous spot. Rocco looked relieved. "Ciao, where were you last night? I waited for you for fifteen minutes and then came on home."

Stefano replied, "Sorry. I saw a guy who had stepped on a mine and all his guts were hanging out. I got really upset and Nico brought me home on his bicycle. Honestly, I didn't think about you."

"Amico, you've got to get over the war. It's done with, get it out of your head."

Stefano, through gritted teeth said, "I am over it. It's just sometimes when things happen, like yesterday, I get upset. Glad you've tossed it away so easily, but maybe you didn't see some of the shit I saw."

"You could be right but we all saw enough bad that we can let it drive us crazy or we can move on with our life. Yeah, I know that's easier to say than to do, but it's true."

That point became pivotal in Stefano's life. He was angry at Rocco at first, but inwardly he realized his friend was right. He was most angry with himself for getting upset over the past. What could he change in the past? Nothing. He had to start focusing on the future. Gradually he would learn to stash the war memories away in a guarded compartment of his brain. Over time, he would close the lid on that compartment tighter and tighter. He was soon to be fourteen, had a job, earned good money, he and Marta were able to buy food and they even had money for clothes and shoes. Wonderful, wonderful shoes! He didn't have his first pair until he was ten years old. He had worn those throughout the war until his toes curled under to fit in the shoes. Now three years later, he actually had work shoes and dress shoes!

Gradually his dreams became happier, hopeful and more vivid. Interspersed were dreams of Lucia, which were always beautiful. In the dreams she came often to visit him at his home and they spent long hours talking about the future and even their future together. The first time he awoke from that dream, he laughed. "What kind of craziness is that? Me getting married? Go back to sleep, Stefano."

CHAPTER TWENTY-SIX

· ·

AS THEIR FORTUNES IMPROVED, Marta and Stefano began to have reason to hope. With his job he was able to earn more money than he had ever hoped to see. Marta was efficient and knew how to stretch lira better than a postman could stretch a rubber band. The circle was finally broken. They could now hire someone to help with the plowing and leveling of the farmland. They expanded the vegetable garden, not only in size but in the variety of plantings. The early spring sun warmed the soil, and everything was again in harmony. Even Stefano's mind was finally at peace.

After the war, changes came very fast to Italy. Technology and machines accelerated the rebuilding efforts, and Stefano saw it first hand when the first crane came into Cassino. Dump trucks could be filled rapidly and the massive rubble piles began to disappear. New buildings were rising by the week and Cassino was again beginning to resemble a city. Not the old city of Italian charm, but a city of fresh new beginnings.

At the Capaldi farm, tractors plowed the fields. Marta and Stefano watched in amazement, and after four days the soil was turned, disked and ready for planting. Stefano remembered it took a week to hand turn the soil for their first little garden. He bought seeds for every grain he could imagine and for vegetables that he had never liked, such as Brussel sprouts and eggplant. Nico teased Stefano that he was trying to feed the world.

Stefano replied, "I never want to be hungry again."

That pretty much encapsulated his motivation. He bought hens and a rooster and looked forward to having chicks to raise, eat and sell. He reminded Marta to be careful how much wine she gave the chicks! Fresh eggs were a treat Stefano had trouble describing.

"Two eggs, with their golden suns floating in the middle of clouds, is the most wonderful sight in a home. To awaken to the sound of eggs frying is beyond compare. It is simply magnifico!"

He was content with his life. Being the mason's helper didn't get any easier, but it became more bearable. He was still short, but he had muscles on top of muscles. The summer days were longer, but that didn't mean he would get home before dark, it only meant they worked longer hours. The construction crews still worked sunup to sundown.

One evening he came in the house and greeted Marta as she stood by the kitchen table, reading a letter. "Ciao, Marta. Come sta?"

She didn't look up from the letter when Stefano spoke, but continued to read. Suddenly she stopped and ran toward him. "Stefano, listen to this wonderful news! This letter is from one of our aunts in America. She and our uncles have made a new petition for us to come to the States."

The news made Stefano forget the aching in his back. He grabbed his sister and they danced about the room. Going to America meant leaving all the memories of the war behind! That was good, but he couldn't forget that a petition had been made before only to be squelched by the war. That experience taught Stefano that nothing was ever simple. The uncles had lived in the States since long before Stefano had been born, but that didn't matter, they'd get to know each other. Stefano was so excited he thought he might have difficulty sleeping, but being a mason's helper was a powerful sedative.

The next morning while going to work, he vaguely recalled the time when his aunt had left for America. From what Marta had told him the night before, it was 1935 and winter. He was three at the time, and he could recall it was confusing to him at the time.

Everybody was excited and supposedly happy for his aunt, but they were crying. It made no sense.

A car came to pick up the aunt and parked in the middle of the road in front of the house. Grandfather, the stoic one, carried the luggage to the car and placed it on top. With ropes he secured the luggage through the rear window frames. Stefano's main thought was, *They're going to get awful cold with the windows open.*

He didn't say anything. At that point in his life he was sort of just there. No one paid much attention to him. The crisp, cold air inspired the aunt to be dramatic and to emote about Monte Cassino.

She peered up at the mountain, opened her arms and cried, "Oh, my mountain, how I'm going to miss you. With your ever-changing, wonderful snow cap. Oh, I know I'll never again see such a beautiful sight."

Stefano stared at the mountain and tried to figure out what had changed. It looked the same to him.

Grandfather was not a man who could relate to such a display. He took his daughter by the arm and ushered her into the car. "Better get along or the snow on the mountain will melt before you leave."

The relatives stood in the road and waved until the car was out of sight. Then they went back to what they were doing before the car came. The family heard very little from the aunt during the intervening years. Marta did comment one time, "I wonder how much she really misses the mountain. She never writes to see how it's doing."

As Stefano walked to work, he thought, *Sorry she hasn't kept in touch, but I'm glad she's in touch now and that's what matters. It's now and the future.*

He was quietly disappointed that after the one letter they heard nothing for months. He was sure it had all been a misconception by Marta and himself, but he couldn't believe it had been an evil prank. Best to concentrate on the present and not think about the future.

The harvest had been good and the basement shelves were laden with enough fruits and vegetables to last through the long winter months, and that winter was soon upon them with an abundant snow blanket on the mountain. The valley had been very fortunate not to have had much in the way of snow for the past two winters. The villagers liked it when they could appreciate the beauty of the snow-covered mountain from afar. That beauty could be appreciated until April or May, rarely into June. The people of the valley were not equipped for snow. They didn't have a lot in the way of winter clothing because they seldom needed it and the homes only had fireplaces for heat. Those fireplaces were bigger than when the fireplaces were for cooking only. Fortunately, once those thick walls were warmed, they emitted a lot of heat.

In his early years Stefano had hated the snow, as he didn't have shoes or other proper clothing. He dreaded climbing into bed at night. The bed sheets were so cold that Marta took pity and ironed his sheets just before he jumped into bed. They had bed warmers, which were like a lidded-skillet with holes in the top. Before bedtime they put embers from the fireplace into the warmer and slid the warmer between the sheets and blankets. It couldn't warm the whole bed at once, but warm feet were the most necessary.

The construction site was shut down for Christmas, which didn't mean much to Stefano. He had memories of a celebration time in early January, when Befana, a hag-like creature, was supposed to come down the fireplace chimney and leave presents for the children. Befana was always covered with soot and traveled about the sky on a broom and carried a big sack of toys. She didn't visit the Capaldi family. They didn't celebrate Christmas either. Mama went to church more often during the Christmas season, and she fixed a larger than usual meal on Christmas Day, that was about it. There certainly was no money for presents.

But it was December 1945, and Marta wanted to celebrate. "Stefano, I want to celebrate Christmas. After all, this could be our last Christmas in Italy."

When Stefano looked up from his seat by the fireplace, he expected to see tears in his sister's eyes. Instead she was standing there with a grin that spread across her face.

"Due to your hard work, we have money now and I want us to enjoy something, not just sit here looking at each other."

Stefano felt there was finally hope for his sister. Was she really letting go just a bit? He stood, crossed the room and hugged her for the first time in a long while.

In his embrace she whispered, "Do you think you could find a Christmas tree for us? No one has Christmas trees, but Uncle Sandro talked about them when he told us stories about the United States. Maybe we'll be there next year, but I want to have a tree now. It will make our house smell so nice."

"Of course we can have a tree, and it'll be the best Christmas tree in the village, since it will be the only one. Why don't you start making plans for what you want to do to celebrate! We'll have a wonderful celebration!"

Stefano ventured into one of the few wooded areas left near their home and trekked about looking for the perfect tree. He had no idea what Marta's ideal tree might be, but he had seen a picture of a Christmas tree in school many years ago. He found several possibilities, but soon realized that although they were beautiful there, was no way he would ever be able to drag a large tree so far. He settled on a soft, fragrant pine that was about two meters tall.

Marta and Stefano made decorations from colored paper, and Marta seemed so happy with the way the tree turned out. Nothing was said about presents, but Stefano wanted to do something special for her. In Cervaro he bought a pair of beautiful wool socks. She was beside herself when she pulled away the tissue paper revealing her gift.

"Do you realize this is the first pair of socks I've ever had that I didn't knit?"

Marta's tears made Stefano uncomfortable, but he smiled and felt happy.

They enjoyed a quiet dinner, just the two of them. Earlier they had talked of having some of their relatives join them, but decided they didn't want to impose. Sandro's family hadn't mentioned any Christmas celebration. Maybe they, too, had had enough closeness.

The holidays passed uneventfully and quietly. Immediately after the New Year Marta and Stefano discussed which crops they would plant in the spring. "I want to expand the wheat and corn," announced Stefano. "We'll have more land plowed this year."

"We must be careful, Stefano. We can't plant more than we can tend unless you could quit your job and work just on the farm."

"Get serious, Marta. How will we be able to pay the workers if I don't continue as a mason's helper? No, that's not up for discussion. I won't give up that money." He was up pacing the floor.

"I understand, but I don't want us to have so much planted that we can't tend it."

"Marta, please start off positive for once!"

Stefano stormed out the door. He had gone only a short distance when he realized that spring had not arrived. He was wearing only a shirt and pants and was soon freezing. His pride would not let him go back, so he practically ran into Cervaro to visit his friend Rodolpho.

The two friends were seated at one of the small tables used for card playing, next to a wood-burning stove. Stefano rested his head in his hands and his woeful look transmitted his mood. "Rodolpho, tell me about women."

His friend roared. He was leaning back in his chair and almost fell over backwards. "Tell you about women? What is there to tell about women? You think you finally understand the game and they change the rules! My little friend, I long ago gave up trying to understand women."

Stefano let his steam subside and laughed. "And here I thought I'd ask the master."

"The master? Sure, I'm the master. Do you know how long it's been since I've had a woman?"

"Uh, I...I didn't...Uh..." Stefano's face was scarlet.

Rodolpho laughed even harder. "My little friend, what I think you need is maybe a little vino. I don't think you're ready for a woman. Who is she, by the way? Don't tell me it's Lucia? Did she say no?"

Now Stefano couldn't stop laughing. "It's no one. I had a fight with Marta, that's all. You're right, I'm not ready for a woman, but I will take that glass of vino."

Rodolpho went behind the bar and poured two glasses of wine, more for himself than for Stefano. He came back to the table and set the glass before Stefano. He sat and raised his glass to Stefano. "Alle donne—to women."

They talked for the next hour. Rodolpho encouraged Stefano to plant whatever amount he wanted to plant. Through another gale of laughter, Stefano said, "No wonder it's been a long time since you've had a woman if that's how you go about your life! I have to remember that Marta is half owner of our farm."

"Hey, Stefano, she owns half of your farm, not half of you. Remember that." With that Rodolpho refilled the glasses.

By the time Stefano left for home the vino had warmed his blood and he didn't notice the cold as he walked. He crept into the house, quietly undressed, slipped into his bed and slept like the dead.

CHAPTER TWENTY-SEVEN

EARLY SPRING BROUGHT MORE news from the States. Uncle Francesco wrote that he was coming to Italy with his daughter, Mary, and would arrive in early May 1946. This was wonderful news and it gave Marta and Stefano another focus other than work, although it created more work.

They wanted their home to be a place welcoming for the visitors even though they wouldn't stay with them, they'd be with Francesco's sister who lived about two kilometers away. Nonetheless Marta wanted to put a new coat of whitewash on the inner walls, hang new curtains at the windows and maybe even spring for a few new dishes. Since they'd moved back into their home they'd never had more than one guest at a time with them.

Marta was her usual worry-wart self. "Stefano, I'm afraid we won't have enough extra eggs. I think I may need to buy a few more chicks and a couple more hens."

"You worry too much. You think you buy chicks now, they'll be grown enough to kill for cooking?"

"And you're too free thinking. Someone around here has to be sensible."

Stefano could feel his red-headed anger coming to the surface, but as Rodolpho had told him, "It doesn't help to get bevuto— pissed—eventually they'll get you back."

He smiled and said, "Tell you what, I'll go talk nicely to our hens and ask them to please lay more eggs for the next couple of months."

Marta didn't find the humor in her smart-ass brother's comment. Stefano decided the best thing he could do at the moment was go to the fields and check on the seedlings. The men they had hired did a great job and he didn't need to check on them, but he needed to check on something!

The month of May seemed to come faster that year. Stefano was still applying the whitewash the day before Francesco and Mary arrived. He had his hands full, working all day as the mason's helper, working in the fields when he came home and following Marta's instructions as to what had to be done in the house.

Word of the relatives' arrival came and Marta and Stefano dressed in their best clothes and walked to meet their uncle and cousin. Stefano was his usual shy self, and Marta was withdrawn. Cousin Mary was affectionate and bubbly, and Stefano quickly surmised she would be good for Marta. Was this a short visit or was she moving to Italy? Uncle Francesco was of the old school, very stern and shared few words.

There was much commotion, much kissing and much talking with the hands, which every good Italian does with gusto. Francesco's sister went all out laying a table fit for a festival. It was an occasion for great celebration. Stefano's eyes widened as he watched the antipasto being placed on the table. Platters overflowed with roasted peppers, cheeses, a variety of sliced meats and at least three different types of olives. There was even a platter of marinated calamari and polpo—octopus. On this day no one sat at the table, it overflowed with the food.

Sandro and all of his family shared the celebration too. It was the first time Stefano had seen Polombo for some time. He had grown in height and had filled out. Polombo was somewhat distant, but warmed up to Stefano in a short time. Stefano never could figure what had happened to their relationship when they had returned from Ferentino. Frankly, he had been too busy to give it a great deal of thought.

Sandro said the blessing, and when he finished, it was all Stefano could do to keep from diving for the table. He reminded himself of the manners he had been taught by his mother, so long ago. Even though they were poor peasants, Mama had taught him the essence of politeness. Patience and politeness or get your ears boxed, you made the choice.

It was at times of family celebrations, that he missed his mother the most. Frequently he felt guilty that he didn't think of her more often, but life came at him at such a rapid rate that he couldn't find time anymore to think about the past. That was true for everything except for his memories of Nonno. Not many days would pass without some fond memory or a quiet communication with his grandfather.

The antipasto, the first course, was followed by delicious homemade pasta with a wonderful tomato sauce. Lamb was the meat course and for so many people it looked like an entire lamb had been prepared. Then there was fruit and a chocolate concoction topped with whipped cream finished off the feast. Stefano had never seen so much food for one meal.

After dinner, Francesco stood before the fireplace holding a glass of wine and stiffly said, "There is an announcement. Mary has come to Italy to be married. I propose a toast to her and Mauro."

Everyone looked around for Mauro, wondering who he was. No one stepped forward. Stefano recalled having seen Mauro once. Somehow he knew the name meant dark, after the Moors. Mauro certainly wasn't dark. Francesco's sister didn't know about the engagement and had not been told until the moment of the toast. It seemed strange to Stefano that the prospective bride, Mary, had not found a way to get word to Mauro that she was in Italy. However, he had long since stopped trying to make sense of what went on in the world.

Later, in a quiet conversation with Marta, Mary told her the story of her love. During the war, Mauro had been taken prisoner-of-war in North Africa and was shipped to America and was held at Fort Jefferson outside of New York City. A friend of Mary's had made a commitment to go talk with some of the prisoners, to cheer them up. The friend had not wanted to go alone so invited Mary to go with her.

Mary was introduced to this young prisoner, Mauro. Their first visit was awkward because Mary's Italian was not that good, even though it was the only language spoken at home, but love has a way of working around difficulties. It was love at first sight and from that point on she made frequent trips to the fort, spending many hours talking with Mauro. After the war, the prisoners were sent back to Italy, but before Mauro went back, the couple made a commitment to each other. He would go and she would follow as soon as possible. And now it had all come true.

On July 7, 1946, they were married in the little church in Cervaro, and there was a small reception in terms of the number of people, but again the food was plentiful. Francesco's gift to the couple was a short honeymoon.

At the reception Mary and Marta talked incessantly. Marta sensed Mary was unhappy about something. When the two young women were totally alone, Marta asked, "What is wrong? This should be your happiest day."

Mary's eyes glistened. "Oh, I am happy. I love Mauro so much. It's where we have to live when we come back. My father, as you know, has purchased a house near here, and he expects us to come live with him. I don't know if I can stand that."

"Will it be that bad?" asked Marta.

"It will be horrible. You forget I've lived with him my entire life. He's so strict and even though I'm married, he'll still expect to tell me what to do. He'll want to boss Mauro, too, and I know that won't work. Mauro had plenty of time to grow up when he was fighting in Africa and then as a prisoner. He is not a reticent Italian boy who only does what he is told. I feel so tense and nervous when they are even together now."

"Oh, Mary, I didn't know your father was so strong willed. Of course, I've only known him for the past few weeks. There must be another answer," said Marta.

"Mauro has found a good job here, but he doesn't make enough money for us to afford a place of our own. We talked of waiting, but Mauro said he had waited long enough and if we didn't get married soon, he would not be responsible." Mary blushed and smiled. "You know what I mean."

Marta excused herself and pulled Stefano away from filling his plate a second time. She dragged him outside and relayed what Mary had told her.

Stefano was mystified as to what he had to do with the problem, but soon understood as Marta said, "Why don't we let them have our place?"

"What, are you crazy or something?" asked Stefano. "And pray tell why this has come up at the wedding and not before?"

"Oh, Stefano, don't be that way. I'm sure Mary and Mauro have talked about the situation, but I'm also sure Mauro has no idea what he's getting into."

"And where are we to live? That's a consideration, you know. We've finally gotten ourselves settled."

"Oh, I'm sure Uncle Sandro will let us live with them for a while."

Stefano wasn't happy with that idea. "Look, I'm very appreciative of what Sandro's family has done for us, but I don't feel comfortable asking for more."

Marta understood what Stefano said but could think of no alternative. The kind-hearted girl was always willing to take on everyone else's problems.

"Stefano, go talk with Mary. Maybe you can get her to settle down, she's almost hysterical."

Why me? thought Stefano as he made a spinning motion against his temple with an index finger. *Merry Mary where are you?*

It was a very short conversation. In fact, it had just begun when Mauro came looking for Mary. "What's the problem? Are you sad that you have married me?" He was distraught.

Mary fell against Mauro. "Oh, no, no. I am so in love with you and have waited a long time to be your wife. We can talk about it later."

Mauro wasn't about to let the moment pass. "No, you tell me what's bothering you now. I won't be able to enjoy this celebration knowing that you're unhappy."

Mary dried her tears with the handkerchief that Mauro handed to her. "I don't want us to live with my father. You've seen how he's acted today. He'll be worse when we come back in three days."

"Oh, my Mary, we have talked about this over and over. We have nowhere else to go now. I promise I'll get us out of his house as soon as I can. Please be patient with me."

Mary forced herself to be composed. "It will be all right. I'll make it work, but I won't let him boss me around any longer." Stefano cleared his throat; he had felt as if he had been intruding on a very private moment. "I have an idea. Why don't you come and live with us for a while?"

Mary beamed and quickly answered, "Oh, yes! We'll do that." She replied so rapidly Stefano wondered if it all wasn't a setup.

Mauro wasn't so sure. He knew how small the Capaldi house was. "Uh, Mary, I don't know if that will work. At your father's house we'll have our own room." The visions he had of the four young people sleeping so close together didn't conjure a comfortable newlywed scene.

"Maybe you're right." The change in Mary's mood was evident.

Stefano couldn't believe what he was hearing himself say. "I have another idea, Marta and I will go across the road and stay with Uncle Sandro. We've stayed with him so long before, he won't mind."

Then Mary and Mauro were beamed. The only person who was not beaming was Stefano. *Am I not the most stupid person in the world? How did Marta trick me into doing this?*

"Oh, Stefano, I'm so proud of you. You did the right thing and I knew once you talked with Mary you'd agree with me. She's like my sister and I wanted to do something for her. I think your original thoughts were very selfish."

"I'm not being selfish. We've only been in our home for a short time and I enjoy the two of us having our own place. I'm not saying it's a bad idea, but come on, how would you feel if I asked Rodolpho come live with us? On second thought, maybe you'd like that."

Marta swatted Stefano over the head with her purse. "You are such a child."

Her use of the word child cut Stefano to the quick. "I know one thing, I'm not going to ask Uncle Sandro if we can live with him again. You set this up, you ask him."

Marta tilted her chin upward and said, "Good, I planned to do it anyway."

And so it was. Sandro said he had more room since Giovanni had married and Polombo was never home for any period. He was staying most of the time with a friend near where he worked. It was tough for Stefano to go back to the room he had shared with Karl. Each time he felt he had closed the cover on the war memory compartment, something else would happen to pry the lid up again.

His second night at Sandro's, Stefano came in from work, walked into the room and automatically said, "Karl, wie gehts—how goes it?" Shaken, he stood in the middle of the room, questioning his sanity, and he looked back out the door to make sure no one heard what he had said.

Within a short time Stefano had acclimated and didn't think of his own home except when he wanted something special and remembered that it was still across the street. Mary and Mauro were most appreciative and told Stefano repeatedly how grateful they were. Marta spent most of her free time with Mary while Mauro was at work. Stefano recognized he was jealous that Marta had a special friend, but he knew that he had Rodolpho anytime he needed to talk with someone. That wasn't very often.

A few weeks into the new arrangement, Mauro tried to catch up with Stefano as they were leaving church. It was a Sunday and everyone was dressed in their best. Mauro called to him, "Hey, Stefano. Wait!"

Stefano turned and walked back to meet Mauro. "How you doing? I couldn't believe how long that sermon was. You ever heard one like that?"

"Yeah, it was kinda long. I want to talk with you about something. Mary and I've been talking and we've decided we can't let you live across the road when your house is right here."

"You found a place of your own?" asked Stefano with anticipation and a wide smile.

"Sorry, no, but we want you to move back into your house. We'd like to continue to stay there for a little while longer if it's okay."

"Mauro, our house isn't that big. Where would we all sleep?"

Mauro put his arm over Stefano's shoulder and said, "Mary and I haven't worked that out. Come on to the house, Marta is there and Mary's telling her what I just told you. We'll talk it out and see what we all think."

Reluctantly Stefano walked on to their house and climbed the steps. He heard laughter coming from inside and when he entered Marta and Mary were sitting at the table. Mary had made coffee and had put four cups on the table and a plate of sweets. Stefano surveyed the table and asked, "What's going on? Looks kind of like a party that everyone knew about except me."

Marta smiled at Stefano. "Silly, no one is keeping anything from you. Come sit and try one of these delicious rolls that Mary baked."

Stefano had to admit the sweet rolls looked wonderful. He sat at the table and said, "There's no big secret. Mauro told me what he and Mary have in mind. I don't know how it will work, but we've lived close with others before and I guess we can again."

Mary filled everyone's cup, and Stefano helped himself to a roll. In his opinion anything can be talked about, but it's much better if it's talked about with a sweet roll in your hand.

Eventually they were able to work out sleeping arrangements so that everyone had privacy. Mauro made it plain that he and Mary would pay their own expenses plus a small amount more. After all, they had paid no rent since they moved in. Even if they had offered,

Marta and Stefano would have refused. You don't charge a relative for a place to sleep.

Weeks passed and the household was running smoothly, with all the occupants sharing the work and the expenses. Stefano was making good wages and Mauro had a new job, so the four of them actually had more money than they needed, which was a remarkable situation for any Capaldi.

CHAPTER TWENTY-EIGHT

BEFORE HE WAS MARRIED, Mauro had lived in Naples with his family. One evening, as they were having dinner Mauro said, "I've written a letter to my brother, Gino, in Naples and asked him to come and pay a visit."

Stefano inhaled his soup, and through his coughing, couldn't believe what he had heard. Clearing his throat he asked, "And where do we stash one more person here? This place is already like a rabbit warren with all the temporary dividers."

"It's okay, Stefano. He'll sleep on the floor in our area. You'll like Gino. He's about four years older than you, and you'll have fun together. I want to get him out of the city for a few days."

"Why not? We've all the room in the world. We have more room here than the new Excelsior Hotel in Cassino!" Stefano didn't say another word during dinner. He ate as rapidly as he could and left the house. It was time for another chat with Rodolpho.

By the time Stefano reached Cervaro and Rodolpho's place, he had cooled considerably, but he was still stunned. He felt badly that he had ruined everyone's dinner, but on the other hand he didn't care, as he felt he and Marta had been taken advantage of one more time.

"Rodolpho, how could Mauro have the balls to invite someone else to share our house? Most anytime now I'm expecting him to announce that he's gotten Mary pregnant and there'll be one more."

"Well, you can't have it both ways, my little friend. Either he does have balls or he doesn't. Since you put it the way you did, I'd say he's got balls, but if Mary isn't pregnant then maybe he doesn't have balls."

As usual Rodolpho had Stefano laughing in minutes. "You are a real coglione—testicle. You don't have another glass of that good vino, do you?"

As Rodolpho got up to go to the bar he asked, "What am I, your jester or your vintner?"

They sipped their wine silently, and when the glasses were empty Rodolpho said, "Don't jump to conclusions. As Mauro said, you might really enjoy having Gino around. Now go home."

Stefano stood and grabbed Rodolpho in a big hug. "Buona notte—good night."

When he got home Stefano wrote a note to Mauro saying he was sorry and that Gino would be most welcome to come for a visit. He placed the note on the table before he left for work in the morning. He was normally out of the house before anyone else stirred.

Gino came and Stefano was caught off guard by how quickly their friendship developed. Being from the city, Gino relished the clear air and the crispness of the fall nights in the country. He was most happy when Stefano got home from work. In the evenings they played cards and on the first Saturday night Stefano took Gino to meet Rodolpho. Gino ordered a beer as though he frequented bars daily. Rodolpho gave Stefano a small glass too. Gino quickly downed the amber liquid and ordered another. Stefano followed suit. Rodolpho brought Gino his second glass of beer and poured about an ounce in Stefano's glass.

"Amici—fiends, when the beer is finished, so are you, especially you, my little friend. Because Gino is here, you come playing the party boy." He turned to Gino. "Take him home before he can't walk."

Stefano protested, "I'm fine. I can walk fine."

"Sure you can, and I'm going to see to it that you leave while you're still able. The last thing I want is for Marta to get on me, and she would with little thought."

Stefano's beer was kicking in. He laughed and said, "Oh, I think you'd like that, my biiiig friend."

Gino was startled by the comment, but because Rodolpho and Stefano were laughing so hard, he knew there had to be an inside joke. He laughed along with them, as best he could, and then the two headed home.

At Stefano's insistence, Gino stayed on for two weeks, and after he left, Stefano was lonely. He didn't realize he could become attached to a friend so quickly.

———————

Good news from Uncle Francesco made Stefano forget Gino. Uncle Francesco summoned Marta and Stefano to his home. That's the way he operated; he sent a summons calling you to an audience. It was as though he was the Pope on Good Friday! Mary accompanied them, not knowing what her father might want, and knowing him, she thought she might need to protect them. Francesco made it plain that he was not happy that Marta had invited Mary and Mauro to share their home. Once he got that off his chest, he got to his real reason for the meeting.

"I've given this long and serious thought. As you know, my brother, sister and I submitted papers for you to immigrate to America. That was a long time ago and everything was put on hold because of the war. The government didn't even consider anyone for immigration during that time. Now that we are at peace, we have to pursue this more vigorously. We again filed papers before I came here, but we have heard nothing"

"Doesn't it just take a lot of time?" interrupted Stefano.

"Yes, it does take longer than you've given me to explain."

"I'm sorry, Uncle Frank."

Francesco stared at Stefano. "Maybe you'll make a good American, you're impetuous like they are, and you used my American name. Now, what I plan to do is to go into Naples to see if I can't expedite matters at the American Consulate. I'm sure the holdup is on this side of the Atlantic rather than America."

"Oh, that would be so wonderful!" said Marta.

Mary teased, "I see. You're tired of being an Italian and you want to try being an American.

Marta caught the jibe. "Well, you got tired of being an American and have decided to be an Italian!"

"Yes, but I had a very good reason for coming here."

"Well, maybe I'll find my Mauro in the States."

"Enough of your jabbering, women. This is very serious. First, I need to know that you want to immigrate and why," postured Francesco, as he paced before the fireplace.

Stefano spoke up for the first time since being told to keep quiet. "Yes, I want to go to America, and it's not because I've heard all that stuff about the streets being paved with gold. In Italy we don't stand a chance. No matter how hard I work I'll always be a peasant farmer or a mason's helper. If I'm lucky, I may become a mason, but I can't see doing that for the rest of my life. I want the chance to go back to school and learn a skill that will let me earn an easier life than I've had."

"And you, Marta?" asked Francesco.

"I'm more torn than Stefano. If I didn't have to worry about where the next lira was coming from and if I didn't feel that I had to manage the farm, I think I could be happy here. What is left of my family is right here."

Her answer surprised Stefano. First of all, he didn't know she felt she had the responsibility of managing the farm. He was in the fields every minute he wasn't on a construction site. Truth told, he spent as much time thinking about the farm as she did.

"Are you saying that if you didn't have to manage me you could be happy here?"

Marta blanched. "That isn't what I mean and you know it. I get so tired doing the housework and then working in the fields."

Mary spoke up again and this time she wasn't teasing. "I think I do my share of the housework, and Mauro contributes a fair share to the upkeep. I don't..."

"Now the three of you stop it," said Francesco emphatically. "I called you here to help you, and not to get the three of you riled up. I think you need to have a family conference and clear the air in that little house. Am I to proceed with the immigration or not? That's all I want to know."

"Absolutely," said Stefano. "And Marta will be going with me, if we get permission. We've been through too much together to separate now."

Marta nodded in agreement at her brother's statement. "I agree. I don't want us to be separated. We've had support from Uncle Sandro, but we basically only have each other. Maybe my brother is taking charge."

Stefano blushed. "I don't want to take charge. I just want to be equal. Is there anything else we need to do?"

"Not right now. The two of you belong together, and I wouldn't want one of you to stay here. I'm going to appeal to the officials at the Italian Consulate on the grounds that you are orphans and should be with your aunt and uncle in the States. There is a little problem though. You know this is Italy and there will be challenges."

"What do you mean 'challenges'?" asked Marta.

Francesco rubbed his thumb and forefinger together. "Their question will be, whether they say it or not, 'What's in it for me?'"

"Ah," said Stefano nodding his head with understanding. "We're going to have to pay lira. How much and at how many levels?"

For the first time Francesco smiled, crossed the room and sat next to Stefano. "You're very astute, have you done this before, Stefano? I have no idea, until I get to the Consulate and get the lay of the land."

"The lay of the land?" quizzed Stefano.

Mary and her father laughed. Mary said, "That's an American expression. Before long, you two will be using American phrases like that withhout even thinking. It means Father will have to hear what the officials have to say and then he'll have a better idea."

"That's okay," said Stefano. "I think Marta has saved some of the money I've brought home. She'll give you whatever you say. Am I right, Marta?" He was fanning his tail like a peacock, he was in control.

"Yes, I'm fine with that."

"I could pay it, but I think the two you should be invested in the process. In that way, I'll know it's what you want to do. Let's be optimistic," Francesco said. "Let's hope it will only take one trip to Naples."

I could be just as invested without it costing me money, thought Stefano.

A few days later Francesco announced that he had an appointment at the consulate and was ready to go. Marta gave him the money he requested and off he went.

He returned assured that the consulate would do everything they could to bring about the immigration permit, but he wasn't convinced. "I talked with everyone I could see and I'm afraid I had to pass out most of the money you gave me. There was a hand out at every office. There's nothing like this in America. The government is much more tightly controlled, so there is less bribery. I don't know what will happen, but I think it will take time."

Stefano and Marta were discouraged, but within a few weeks they had fallen into their usual routine and thought little about the Naples Consulate.

Stefano went to work every day with Nico, and Marta continued running the house and supervising the farm. They had a good harvest and canned the tomatoes and vegetables as though they were definitely going to be in the village for another winter. In October the shelves were once again brimming with the bright colors of the summer garden. Most of the canning was done on weekends when Stefano would be available. He thought it was easier on the construction site than having Marta tell him to light the fire outside, to lift the jars, do this, or do that. But when it was finished, he was as proud as was she.

Francesco came back to them at the end of October and said he'd been told to come back to the consulate. Once again Marta gave him money and off he went to Naples. At the consulate Francesco pleaded as if he was asking for mercy before being led to the guillotine.

He spoke with the chief of immigration, after having passed through two other bureaucrats who had taken most of the money he had brought with him. Each one had said that there were fees for this or that. The chief seemed sympathetic.

"Sir, I implore you to push through the paperwork for these two children. They are alone, having lost their parents when they were merely eight and fourteen years old. They have not only suffered the war like most Italians, but they also lost their home to bombing. They've been sharing their one room home with some other struggling young villagers. They divided it with a curtain for some sense of privacy. They are survivors and complain hardly ever. They will be very good citizens in their new home if they only have the chance," pleaded Francesco.

The chief didn't respond, he kept shuffling papers on his expansive desk. Francesco stood before the desk, with his hat held by both hands before him, not his usual stance. If he was more supplicating he would have had to be on his knees.

"Signore, you must know that there are hundreds with the same story as your niece and nephew. We only can do so much. The U.S. Government will only allow us to send but so many on each ship."

Francesco pictured lira signs in his mind as the chief spoke. There was little money left for a last bribe, but it appeared the time had come. "Sir, I am prepared to pay to have all the forms completed."

The chief stopped reading, looked up with a most unhappy expression on his face. "Signore, are you offering me a bribe?"

"No. Absolutely not. It's that I don't want the office to think that I'm unwilling to pay any fees that are necessary."

The chief looked straight into Francesco's eyes. "I understand that you have handed money to some people in this office, and if I knew who they were, I'd have them fired today. However, I won't ask you to give names since you will still have a lot to do here before the young ones are allowed to leave."

Francesco was sure he had blown the deal. "I apologize for the misunderstanding, sir. I did not mean to insult you."

"Relax, Signore. As I said, I understand and I do appreciate what you are doing for this niece and nephew. Let me say this, I think you can tell them that they will most likely be summoned to come in for their physical examinations in the near future."

With that the chief stood and offered his hand to Francesco, who shook the hand almost violently. "Thank you, Sir. I do appreciate all of your help."

Francesco returned to the village and told Marta and Stefano what had transpired at the consulate. He left out the part of attempting to bribe the chief. He returned what money that was left and told them to be ready to leave for Naples whenever the letter arrived.

When he left, Mary and Marta danced around in a circle. Same old story. Dance in a circle, go back to your chair along the wall and wait. Stefano went outside where he could be alone. He went to his favorite tree stump where he had a long talk with his grandfather. Meanwhile Mary was telling Marta about all the wonders awaiting her in the States, like running water, electric lights and most of all, heat to warm the house.

"Marta, you're so lucky to be going to America. I wish we were going with you, but I must wait for Mauro to receive his papers and I'm afraid that will take longer than it has been for you and Stefano. What the officials see is that Mauro has family in Naples, he has a job and we have become somewhat established here. They don't really care that it's not our house and when you leave they will assume it's ours. Mauro and I have talked and we hope you don't sell the house too soon. That's very selfish of us, but we don't know what we'll do if you sell this place."

Marta laughed. "Sell this place? Look around you. It's basically one room. No one will want to buy it."

Mary answered somberly, "Open your eyes. There're many people who don't have one room. We wouldn't have a place if not for your generosity."

"You will have a home. Your father will soon be returning to America and you could go live with your aunt."

"Can you imagine living with that old bat? She's worse than my father! She would probably want us to sleep in separate beds. She stopped here one day, unannounced, walked in when Mauro was kissing me and gave us a lecture on public displays of affection!"

The two girls were in near hysterics when Stefano and Mauro walked in. Mauro took Mary in his arms, kissed her and asked, "And he is so funny, your husband?"

Mary drew back and looked at him to see if he was joking. He was smiling broadly and winked at Stefano. Mary jabbed him in the ribs and scolded, "You're always teasing me. Marta and I were laughing about them going to the States."

"I don't think that's funny," added Stefano. "I hope it's fun, but I don't think it's funny."

"Don't worry," assured Marta, her face blush-red. "It wasn't like that at all. What shall we have for supper? I've cooked some lamb and we can have whatever vegetables we like."

Stefano didn't like being dismissed in such a fashion, was still smarting from the fact that Mary and Marta had used the last of the coffee that morning and said they forgot him. No one likes to be forgotten.

Mary teased a little more. "Come on, Stefano, I know we didn't save you coffee this morning, but you won't have to worry about the last of the coffee in America. There is always plenty of coffee."

That didn't help Stefano's feelings. "That's probably true, but shall we all remember that we're not in America, or we weren't the last time I looked outside."

With that comment Stefano went to the door. As he closed the door he heard Mauro say, "Don't worry, I think his hormones are in an uproar."

Another pissed moment. He decided to go into Cervaro and have a talk with Rodolpho. It wasn't Stefano's day. When he got into Cervaro he was told that Rodolpho had gone into Cassino. Stefano was now truly pissed. After walking all that distance, his friend wasn't even at the bar. If his hormones were in an uproar before, they were about to boil over now.

He sat on the steps leading to the bar and had a long talk with himself. At the end of his internal monologue, he concluded that he was more hungry than pissed and headed back home. When he arrived, no one asked where he had been or mentioned the previous conversation. The meal was delicious, and he ate his full share.

Within the month, the letter arrived directing Marta and Stefano to report for their physical examinations in Naples. Marta was very excited, but doubt clouded her thoughts, as usual. "Suppose we don't pass the physical exam?"

Stefano shook his head in disbelief. "What do you mean we could fail the physical? What have I been doing for the past two years? I haven't been sitting on my butt."

Marta stiffened. "Stefano, don't speak in that manner."

"Marta, for God's sake, ease up. I've been mixing cement by hand, climbing ladders, walking miles back and forth to my job and then working here. There is no way I'm going to fail a physical. And you're not going to fail either. You work hard and for the past several months have eaten very well. You will pass. Now, no more negative talk."

Finally, the day arrived for the physical exams. They scrubbed themselves, dressed in their Sunday clothes and walked into Cassino where they could catch the bus to Naples. Stefano was leery of the bus ride. He'd only ridden on a bus one time before and that wasn't a good scene. He had vomited copiously after ten kilometers down the road. This time the trip was uneventful and he enjoyed watching the scenery pass, scenery he had never seen before.

When they arrived at the office for their exams they were separated and told to wait for the nurse. The building was both old and chilly. The walls were paneled wainscot high, painted hospital green, and the plaster above was whitewashed. The floor was covered with tiny black and white tiles. The overpowering smell of antiseptic permeated the room and irritated Stefano's eyes.

Finally, the nurse arrived and asked him to follow her to a small office. When she had closed the door she sat at a small desk and gave Stefano the nicest smile he'd ever seen, next to Lucia's. She questioned when his last exam had been and was taken aback when Stefano replied, "I've never had a physical exam. Actually, I've only been seen by a doctor once. I only know what I was told by my sister, it was when I was very young."

The nurse recovered from her surprise and took Stefano back to the examination room. She pointed to the table and said, "After you've undressed, please sit on the table. The doctor will be in very shortly."

When the doctor entered the room, he was accompanied by the same nurse, whose smile melted the boy. Stefano had thought about her a lot while he waited. He was glad he had taken off his shirt but left his pants on. A little cover-up was in order.

The doctor wasn't concerned that Stefano wasn't totally undressed, but proceeded to ask a few questions and then commented that he was impressed by Stefano's general musculature.

Stefano smiled and said, "I suppose that's what happens when you work as a mason's helper."

The doctor replied, "Well, it seems it hasn't done you any harm." He looked in Stefano's mouth, ears, nose and eyes. With his stethoscope he listened to Stefano's heart and lungs.

He stepped back from the table and said, "Okay, now slip off your pants. You may keep on your underpants."

Stefano blushed. "I don't have any underpants. We've never been able to afford them."

The doctor didn't comment other than to say, "That's okay, just slip off your pants."

Stefano turned and looked at the nurse, who picked up on his self-conscious expression, "Doctor, I think Mr. Capaldi would be more comfortable if I waited outside."

With that she disappeared through the door. As she went out, so did the scarlet color from Stefano's body. He removed his pants and stood by the table.

"Okay, let's check you for a hernia," said the doctor.

"What's a hernia?" asked Stefano.

"It's a bulge you get down here, the doctor said," as he point to Stefano's groin.

Stefano was mortified again, blushing from head to toe. No one had ever touched him down there except Mama when he was a very young boy, and that was for a bath. Could the doctor know that he frequently got bulges down there and had done so most recently, a few minutes ago, when he'd been thinking about the pretty nurse?

With that, the doctor inserted a finger up Stefano's scrotum. Stefano jumped back against the wall. "What're you doing?" He grabbed his pants from the table and was about to step into them.

The doctor didn't laugh out loud, but looked as if he was about to split. "Sorry, young man. I should have told you what I was going to do. I have to do this, and it really isn't uncomfortable. I have to be able to write on the form that you do not have a hernia. Shall we try again?"

Stefano was not so sure about the situation but was determined he wasn't going to fail his exam. "Go ahead. I'll stand still."

Within fifteen seconds it was over with. "Now, was that so bad?" asked the doctor.

"No sir, I'm sorry I jumped."

"I think I may have jumped too. Again I apologize for surprising you. Now lie on the table so I can examine your abdomen and we'll be through."

Ten minutes later, the doctor opened the door and called in the nurse. "Mr. Capaldi is a fine specimen of a man. You can take him back to the waiting area while we determine if he should have any inoculations."

Marta joined her brother in the waiting area, where they were told they did have to have "shots" for tetanus and smallpox. That bit was accomplished over the next half-hour and they headed back to the bus station. It was done. They simply had to wait to fit within the quota for immigration. Stefano felt he had waited his entire life.

The cold weather wreaked havoc with the construction business. There were days when they couldn't work because it was too cold for the cement to cure. Stefano welcomed those days—handling mortar and stone in frigid weather was not his idea of teenage fun. He talked with Nico about leaving the job.

Stefano was shy about approaching Nico because he respected his boss and the man had great faith in him and had given him a break when no one else had. "Nico, I have to talk with you about something."

"And what is that?" asked Nico.

"I hope to be going to America soon and…"

Nico reached out and took Stefano's hand. "Congratulations, my man. You don't have to hesitate to tell me. I've seen it in your face for the past couple of weeks. I knew this time would come, but I'd about given up for you. You've been a good man and I'll miss you. Good luck."

"I know it's not much time, but this Friday will be my last day."

"That's okay. I have five days to find your replacement. There's a man who is about 25 years old who wants a job. I think he will be good, but I won't expect him to work like you do," Nico said with a hearty laugh. "You're one tough little red-head."

Coincidently, on Stefano's last day they received the letter notifying them that their passports were enclosed and that they would sail on December 29, 1946. It was a joyful event all around. Mauro went into town and brought back Frizzantino—a local sparkling wine—and Marta made a huge chicken cacciatore dinner.

Mauro was happy for his friends and wanted them to have a happy departure. "I tell you what we'll do. We'll all go to Naples a few days before you sail and we'll have a great time. You'll see Naples and eat some Neapolitan food, good food to fortify you for the journey."

Everyone loved Mauro's plan and the consensus was that they would leave on the 26th. Mary was determined it would be a full-fledged Christmas. She exclaimed, "We have to have a tree with decorations, gifts and a feast. It'll be a prelude to what you'll experience next year at Christmas time."

"We don't have real decorations. Last year we had the first Christmas tree in the village and we made paper decorations," said Marta.

"Ah, but we will have real decorations this year," said Mary. "We have to have everything. A tree, lots of food and little presents for each other."

Mauro added, "We'll have a wonderful Christmas and then the next day we'll leave for Naples. Sadly, it's not the same city as it was before the war. So many of the beautiful structures were bombed, but there's been a lot of re-construction and now many new modern buildings. Best of all, though, are the fantastic views of the bay. Even a war couldn't extinguish those."

On the Saturday before Christmas, Mauro and Stefano tramped through all the wooded areas they could think of. There had not been a great deal of growth since the deforestation of the war, but they found one of the trees Stefano had rejected the year before as being too big for him to get home. For the two of them it would be no problem. Yet, by the time they got home they were exhausted from wrestling with the evergreen tree.

The next item was decorations. The four walked into Cervaro and were met with stares when they asked the shop keepers for Christmas tree ornaments. Later that day they decided to persevere and walked the 10 kilometers into Cassino where they were met with the same stares. They finally settled on meters of ribbon, which they would tie into bows. They all agreed that they spent more than they should have. Youthful enthusiasm sometimes clouds common sense.

That evening Mauro and Stefano made a support for the tree and it stood next to the fireplace. They all took turns tying the bows on the tree, which could have used four times as many bows, it was so large, but everyone was very pleased with the final result. They joined hands and stood admiring their beautiful Christmas tree.

Mary became teary-eyed. "I wish we were all going. I will miss the American Christmas so much."

Mauro placed his arm around her waist. "It won't be long. I'm sure by this time next year we'll be joining Marta and Stefano in America."

The next week seemed to pass rapidly. Marta bought a cheap suitcase, large enough to hold everything they would carry with them. They didn't have many clothes, so there was room for the sentimental items. Marta had some embroidered pillow cases and sheets left to her by their mother. She was amazed that they had survived in the basement of their home when it had been bombed. Dust galore had settled on the brown paper wrapping, but not a tear.

It was during the packing that Marta became very emotional about leaving their home, Cervaro and Italy. It may not be much but it was home. Stefano had the solid gold pocket watch left by his father. The watch had accompanied Stefano wherever he had gone during the war. He always kept it in a white cloth, tucked away where he felt it was safe. He stroked his large straw hat that he had worn long after it was too small for him. It was bleached almost pure white by the constant unrelenting sun, except for a brown stain where the brim met crown. The sweat had been as unrelenting as the sun.

He thought back to the many days he had worn the hat and tried to remember certain details, but they were gone. He smiled as he placed the hat on the pile of discarded items thinking that maybe, just maybe, he had surrendered the past into the past.

He had a sudden thought, picked up the hat and walked into the garden. At his tree stump, he placed the hat atop it and silently backed away with misty eyes capturing the scene for all his life.

They knew their property would be in good hands. Mary and Mauro would continue to live in the house until it was sold, and since few people had any money, it might take a while. The farm would be partially worked by Sandro and he would lease out the rest for them.

They trusted Sandro implicitly. He had cared for them so well during the war. Arrangements were made legally to give him power of attorney to care for their holdings. Deep down they didn't care if they ever saw any money from the property. If Sandro could use it, good. Not that they couldn't use the money, but they owed him so much.

There had to be another farewell. Stefano made his way into Cervaro and straight to Rodolpho's place. As it was the holiday season, the bar was crowded and many of the patrons had certainly had their share of vino. Rodolpho and the woman who worked there were as busy as four hands can be. To Stefano's friend the business could wait. When he saw the young man come in the door he immediately came around the bar and extended his hand. "Hey, mia Amico, how are you? You know, I was afraid you were going to leave before I got to see you."

Over the din, Stefano yelled, "There is no way I would do that."

"Good, let's go upstairs." He called to his helper and pointed up. She nodded, and then he led the way to his private quarters. Stefano had never been invited to Rodolpho's home before and was surprised how nicely the place was furnished and decorated.

The older man went to a cupboard and removed a bottle of red wine which he uncorked and set on the table. He gathered two glasses while Stefano looked around.

"Your home is very nice, Rodolpho, I'm honored that you brought me here."

"I've been very fortunate, my friend. I did not bring you here before because I was reluctant for you to see it."

"Why would you be reluctant? It's beautiful."

"Thank you, but I know how difficult your life has been. I didn't want you to think I was showing off."

"As you would say, 'Hey', I'm only happy for you. You work very hard and deserve to live nicely. Now I'm going to America and will make a better life, too."

Rodolpho came to Stefano and hugged him. "There is no question in my mind. You've said it exactly as it will be. Now, come, sit and have a glass of vino." He poured two full glasses of the dark red nectar.

"I guess I should have said I was leaving earlier. This is the first time you have ever given me a full glass."

Rodolpho laughed. "I always gave you what I thought you could handle."

"Well, now that I've got a bigger muscle to handle, I can have more, right?"

Then they both laughed as they had done so many times in the past. Stefano's eyes teared up as he said, "Rodolpho, I'm going to miss you and our conversations so very much. You always treated me as a person and not as a little boy. I'll never forget you, mio amico."

Rodolpho raised his glass and touched Stefano's. "Per se salute— to your health."

Silently they sipped their wine. Stefano knew there were many things he wanted to say but was trying to hold himself together. When their glasses were empty Rodolpho reached for the wine bottle. Stefano held up his hand. "I better let you get back to work. Somebody has to pay for this place."

They stood and embraced for a good while. Then Stefano turned and walked to the stairs and without looking back said, "Ciao."

Mary and Marta baked cantucci—biscotti—apple tarts and cookies. The one apple tree, left partially standing after the war, had two branches which produced delicious apples. Few in number, but great in flavor. They had been harvested and stored in the basement for special occasions. Well, there were a couple missing which Stefano had enjoyed when he picked the harvest.

CHAPTER TWENTY-NINE

．．

ON CHRISTMAS MORNING STEFANO along with his extended family, went to eight o'clock Mass. Afterward, Stefano insisted that everyone come to their home for cantucci and coffee.

Sandro asked, "Why don't you come to our place?"

Stefano was on top of that in a hurry. "I know what you're thinking, Uncle. There's no way everyone will fit into our tiny house. We'll be crowded, yes, but it'll be fun and it's very important to us. And besides, you know that Marta makes the best cantucci in all of Italy."

"Yes, please come," said Marta.

"Very well, but we'll all have Christmas dinner together at our home," said Sandro. "Let's see how good those cantucci are."

Marta walked close to her brother on their way back from church. She reached out and took his hand. His first instinct was to pull back. After all, he was now fourteen.

Marta held on. Softly she whispered, "Thank you for saying I make the best cantucci. I think that's the nicest thing you've said to me in a long time."

Momentarily speechless, Stefano finally muttered, "I think I've been mean at times. I don't mean to be."

"I know," replied Marta. "It's the way young men are. They're not supposed to treat their sisters too nicely."

Stefano was relieved to see a big smile on Marta's face. "I promise I'll be better. We've got a big journey, just the two of us one more time. I do appreciate all you've done for me over the years."

Marta squeezed his hand and then let go. "We've done it together. Each of us did what we could and we managed. Now, that's enough of this sentimental talk. Let's enjoy this, our last day in Capaldi. After church I saw you speaking with Lucia. Were you saying goodbye?"

"To be honest, that was my intention, but when I was talking with her I invited her to our house and then to have the meal at Sandro's."

"Oh, Stefano, I think that's wonderful. Is she coming?"

"She said she would ask her father."

Christmas was wonderful. It was beyond crowded at Marta and Stefano's, but that added to the joviality. Stefano was right, Marta's cantucci were the best and Sandro agreed.

Sandro's family left and the four young people cleaned up. In the early afternoon they packed up everything they had planned to cook and took it across the road to join their relatives. The women cooked, the men talked, played cards and drank wine. For the second time in his life Stefano had too much vino. He decided he had best take a walk in the cool air to clear his head before dinner.

Not surprisingly, he went back to his favorite tree stump to bid his grandfather goodbye. "No matter where I go, I'll never forget the times we had together. I've missed you, and I've missed all the things you probably would have taught me. Oh, oh, don't get me wrong. I appreciate what you had time to teach me. I'll keep on missing, you and if I have to tend any sheep and goats in America, I'll do it, just like you taught me."

Stefano wiped his tears on his coat sleeve and started back to Sandro's. After a few steps he turned and looked back at the stump. "Goodbye." Again, wiping his tears, he picked up his pace and returned to the party.

Christmas dinner began with chicken soup with homemade egg noodles, followed by a simple pasta course, roasted chicken with several vegetables and, of course, followed by a desert of tiramisu, which Stefano considered a cake sent by the angels. It had to be made right and his aunt must have talked with the angels personally. She made her own little finger cakes, soaked them in just the right amount of espresso, added the mascarpone and whipped cream, for a true Christmas extravagance. There were probably more calories in the dessert than the rest of the meal combined, including the wine. Stefano never counted calories, so he had a second serving of the Angel's cake.

Lucia did not come to the celebration.

CHAPTER THIRTY

EARLY ON THE MORNING of December 26th the little Fiat 1500A arrived from Cervaro. It was the only taxi in the town and had been reserved a week in advance. The little car was designed to hold four people and today there were four adults, plus the driver. Everyone wondered how they'd fit them all in the mini-machine, much less the chickens.

Stefano had chosen two fat chickens and tied their feet together. He tore a hole in the bottom corners of a paper sack, put the chickens in head-first and stuck the heads out through the holes. Simple, compact and sanitary for the trip.

The driver figured a way to secure the suitcase to the roof, but he was aghast when the produce and chickens were brought out. His first comment was, "I think I'll have to make two trips."

To which Stefano replied, "Okay, I'll wait for the second trip, but you only get paid for one."

The driver gave Stefano a surly look, but added, "We find a way." He went back to his loading the luggage as the family said their last goodbyes. It was most hard for Stefano to say goodbye to his Uncle Sandro.

Stefano hugged his uncle as hard as he could, "Thank you for so much. I..."

Sandro cut him off. "From the strength of that hug, I think you are now well on the way to taking care of yourself. You no longer need me, you're more of a man than many twice your age."

He took Stefano by the shoulders and turned him toward the car. From that point on Stefano knew he best not look back. He climbed in the middle of the back seat and immediately had the bag with the two chickens thrust on his lap by the driver. Mary got in on one side and Marta on the other. Mauro was in the front holding the box of fruits and vegetables. The two women were mainly sitting on one hip each, facing Stefano, and he was quite sure he was going to be smothered either by chickens or by breasts before he reached Naples.

After a two-hour drive they arrived at Mauro's home in Naples. Immediately Gino grabbed Stefano and said, "Welcome to Naples, my friend! I have much to show you."

Mauro had two brothers, Dante and Gino, a sister and mother. Naturally being a good Italian family, they had their boisterous greetings and then they sat down to lunch. It was a modest meal by the usual Neapolitan standards, but with nine around the table it was a jovial affair.

Following lunch Mauro insisted they all go for a tour of the city. Before they left Marta gave Mauro's mother and sister instructions on cleaning a live chicken. The city folks had only bought cleaned chickens from the butcher shop. Marta was determined to be patient although she was amazed that a woman didn't know how to prepare a chicken. "First you have to cut off the chicken's head."

It was a toss-up which had the most startled expression, the mother or the sister. Stefano laughed, "Don't worry. Mauro, show me where I can kill the chicken and I'll do it."

They went outside with one of the chickens and Marta continued her instructions. "Then you boil a big pot of water, dip the chicken in several times, but don't let it stay in the water. Then you'll be able to pluck the feathers." As she was finishing, Stefano returned with the killed chicken in a large basin which he placed on the table and they said their goodbyes. Mauro called from the door, "We'll return around seven for dinner."

Their first stop was the bay, where Mauro used to swim as a boy. The city intimidated Marta and Stefano, but they felt perfectly safe with Mauro. After they relaxed, the touring was exciting, so exciting that they were exhausted by six-thirty and they took the trolley back home.

When they arrived home, Mauro's mother announced, "The chicken is in the pot. You see, I can cook a chicken that's not from the butcher."

The four visitors were very impressed, but then Marta asked, "What is that odor?"

Mary sniffed and went to the stove. She lifted the lid from the pot and was overwhelmed by the odor. She slammed the lid back on the pot and Mauro took a towel, lifted the pot, and carried it outside while Mary opened the windows to air out the house. Mother had plucked the chicken, but hadn't gutted it.

Mauro came back from disposing of the chicken and apologized for his mother, "She wouldn't have had the least idea. The butcher has always done that for her." The other three could only laugh.

Stefano said, "Don't worry. That's why we brought an extra one." In short order the other chicken was prepared and while it cooked, they sat around the table, drinking wine and getting to know each other better. By the tie the chicken was baked, the adults were fried. It was a great meal, Mother decided to bake rather than use the gut pot, as Mauro had called it. As soon as dinner was finished, Stefano asked Gino where he could go to bed, he was beat.

The following morning Mauro got everyone up early so they could have a full day in the city. They had coffee and cantucci. Stefano thought the cantucci were good, but not as good as Marta's. Mauro told his mother they would be bringing home the main dish for dinner and, "Please, don't cook another chicken. Tonight, when we return, I'm bringing fish. Prepare something to go with fish." Then as he hugged his mother he whispered, "And I promise we'll clean the fish."

His mother slapped him on top of his head, laughed and wished them all to have a wonderful time in the city. Gino went with them and they began to explore. They visited a store that had a large display of jewelry. Marta and Mary each bought a piece, nothing expensive, 14 carat gold. Marta was very reluctant at first, but at the urging of Mary and Stefano, she bought a pair of earrings.

At lunchtime they stopped at a pizzeria, and Stefano was mesmerized by all the choices. He had never had store-made pizza. In Cervaro pizza was made when fresh bread was made. Fresh tomatoes, basil, oregano and sometimes a little onion were placed on flat bread and baked. Rarely, if available, they'd sprinkle a little Pecorino Romano cheese on top. Sometimes they took a large cabbage leaf, cleaned it, and spread a layer of the cornmeal mixture inside, brushed it with olive oil, added the tomatoes and seasoning and baked it. The cabbage leaf would burn, but it was so hot and delicious.

The pizza they were served was covered with mozzarella, which Stefano had never eaten. Acting like a clown, he stretched the cheese up and up to his mouth and wrapped it around his nose. Everyone thought he was hilarious, except for Marta, but eventually even she had to laugh.

After lunch the group wandered down to the sea to a specific fish market, where Mauro said he had always shopped for the freshest items from the bay. Stefano stared bug-eyed at the box after box of water creatures.

A fishmonger called as they walked into the building, "Mauro, where have you been? We haven't seen you in ages."

Mauro smiled and walked over to where the man was working. He leaned across the boxes of fish and extended his hand. "I've been busy, Giuseppe. I got married." Mauro turned and took Mary's hand. "And this is my wife."

"Oh, how did you get a pretty lady to marry you?" Giuseppe turned to Mary. "If I was you, I'd watch this one. He always had a roving eye for the ladies when he came here. Most of the time he didn't buy anything, he just came to enjoy the scenery."

The group laughed as Giuseppe continued to harass Mauro, and he could give it back. "Giuseppe, Mary and Marta are probably the only pretty girls who ever came to this place. You're so ugly you scare them away."

Giuseppe threw up his hands and said, "Okay, okay, you got me right in the heart. What can I sell you? If you're going to hurt me, let me hurt your pocket."

"What do you suggest?" asked Mary.

"Today, only the eel. It's so fresh it walked in from the boat." Giuseppe picked up a huge eel and held it out while it wriggled violently. "You see, plenty of life left."

"Then we'll take the eel, but not that one. Give us three of the smaller ones."

The monger placed three eels in the scale tray, noted the weight and then slid the creatures into a sack. Mauro paid him and took the sack, which he handed to Stefano to carry. From the market they headed for the trolley.

Stefano carried the sack against his chest as they walked along. Suddenly he yelled and dropped the sack. Mauro turned, looked at the sack on the ground and asked bewilderment, "What happened?"

"It felt like a nest of snakes crawling on my chest," replied Stefano.

"Oh, my God. What do you think they're going to do? They don't bite." He stooped, picked up the sack and handed it to Gino, who was laughing himself silly.

Stefano reached out for the bag and stiffly said, "I can carry the sack. It just surprised me, that's all." He walked several steps in front of the others, and nobody risked saying anything else. They walked in silence to the trolley, but by the time they were home, their lighthearted mood had returned.

After Mauro had cleaned the fish he turned them over to his mother, who was right at home with the eels. She put them in a big pot which had been properly scrubbed. Stefano wasn't convinced that eels were something that should be eaten. He ventured into the room where his bed was and sat looking out the window. When he was called to dinner, he was very happy to see there were other dishes. He was cajoled to try the eel and found that it wasn't bad, but after the one piece, he ate rice, beans and escarole.

After dinner, Mauro said, "Now I have a surprise for you. Have you ever been to a play?"

Marta and Stefano shook their heads.

Stefano asked, "What's a play?"

"It's like a movie except all the actors appear live right in front of you."

That didn't really impress Stefano much since he had never been to a movie. It turned out to be pretty boring as far as Stefano was concerned, and he found himself drifting off to sleep from time to time. Marta later admonished him for being an unappreciative guest.

On the last day before embarking, they were greeted by a brilliant, sunny day. There was a nice nip in the air, but it was beautiful. Gino was anxious to give his friend another new experience.

"Stefano, let's go for a scooter ride today. It will be a great way for you to see more of the city and we may even go outside the city."

"That would be great. I'll talk with my sister."

Marta was uneasy at the thought of seeing her brother taking off on a scooter. Stefano was going to say that he was going anyway when she acquiesced. She admonished Gino to drive carefully, as Stefano rolled his eyes.

They rode past a soccer field where Gino had played. He gave Stefano a rundown on the season, adding more than a little self-aggrandizement. They rode along the sea on a path for bicycles and scooters. They went as far as the path extended and then came back along a ridge where you could see out over the water. The harbor was very busy with many large and small ships.

Gino suggested they have pizza for lunch, which Stefano ordered as if he had been doing it all his life. He had his first Coke, which he thought was tasted strange and fantastic at the same time. Over pizza, Gino brought up his favorite subject, girls. After all, he was 18 years old.

"Say, amico, you got any girls on the line?"

Stefano flushed, "Not really. There's this girl back in Cervaro. I think I pointed her out when you were there, that Sunday at church."

"Oh, yeah. She was really stacked. I've got a couple I go out with. You know, girls like soccer players."

"I bet they do. I was shy around Lucia, and now it's too late since I'm leaving for America."

"Never pass up an opportunity, amico. Remember, if you don't get it with each girl that comes along, it's just one more piece you'll never get."

Stefano wasn't comfortable with such direct talk concerning girls. Somehow with Rodolpho it had been different. The way Gino talked, it didn't seem right. Gino hadn't been brassy when he was in Cervaro, maybe he felt the need to show off on his territory. Stefano tried to change the subject.

"You going to be playing regular on the team next season?"

"Oh, sure. I'm their best striker. Wish you were going to be here longer, I'd fix you up with a nice girl. Hey, you want to go out tonight?"

Stefano shook his head. "I don't think I'd better. We leave early tomorrow and I don't know what it'll be like on that ship. Hope I don't get seasick."

Gino looked at the ceiling, raised his hands upward and asked, "What am I going to do with this guy?" He then leaned across the table and whispered to Stefano. "Did you ever get a feel of those big tits?"

"No! We'd better be heading home. Marta will be worried about us. Have you ever thought about immigrating to America, Gino?"

"Now, why would I do that? I got everything here that I want. I'm on the best soccer team in the area, I live with my momma and I got the world's best—looking women. Why would I want to go to America?"

Stefano couldn't imagine that America would have the space to hold such a fat head. "You about ready to head home?"

Gino went to the counter to pay for lunch. When he returned he shook off his disbelief and said, "Okay, let's head back to il palazzo—palace."

At home, Gino smiled when he heard Stefano describe all they had done and the great lunch Gino had so graciously paid for. Gino thought Stefano was very immature, but he had no idea what the past years had been like for his young friend. It had been no bed of roses for the people of Naples, either. The bombing had been ferocious, but Gino had not witnessed death up close as Stefano had.

That evening they all went to a renowned seafood restaurant which projected out over the bay. They started with antipasto, which Stefano only picked at, he just couldn't bring himself to eat raw sea creatures. He ate the cheeses, olives and sliced salami. Frankly, he didn't want to eat any creature raw. The antipasto was followed by pasta with clams and mussels, and finally grilled red snapper. After dinner they took a short detour on the way home, stopping for gelato. It was a terrific evening and would provide many memories for the two as they crossed the Atlantic Ocean.

CHAPTER THIRTY-ONE

ON THE MORNING OF 29 December, 1946, Marta and Stefano arrived at the dock at 10:30 a.m. and the SS Oceana looked as if it had just been painted. The ship was of the C-4 A-S-3 class, 523 feet long with a 71.5 foot breadth. She had a single funnel and a single screw. Stefano had envisioned a much larger ship, although looking at the vessel from the dock, she looked massive. They boarded the ship, and from the upper deck, after much searching, they finally spotted Mary and Mauro, waving, amongst the masses doing the same. It seemed the Oceana had been waiting for them to make a final disconnect from Italy. The ship's horn bellowed, and as it did, the mooring lines were cast off. Their adventure had truly begun.

Attendants sorted the crowds of people on the decks as rapidly as they could. Marta had not realized she would be separated from Stefano. She made some feeble gestures of protest which were duly ignored. She was ushered below with the women to the middle section of the ship. Stefano was told to follow the men to the forward section. He was not at all concerned with the separation, and in fact he thought it was going to allow a little breathing room.

The quarters consisted of one large room with bunks racked four high. When you were in a lower bunk, you touched the bunk above you if you tried to lie on your side. The area smelled of fresh paint and at first it was almost overwhelming. The consensus was it was a good sign, because it meant he place was clean.

Marta and Stefano were told they would be able to join each other for meals which were served in the mess hall, military style, on metal trays. Meatloaf, mashed potatoes and vegetables were placed on the tray, not Italian fare but good. They sat at a table with a bench, each of which were bolted to the floor, and enjoyed their meal. They weren't really hungry after all the food they had had in Naples, and in fact it was good that they could eat what they wanted. They had never had that much food consistently for three days.

The first leg of their journey was short and in very calm waters. On a short stop in Palermo, Sicily, Stefano observed the on-loading of more supplies. He was fascinated by the operation of the cranes and booms. The stopover at the pier was less than four hours, and then they headed for the open Mediterranean.

Marta was in a good position, as her quarters were mid-ship, but Stefano didn't fare so well. Being forward, the ship's motions were exaggerated. He decided to take a walk around the deck to take in the sights, which consisted of water, water, water and a rare seagull. He had about decided that it was getting too rough to stay outside when a sailor came along and spoke to him sternly, "Get below. We don't want a man overboard drill in the first 24 hours." The sailor pointed toward a hatch and Stefano obediently went inside. If this was the beginning, Lord help the future.

Below deck and back in his bunk, Stefano could feel the awakening in his stomach, the awakening of a feeling he had hoped to avoid. It was fortunate he had been placed in one of the lower bunks. He grabbed his bucket and began to heave. For three days he lay on his bunk, rising only to vomit and to make head calls. The head calls were mainly to empty the bucket. Seasickness is one of those things that the less you try to think about it, the more prominent it becomes.

Marta became frantic, as she hadn't seen her brother for three days and none of the other passengers she questioned could tell her anything.

She finally found a sympathetic attendant, with whom she pleaded, "For three days I haven't seen any sign of my brother. I'm terribly worried something has happened to him."

"Rest assured, if something had happened to him we would know."

"But how would you know? None of the other passengers know anything about him and they'd be the ones to tell you."

"Okay, take it easy. I'll go take a look in the men's quarters."

When the attendant finally found Stefano he was both surprised and angry, knowing somebody had not been doing proper bed checks. He carried a very limp Stefano straight to sickbay and the nurse there told Marta that her brother was fine, just dehydrated. Just dehydrated, but so short of fluid they had difficulty finding an adequate vein to start an IV. They gave Stefano intravenous fluids over the next four hours, and the next day he was feeling much better and the nausea was gone. Stefano was so thankful that his nausea had been treated before they encountered really bad weather, including a storm so violent that the captain cut the engines and allowed the ship to free-float for two days. The crew spent most of those two days reassuring the passengers that they would be all right. Marta knew that Stefano had recovered when, during the worst of the storm, he was in the dining mess eating quite well of the little food the cooks had been able to prepare in the storm.

Finally the sun came out and the sailing was smooth from that point on. They eventually saw a seagull and one of the other passengers said, "If we see seagulls, we are not so far from land. They arrived in New York on the morning of 16 January 1947. All of the immigrants, including Marta and Stefano, stood on deck and were treated to the marvelous sights welcoming them to America.

The many tall skyscrapers were jammed so close together it appeared like one mass to Stefano. He couldn't comprehend that a city went on and on, as far as the eyes could see. The noises of the city blended in with the toots of the tugs and the roar of fellow passengers on deck. Stefano had hugged the rail for hours, from the time he could see land in the distance. Several times larger people tried to move him aside, though he was not as tall, he remained an immovable mass. He was so secure that when Marta tried to join him he simply expanded, edging those on either side to move away until he made room for his sister.

Mary had told her cousins about the Statue of Liberty, but she had not prepared them for the sight they would see. The Lady glowed that morning. The sun's rays reflected off the verdant skin of the statue, and Stefano felt the sun was rising within him, the sunrise of a new life.

Fascinated, Stefano peered over the side of The Oceana and watched the tugboats approach and began to nudge the huge ship toward Pier #31 on the west side of New York. The passengers had never witnessed such a mass of people. The docks were covered with people of every size and shape, squeezed together, looking up, trying to spot a familiar face. Everyone waved as if that would identify them to their loved ones on deck. Of course, most had not seen their relatives for years and each person was bundled head to toe to fight the cold. Recognition was not easy. Most of the people on deck were waving too, which Stefano found somewhat amusing. To join in the mood he turned to Marta and asked, "Don't you see our aunt down there?"

"Where? Where?" Then she looked at the huge smile on her brother's face and knew he had been teasing her. She slapped him on top of the head and then pulled him to her. They comforted each other as they debarked into the throngs.

The relatives were among the masses, and were confused by the process but were eventually able to sort out in which queue to find the teenagers. There was a lot of pushing and shoving, along with a gross amount of confusion for Marta and Stefano. It seemed as if a hundred people were all demanding answers at the same time.

The translators were doing their best, and it was as though a special miracle occurred when Marta heard her name being called, followed by a long sentence in Italian. It was an aunt. From that point on the processing moved along swiftly, and the two young ones soon found themselves being whisked to a large motorcar and off to their new home in Connecticut. The drive to that new home was long, but they were so enthralled by the scenery, it seemed very short.

That evening many relatives were invited in to greet the new arrivals and dinner seemed to Stefano to go on forever. He was exhausted and he longed to crawl into a real bed and have a good night's sleep.

The relatives lived in a home like neither Marta nor Stefano had ever experienced. They were generous to have invited the young people to live with them, but it was quickly made clear this was not to be a long vacation.

At breakfast the next morning, their newly met uncle, asked, "Stefano, how far did you go in school? You should be at least in junior-high."

Stefano looked down at the table and said nothing. Marta started to answer for him but was interrupted by the uncle. "Young lady, I will ask you questions soon enough, this time I am speaking with Stefano.

By then Stefano had recovered his voice and knew that he probably wasn't the first one in the family to have little or no education. "I would say I had about what you would call third grade."

"That's nothing to be ashamed of, young man, but it will have to be changed. America is a country that expects hard work, but if you are ever going to get anywhere you will have to have much more education. Consuela will go with you to the schoolboard office tomorrow and talk with them about where you will need to go."

"Please uncle, I don't want to go anywhere, we just got here and we wandered around for so many months during the war."

"No, no. You will not have to go away to go to school. There are schools close to home. You may find that you actually like it." He wanted to laugh but recognized the young man was way too serious for joking at the present time.

So within a short time Marta and Stefano were enrolled in school, having to study like crazy. English wasn't a problem to them and both were soon carrying on fluent conversations in English, everywhere except home, as only Italian was spoken in the home.

As the years passed, Stefano eventually was aware that the military system would often pay for advanced education. He bided his time and as soon as he approached the age when he could join the US Navy, he did so. His intelligence got him through basic training with little problem while he continued his general education. Soon he was sent to Europe where he served as an interpreter.

Upon his discharge he acquired a job with the Federal government, where he continued to utilize his Italian in the field of intelligence. Though he tried, Stefano was disappointed that he was never able to find any trace of the American pilot, even with all his intelligence connections. The big question always lingered in his mind, did Richard lose his life or had he returned home to America?

After marriage, Stefano established his home in Maryland, had one child, a daughter, and lived a very full life.

ACKNOWLEDGEMENTS

There are many people who aided me in putting this work together. I'd like to thank the following for their time, effort and knowledge: Terry Martin for his insight into the story. Joe DeVincentis for his living knowledge of what life was like in Italy during WWII. John Edmonds, an interpreter living in Milan for his varied help. Adrian O. Eissler, Esq., with whom I've written two medical/legal thrillers, I thank, as always, for his insight and advice. Gretchen Cosgrove, to whom I owe much appreciation, did a final reading of the manuscript. Special thanks to Colleen Anders for the long task of line-editing and Susan Hagerty for readings and straight up opinions. I'll always be thankful to Anne Ward for her continued readings, love and patience over the many years.

I'd be amiss if I didn't thank the kind people of Italy, who helped repeatedly during my research visits to their beautiful country.

Thanks to all the people at iUniverse, especially Joseph, David and Kathi.

Printed in the United States
By Bookmasters